WITSH

WITSH

Mari Ellis Dunning

HONNO

First published in Great Britain in 2025 by Honno Press
D41, Hugh Owen Building, Aberystwyth University, Ceredigion, SY23 3DY

1 2 3 4 5 6 7 8 9 10

A catalogue record for this book is available from the British Library.

Published with the financial support of the Books Council of Wales

ISBN 9781916821361 (paperback)
ISBN 9781916821378(ebook)

Cover design by Ifan Bates
Typeset by Elaine Sharples
Printed by 4edge Ltd

'[In Wales] the introduction of a new loan-word – *wits* or *witsh* – directly borrowed from the English "witch", appears to have had a considerable semantic impact [...] Actions for slander clearly show that the loan-form "*wits*" or "*witsh*" were almost invariably used in colloquial speech in the seventeenth century when making accusations of witchcraft.'

— *Welsh Witchcraft, Richard Suggett*

'As for witches and wizards, we just cannot do without them, for they do great good, in most folks' opinion, for livestock and men.'

— *Dau Cymro yn Taring, Robert Holland, 1595*

The Villagers

This is how it began: with the wet nurse stumbling from her doorway shouting, her panic sweeping the village like a contagion. We rushed, feverish, to find the magistrate, interrupting his talk with the minister. We told him, *go, now. Find her, before it's too late.* It didn't take him long after that. He had the speed of his horse. We listened as the muscular hocks galloped across the moors, imagined we could hear the thundering of its hooves. Some say the magistrate muttered prayers under his breath as he approached, his hands twitching on the horse's leather reins. Some saw him, dismounting at the edge of the woodland, tying the beast to a gnarled tree trunk. Some say its nostrils flared, hot breath seeping from it like smoke – in that moment, more dragon than horse. Some say the ground squelched beneath his boots, a rug of moss and long-grass, that he felt the sweat settling in the creases of his palms, the uncomfortable turning in his belly. We heard she was asleep when he found her, slumped beneath an alder tree, her mouth hanging open, her eyelids twitching furiously. Some say the blanket she cradled was red. Red. Red. He cleared his throat to wake her: *Mistress Maredudd. Please. Come with me.*

1

1597, Llynidwen, Brecknockshire, Wales

I was crouched near the river when the bleeding began. The blood leaking down my thighs, thin red ribbon creeping a path along my skin and seeping into my stockings. So. Not simply bad sack then, or a cut of undercooked meat, as I'd hoped.

I looked to the horizon for Hywel and his horse but couldn't see them. My husband was likely a long way off by that point, snaring a poor fox or shooting a stag. My stomach churned with a gnawing pain. The idea of a lolling animal carcass, its neck bent like a hook, brought spittle and bile to my mouth.

This time, it had begun only as a small pinch, as though there was a crow trying to peck its way free, but overnight it had become more intense, more difficult to bear, as if something were biting me from the inside.

When the morning came, I snatched up my riding cloak and rushed outside, hastening through the gardens and towards the moors where the grass was stiff and glistening. The urge to get outside, to be in the vast expanse of nature instead of confined within the walls of my home, had been pressing, like a hunger. The cool air was welcome, the crunch of ice beneath my boots satisfying.

A sudden, agonising spasm had brought me to my knees at the river's edge; I feared something was clawing at me, pictured something sinful, a tiny child with teeth and talons cocooned in my belly, fighting desperately to get out.

I sat on the grass at the riverbank, a frosty dew cooling my fingertips, my head reeling with the familiar smell of coins, the slick give between my legs.

Closing my eyes against the bright light of the October sun, I listened to the steady rush of the river for a moment, trying hard to focus on my breath. When I opened them again, a kite had landed on the opposite side of the river. It sat, wings folded, staring at me. Up close, it was bigger than I imagined such a bird would be, even with its wings tucked so neatly at its sides, and just for a moment, I forgot the pain. *Shoo.* I hissed at it. *Go.*

The water was ice-cold as I palmed it from the river to clean my legs. When I was finished, I lay down, and stared at the smear of blood on my hand. It reminded me suddenly of crimson paint streaked from a paintbrush. As a wedding gift, Hywel's parents had commissioned our portrait. That was the first time I'd seen wet paint. We'd posed for hours, holding ourselves stiff for the painting that now hung huge and proud above the fireplace in the hall. I hated the way I looked in it. Like a child dressed in her mother's clothing. Like someone playing pretend.

After a long while, I peeled my body from the frozen ground, stiff and exhausted, using my underskirts to rub my legs dry. The kite was still sitting by the river, watching me with its black marble eyes. It was so close I could see the golden sheen of its feathers. *Shoo,* I hissed again. Still, it didn't move.

I turned to face my home. The manor loomed over the moors, its windows like so many watchful eyes cast in stone, glowering straight at me. The lowering sun threw a dark shadow across the grass, as though the house was reaching out to touch its lands, the hill, the distant line of trees that led towards Llynidwen.

I wondered if the people in the village could see Faen Maredudd from their own homes. If they could sense it, perched high at the brow of the hill looking down at them while they spun their worsted or brewed their ale. If they felt this same chill creeping along their spines when its huge form blocked out the sun.

Back inside, I made my way through the hall, rushing past the turning for the kitchen, where I knew servants would be busy chopping and peeling and cutting and seasoning. Before heading outside, I had sent Ruby, my maid, to help with supper preparations, so that I might be left in peace on my return. Thankfully, she was nowhere to be seen.

Upstairs, I locked the bedroom door, rooted around for a rag to soak up the blood that was still seeping from me, and threw myself on the bed. I curled up in a ball on top of the coverlet, a fox cub, safe and snug in its den.

I drifted into an unsettled sleep, my dreams full of the stampeding hooves of frenzied horses and awoke groggy and hot to a quick banging noise. Horses' hooves...? No. Someone was rapping at the bedchamber door.

'Doli? Open the door.'

I sat up slowly, swinging my legs over the side of the bed and clutching my head. Shadows stretched across the room – it must have been nearing sunset. I took a deep breath, waiting for my vision to clear.

'Doli?'

'Hywel, I'm feeling unwell,' I said, staring at the keyhole of the closed door, hoping he would go away.

'Why? What's wrong?'

'It's nothing. Nothing for you to worry about, at least,' I said, rubbing my temples. 'I need to sleep.'

There was a pause before he asked if he should send for a physician. I told him there was no need. He stayed silent for a moment, and I waited, praying he would do as I'd asked and leave me alone, rather than ignore me and send for someone anyway. A physician would be of no use to me. It was far too late for that.

The last time a physician was called for, he had travelled to us from Hereford, arriving in a shroud of rainwater, advising bed rest and *quiet activity*. He'd barely dismounted his horse before suggesting it had been my fault, that I should have taken to lying in. That had I not preoccupied myself with pruning and digging in the gardens and walking along the moors, things may have been different. I hated him. What sort of woman could stand being confined to her bed for months?

Hywel's voice came again through the door, asking if I wanted broth. My stomach turned at the thought of hunks of grey meat bobbing like corks in scalding water.

When I called back, my '*no*' was unexpectedly thin and high. Why wouldn't he leave me alone? Hywel had been away on business so often recently, frequently spending the night elsewhere. When he was home I felt overwhelmed by his presence. Yes, he was caring, protective, but sometimes ... it could be suffocating. Though I would never have dreamed of telling him so. I knew how fortunate I was to have such a devoted husband. A husband who always seemed to know what was best for me. My mother liked to remind me, almost every time I saw her, that most women of my rank, whose marriages were so often arranged as a matter of business and convenience rather than love, would be grateful for a husband like mine. *You must remember your good fortune, Doli.*

Hywel called through the door again, repeating his question about broth.

'I'm fine. I'll see you downstairs soon for supper.'

He didn't respond immediately, and I closed my eyes, waiting. Hoping he would leave.

'Alright. Send for Ruby if you need anything. She's down in the wash house. I'm riding into the village on business.'

I briefly wondered what business he could be attending to so late in the day – tenants, more than likely – then let myself breathe a sigh of relief, dropping back to the cool comfort of the feather mattress. I closed my eyes. Then, there was a cough, and before I heard his feet marching back down the passageway, he called, 'please, don't lock this door again.'

Still tired, I tried to go back to sleep, pressing my face to the pillow and squeezing my eyes tight. I tossed and turned. I ached. My stomach began cramping again.

It was no use. I got out of bed and looked through the window, squinting towards the river. Far in the distance, over a copse of trees, I could see the faint outline of some of the houses in the village. Hywel owned most of the houses in Llynidwen, which is likely what was keeping him occupied all evening. Who knew when he might return home.

A poem began to take shape in my mind, the letters forming in black ink behind my eyelids.

Mother's love is stamped forever like a waxen seal,
it's another kind of pain, listen to what I feel...

But it was no use. The words wouldn't come. They never did when something like this happened, not at first. I knew I needed to wait for the initial sting of the loss to settle to a dull ache in the hollow of my belly. Then, I might be able to write.

After a while, I was cold, and lay back on the bed, pulling the coverlet over myself, hoping sleep might take the bite from my stomach, and the sadness from my heart.

It was black as pitch by the time Hywel returned, hail pelting at the windows. I went downstairs to greet him – he would grow suspicious if I continued to hide in our bedchamber.

I took his cloak from him, shook the water from it, and watched the droplets collect in the doorway before a servant carried it away to be dried near a fire.

'How was your trip to the village?' I asked.

'It was fine, my little mouse,' he replied. His brown eyes looked almost black in the darkness, and I thought then of the red kite with its huge black eyes. How it had stared at me as I lay shaking on the grass. 'One of our tenants has expired. A sad business. The family haven't been able to pay their rent, of course.'

'What will they do?' I asked him.

He was rubbing his arms, trying to brush the cold from them.

'Well, I went to see them this evening. The widow looked petrified when she opened the door. I do believe she and her daughter thought I'd come to demand payment.'

'But you didn't, did you, Hywel? How will they manage? Where will they go?'

He smiled indulgently at me.

'My Doli, always thinking of others. No, of course I didn't demand any money from them. They are grieving the loss of a good man. I've given them two weeks grace – the daughter should be able to find work during that time. I even took a few pigeon pies for the smaller children. They were most grateful. Particularly given the scarcity of food in the village at the moment.'

Hywel didn't tell me about his business affairs often – he didn't like to bore me with what he called *acquisition and property,* but I found it fascinating to hear about his deals, his conversations. And I was always interested to hear about the villagers, who lived such different lives from us, though they were so close, just the other side of the river.

'You're a good man,' I told him, leaning up to kiss the smooth curve of his chin. There was something unfamiliar in it, something about the way he smelled, or tasted. Like salt and damp earth.

'How are you feeling? Are you well rested?'

'I —' I began, then stumbled over my words, not sure what to tell him. 'I am rested,' I said, finally. I had done nothing but sleep these last few hours, so it was an honest response, despite the pain still lingering in my stomach and the heavy weight that had settled in my chest.

Hywel smiled, pleased, and touched his hand to my cheek.

'Come, it must be time for supper,' he said, taking my hand and leading me towards the hall.

My stomach turned as the servants carried out steaming plates piled high with food. Raisin pottage and meat pies, followed by pheasant and small tarts balanced neatly on a stand. I tried, but I couldn't bring myself to eat.

'What's wrong, Doli?' Hywel asked me, spearing a stringy chunk of beef with his dagger. 'I thought you were feeling better. Aren't you hungry?'

'Not particularly,' I said, watching the pink meat catch between his teeth. As the grease settled on his lips, threatening to run down his chin, I found myself back at the riverbank, watching that slow tendril of blood winding its way down my calves, smearing my damp stockings. My stomach churned.

I couldn't find the courage to tell him. It would taunt him as much as it haunted me, nagging and chattering like a crow at my side, reminding me of my repeated failures. My failure to carry out my duty as a wife. As a woman.

I couldn't do much more than play with the food. Hywel suggested I try something sweet instead, but the pastries and comfits were like dirt in my mouth.

'Doli, you're not yourself. You've barely eaten. You're picking like a little sparrow.'

I tried again to speak, but couldn't get the words to part my lips.

'There's no sense in lying to me. I'm your husband. I know when something's troubling you, darling.'

Was there an edge to his voice, a suggestion that I must tell him what was wrong? That this conversation wasn't negotiable, after all?

I took a deep breath, dropping my spoon to my plate with a clatter that made me flinch, and spoke. I told him what had happened. That it had been like the last time. *My stomach began to cramp, the pains came in waves and then...*

I trailed off, letting the words hang in the air between us. Vowels and consonants dirty as flies over the cooling pies and sweating meats.

I anticipated his usual anger, braced myself for the blow of it. I was ready for the accusations, the questions about what I had done, or had not done, to make this happen. But they didn't come. Instead, his face betrayed only a pained disappointment.

Then he stood up, and came around the table towards me, pressing my cheek tightly to his chest. I felt the hot sting of tears in my eyes, my throat tightening. He told me not to worry.

'When the time is right, and fortune dictates, it will happen. It will be as God intends. For now, we must continue to pray, every day. God will guide our way.'

Peering up at him, his face half in shadow, I asked, 'Do you really believe that?' I found it almost impossible to imagine, after all this time. After all, I had prayed and prayed. I'd prayed until my knees were sore and my mouth dry, and it had never done me any good.

He only bent to kiss the crown of my head in response. A weight lifted from my chest and in that moment I felt my shoulders slacken, my body soften into his like meltwater.

The first time it happened, early in our marriage, we planted a rosebush in the garden as a way to remember. The servants had offered to do it for us, but Hywel and I enjoyed working together, side by side, clawing the soil loose and working the cuttings low into the earth. It took a week to scrub the dirt from beneath my fingernails, but I didn't mind. Now, each time I caught sight of the bush through the bedchamber window, I found myself smiling at the memory of Hywel and I working together, even as the grief stuck like a fishbone in my throat.

Still, despite his reassurances, when I looked at the pottage cooling on the table, cold and congealed, I could see only bloodied sheets and stained skirts. I remembered the water turning pink beneath me, the feeling of giving everything in me over to the land.

When night fell, I couldn't rest. I tossed and turned in bed, feeling the heat rise from Hywel's body beside me. The linens sat warm and thick on my chest.

Perhaps if our conversation at the dinner table had gone differently ... If he had been angry, or blamed me, as I blamed myself, I might have carried an indignant sort of anger of my own, might have gone on as things were, without confiding in anybody else. But his kindness, his understanding, left me more despairing than ever, more desperate than I had ever been to make things work. In that moment, I wanted nothing more than to carry a child – a child Hywel could call his own – to give him a son and heir. To be the wife and mother I was supposed to be.

The Villagers

We went to her alone or in pairs, teeth chattering against the cold. The wind whipping the moors, a frenzied sweep along the river. We shuffled in, eyes widening in the dim of the cottage, smoke curling at our heels. We dropped our satchels at our sides. Often, she would offer ale, but we rarely took it, not wanting to increase our debt to her. We asked for help to protect the livestock – each year, the snow was certain to take a number of our cattle. She handed us a charm scrawled on paper, told us to hang it in the rafters with some cheese from our best cow. Sometimes, the charm would work. Sometimes, it would not. We called her *swynwraig. Hudoles. Witsh.*

A week had passed since the bleeding began, and I found my thoughts caught like a rock in a current. I couldn't help but think, again and again, of the hordes of children in the village, brothers and sisters piled into tiny cottages, sleeping all together on pallets and straw beds, helping their mothers tend the land or churn the ale. Those mothers... how did they manage to carry so many children to term? To survive childbed time and again? To watch their children grow until their limbs were browned and strong as tree trunks?

They certainly weren't *lying in*. They had neither the time nor the luxury. And yet, they bore healthy children over and over, children that helped them fetch firewood or carry their washing to the river, who stood in the church kicking their siblings or squabbling over sticks. Children who had to be hushed, a hand fondly smoothing the backs of their heads, as the minister spoke from his pulpit.

It was at church, one dreary Sunday in late October, that I thought to consult with *her*. On that particular day, our usual minister was accompanied by another man, with eyes dark as a raven's. On his jerkin, he wore a round silver brooch.

As I listened to him deliver his sermon, given in English words most of the congregation wouldn't understand, I let my mind wander, looking around at the faded paintings that had begun to seep through the whitewashed walls in recent years. Muted reds and yellows leering through in blotches, revealing figures from the past. Figures of the old faith, like colourful ghosts all around us, lurking beneath the whitewash, as though to say: *look; we're still here.*

It wasn't until Hywel nudged me, jolting me from my thoughts, that I returned my attention to the man at the front of the church, and tried to focus on his words. He was speaking, then, about *swynwragedd* – soothsayers and enchantresses – insisting their use of holy water and salves were as wicked as sorcery and malice. This was new. Our minister usually spoke simply of kindness, and of caring for our neighbours. It seemed strange to me, that this man had come to speak with such passion and disdain for women who brewed salves and tinctures, who attended births and aided women in their recovery afterwards; women who offered charms and prayers and, sometimes, had the ability to find lost objects, or reveal the name of a betrayer.

At my side, Hywel was nodding his head, slow and subtle, as though in quiet agreement. I frowned at him, questioning, but he didn't turn to look at me, his face focussed only on the man at the pulpit, whose peculiar words were jarring in the church that was so familiar to me.

After all, all villages had healers. Even Llynidwen must, though I'd never met one myself. While the man continued to rail against witches, I began to imagine myself leaning in close and whispering to a woman cloaked in mystery, asking if she could help me to do what no physician ever had. To succeed where prayers had failed.

But it was hopeless even to think of. I had such little involvement in the village, I wouldn't know where to start. Even if I did, the villagers talked and whispered, relentless in their pursuit of gossip. The stories would spread among the congregation before I could stop them. And what would Hywel think? He believed only physicians should attend the sick. Only licensed midwives should be permitted to care for women in childbed. He believed, as so many did, it was best to avert your gaze; to burn the sheets; best not to speak of loss.

As October drew on, I felt I was living in a strange dream-state, wandering through my days in a haze of confusion and grief. The loss had left me depleted, and I found I couldn't settle into anything. I would pick up my embroidery, only to clutch it for a while before placing it down again, or I'd tug on my boots to go out to the moors, only to find myself staring at the dormant rosebush in our garden until the sun was beginning to set, lines of poetry singing in my ears:

Is there a reason only God can see,
that without farewell you should leave me?

15

Ruby knew something was wrong. She must have seen the blood-soaked rags by now – more saturated than they would ordinarily be. She kept a careful distance, looking on with a watchful eye, without asking what had happened. I was grateful for that.

One afternoon as we neared All Hallows, though the air was bone-bitingly cold, the wind ripping through the moors, I suggested a walk around the gardens with Ruby. She agreed, disappearing for a moment then returning with our walking cloaks. Wrapped like parcels against the cold, we stepped outside, passing first the dovecote, then the herb garden, where mint sprigs shrivelled and hardened, waiting for spring.

Ruby mentioned something about the weather, about the frost settling on the muddy flower beds, but I wasn't really listening. I was quiet, bracing myself to ask the question that had buried like an earthworm deep inside of me since the sermon.

'Ruby,' I said, my breath rising like mist as I spoke. 'What do you know of *swynwragedd*?'

'Wise women?' There was a hesitance about her. It sat in the way she lowered her voice, and leaned in conspiratorially, even though there was no one in the gardens with us, besides the blackbirds that darted beneath the hedgerows as we approached, and the robins that perched in the trees overhead. 'You should be careful, speaking like that, even with me.'

'What do you mean?'

Her answer surprised me. It was true – Llynidwen, being nearer to the marches, was different to the village in which Ruby and I had grown up, which sat several miles to the west. Llynidwen saw more pedlars, more trade. Its people were more likely to call for a physician than a minister. Nonetheless, I had found that the slow, settled lives of most Welsh villagers were the same no matter where you travelled in the country, and the people of Llynidwen were as likely to seek a blessing from the clergy as any other village folk were.

'It isn't sensible —' Ruby glanced at me. 'To speak of wise women at the present time.'

'The present time?' I pressed, as we passed the dormant rosebush and headed towards the gate that led out of the gardens and onto the moors. There were no flower heads left, the bush was no more than a knot of brown branches.

'We're living in strange times, mistress,' Ruby said. 'People are beginning to grow suspicious of wise women and soothsayers. There's talk among the villagers of witches.'

'*Witshes*?' Again, her answer had surprised me.

'There's a soothsayer that lives near the village. Her house is on the outskirts close to the lake. But there's talk. People are saying, lately, that she's not a Godly person. There are rumours...' Ruby looked in the direction of the moors, where the stream met the river and wound its way towards the village.

'Rumours?' I pressed. I couldn't help but picture rumours as little living creatures, darting around like the tadpoles that swarmed the stream each spring. 'What do you mean?'

'People say Sara Gwen is a *witsh*,' she said simply.

The name sounded familiar to me – *Sara Gwen* – but I couldn't place it. Besides, I couldn't imagine anyone living in the village could be a real witch, capable of magic beyond healing salves and prayers. Witches – real witches – were said to meet with the devil at night. To dance naked with him. I felt the heat rise to my cheeks at the very thought of it.

'Not only that,' Ruby went on, as we passed through the gate. Now we were beyond the bounds of the house and its grounds, a weight seemed to lift from her. Her hesitance dissipated like the fog on our breath, and I had the sense she was enjoying herself, basking in this reversal of roles, in her ability to educate me, for once. 'She's a church papist. Everybody knows when she does attend service, it's only to avoid recusancy fines. Her home is filled with Catholic relics. At least, that's what's being said.'

What does that matter? I nearly said the words aloud, but didn't. In truth, Ruby was more like a sister to me than my own sister, who was ten years my senior, and had moved to live with her husband when I was still very young. When my sister left to begin her own family, my father had arranged for Ruby to come and live with us, to act as a companion for me and a help for my mother. Her father had done some business with mine, and they became friends, so the arrangement was easy enough – I gained a friend and confidante, of sorts, and her parents were able to take a tenancy in a bigger house with the salary Ruby sent home. I couldn't imagine how I would have managed the move from my family home into Hywel's without her by my side.

But still, I was always acutely aware of the need to remain proper in her company. Though she had been my companion since childhood, she remained in our employ. I didn't want to suggest I might harbour any Catholic sympathies. I didn't want to say anything, for that matter, that might make its way back to the kitchens, or be echoed in the alehouse.

'Ruby, you must keep what I am about to tell you to yourself.' I glanced at her, noticing the shadow waxing across her cheek now that evening was drawing close. It was growing colder, but we had to have the conversation now before heading back inside, where it felt as though the walls were always listening, the doorways speaking in creaks and sighs. I took a deep breath. 'I'm in need of a wise woman to help me to...' Here, I paused, considering my words. 'To do what I have not yet been able to. To carry Hywel's child. To bear a healthy heir.'

Ruby was silent for a while, watching the robins flitting in and out of their nests above our heads. Their middles were tauntingly round, swollen with fat stores for winter.

'Ruby? You must understand. Physicians have been of no use. No midwife has helped me. I have prayed and prayed until my lips were dry, my knees sore. I've asked God. I've begged. It has done nothing.'

'Forgive me mistress,' she began. 'Perhaps the problem lies not with you —'

I interrupted her – 'I'm afraid I don't understand you.' *Don't say it, Ruby. Please.*

'Only, perhaps the problem lies elsewhere.' She shifted uncomfortably.

'Don't be absurd Ruby. The problem cannot lie with a man, if that's what you're implying. Hywel has put a baby in me several times. The children don't quicken. When they do, it doesn't last long. It's me – my body – that has failed us, each time.'

I didn't need to tell her she had spoken out of turn.

'Now, tell me more about this soothsayer – Sara Gwen?' I asked, as we turned to retrace our steps in the rapidly gathering dusk. Suddenly, we were faced with the huge shadow of home, darkening the grass at our feet.

'There isn't much more to tell,' she said eventually. 'She has worked as a midwife, though an unlicensed one, I know that much. But, mistress, you *must* stay away from her. As I said, there is too much talk at the present time.' Too much talk. Talk was currency in Llynidwen, where filthy beggars carried rumours like coins from farmhouse to farmhouse. The right words could pay for milk, pottage, flour. I knew I needed to be careful. But even so, I couldn't believe a real witch had been allowed to cast charms and curses over the village without recourse.

When I didn't say anything, Ruby continued.

'She lives beside a great rowan tree. There's even been rumours of her carving a broomstick from its branches.'

Without meaning to, I laughed. Ruby was not usually so quick to judge those who didn't attend church service, or held the old faith.

'Are broomsticks not still used to show that there is fresh ale for sale within? Perhaps she likes to keep her floors swept and clean? I didn't think you believed in fairy tales and children's stories of witches and ghouls, Ruby.'

I sounded more confident than I felt. I knew as well as anyone – rumours didn't come from nowhere.

She stopped walking then, and turned to look at me.

'Perhaps you've misunderstood me, mistress. Sara Gwen is

capable. She can help those who go to her. She must have a great power. But the villagers are powerful too. Talk is rife. I've heard whispers and rumours – so many of them. There's been trouble in the marches. Hangings, over the border. Women swinging. You don't want to be tangled up in any of it. It's too dangerous. And the master would...' she trailed off, but she didn't need to finish her sentence.

'But Ruby, what if –'

The look on Ruby's face stopped me from finishing my sentence.

'Mistress. If what they say is true, Sara Gwen is a powerful woman. But power must come from somewhere.'

'I won't seek her out, Ruby, please don't worry. I was only curious.'

Ruby's shoulders slackened – she was visibly relieved by my promise. As we passed the dormant rosebush again, I ran my hand along the length of a brittle stem.

Ah.

'What is it?' Ruby asked.

I held my hand out to her, showing her the bead of blood billowing there. 'I pricked my finger.'

The sudden sight of the blood left me dizzy. I held my thumb to my lips, sucking it clean, and found that the taste didn't bother me as it once would have.

Over the next few days, Ruby's words chimed like music in my ears: *perhaps the problem lies elsewhere ... she's a capable woman ... Power must come from somewhere...* Despite Ruby's warnings, I couldn't free myself of the thought of seeking out Sara Gwen. In truth, the possibility that someone might have the power to help me, after all this time ... it was a temptation I couldn't resist.

It was snowing, the white specks cascading around me as I crossed the moors, my boots sinking in the wet ground. My feet were heavy and slow, my toes bitten with frost. I followed the river south, towards the village, but didn't continue on the path that would have led to the farmhouses and market square, as I was accustomed to doing. Instead, I turned, taking the path that continued alongside the river, wrapping itself around the village. Each time the thought of Hywel learning about the visit entered my mind, I swept it away, walking more quickly as though I could outpace the worry.

I couldn't be sure, but something Ruby had said had given me a good idea as to where the house might be. There was only one rowan tree at the edge of the open heathlands. I reasoned it was as good a place as any to begin my search.

Here, the houses were further apart, the space between them stretching with cold, cracked earth and hard snow. Icy wells collected frost at their lips, and I idly wondered how the scattered families along this path collected enough water to drink when the cold set in. Above me, red kites swooped and circled. The dark cut of the birds in the sky was like letters inked over a page, poetry.

After walking for some time, I found the rowan tree I'd been looking for. The house was just as I had pictured – a white stone cottage tucked neatly beside the tree, bordered by a small fence. The gate creaked, resisting my attempts to push it open. As I walked towards the front door, my skirt snagged on overgrown brambles, small glistening thorns hooking the material as though trying to hold me back. A single rat darted from beneath the hedges when I tugged myself free, and for a moment, I wavered. Was this the right thing to do? Even now, I wasn't sure. After all, if Sara Gwen was a witch, this was a sin. I looked upwards at the rolling clouds, as though expecting to see the great, looming face of God looking down at me.

Too late. The door swung open before I could decide whether or not to rap my knuckle against it, as though the woman behind it had known I was there. Waiting. *This was her then.*

Sara Gwen was younger than I had imagined – perhaps in her fortieth year – and taller too. There was a certain strength about her, something that lay in her broad shoulders and straight nose, and I felt instantly nervous, suddenly conscious of how small my frame was in comparison. Hywel had always said my big eyes made me appear like a child's doll, rather than a grown woman. When we first married, I liked it, being his little doll. But by now, on occasion, there was something about the sentiment that troubled me.

'Can I help you?' Sara was staring at me. It was then, on that first meeting, that I noticed her eyes. They seemed to change colour as they caught the light.

'Yes,' I said, drawing my cloak firmly about my shoulders and trying to stand a little taller. Prouder. 'I think so.' As she stood back and gestured for me to enter, a rat lunged over my feet, trailing blood across the earth behind it. I squealed. Regained myself. 'Yes, may I come in?'

The cottage smelled of freshly cut mint, wet earth and something else less pleasant. A large pan sat above the fire at the centre of the room, just beginning to boil. The water burbled and spat.

Sara's cottage was the smallest I had set foot in. I had considered my childhood home to be humble – I'll never forget moving to Faen Maredudd, with Ruby like a faithful spaniel at my side, and discovering the maze of passageways and bedrooms, the multiple staircases – but this was smaller by far.

She gestured for me to sit at a small table near the fire, and I slipped my cloak from my shoulders, looking around for somewhere to place it before folding it over my lap. As I took in Sara's thin smock, I wished I had left my cloak on. My dress of taffeta and lace – a gift from Hywel, was out of place, here. Perhaps I was, too. *I shouldn't have come.*

She seemed to be waiting for me to speak, but I struggled to find the right words. The polite thing to have done, of course, would have been to introduce myself, but I was hesitant. Anxious.

'I heard that you —' I trailed off, looking away from Sara and staring instead towards the fire.

She stayed quiet, waiting. I felt her eyes on my face, as though she was studying me, and squirmed quietly in my seat. I couldn't shake the feeling that she already knew who I was. What I wanted.

'I heard that you might be able to brew me something —' I tried again, my face still turned firmly towards the fire, fixed on the flames licking the pan. 'Something to aid...' I took a deep breath, closing my eyes. I was conscious now of my stomach, flat as a river stone. I could not express how much, in that moment, I wished it would bloom to fullness, grow round and large as a drum. Heavy with new life.

'Ah,' Sara replied, nodding, though I hadn't finished speaking. Her voice was soft as butter. 'Yes. I thought that might be the case.'

Surprised, I glanced up. The amber flames danced and gambolled in her eyes, like foxes in the night. Suddenly, I felt the words tumbling from me before I could stop them. In the weeks that followed, I wondered if she had been performing some sort of sorcery to extract the secrets from within me. It was so easy to speak to her, to confide in her. Once I started, I couldn't stop.

'I have been with child in the past, several times, but it's never progressed. At least, the babes have never made it far beyond the quickening. I'm nearing three and twenty and I fear if I haven't managed to birth a healthy child by now —', here I stopped, looked around, almost scared to speak the words out loud – 'Well ... maybe I never will.'

Sara smiled. Made a dismissive noise. A cluck of the tongue.

'Tssk. You're practically a child yourself. I've helped women much older than you to carry perfectly healthy babes.'

The relief was intense and immediate.

'And can you help me too?'

She looked me up and down, and I wondered how I must appear to her – the long, light hair pulled tight behind my ears and hidden beneath my cap. Leather boots, freshly greased with calf oil that same morning, now warming my feet despite the meltwater on top, and the dirty snow crusted beneath them. The taffeta dress I was so desperate to hide.

'I will do what I can,' Sara replied. 'Tell me, what is your name?'

'Doroli. Doli.' My name sounded strange and out of place, uttered in the small, dim cottage. 'But please, you can't tell anyone that I was here, or what I've asked of you.'

'Of course not,' Sara said. 'I do not speak of others' business.'

I searched her face for sincerity, trying to decide whether or not I could trust her. Whether she was a wise woman or a witch. Whether or not there was any difference.

'My husband cannot – must not – know,' I said, more firmly. 'It's of the utmost importance.'

Sara raised a palm to silence me. I was taken aback by the brazenness of her gesture. No woman had ever silenced me before. But she smiled, and after a moment, I decided that the gesture was well-meant. Reassuring.

'The master will never know,' she said gently. So, she did know who I was. 'Nothing discussed within the walls of my home ever crosses that threshold.' She indicated the doorway with a tip of her chin. 'Not through my lips, at least – that, I can promise you. Now,' she said more briskly. 'Tell me a little more about the problem?'

I told her about the pregnancies that had come before, the way my belly began to grow then flattened again almost immediately. The way my body stubbornly refused to hold the shape of motherhood. The blood. The sweat. The pain like a dagger at my stomach. My words were like water tipped straight from a bucket, flowing and clear. It was freeing, the way the truth spilled from me. It should have felt strange to be having this conversation with a stranger, to be speaking so openly about my marriage and my troubles to anyone other than Hywel, or perhaps Ruby, but as I spoke, I felt a dizzying sense of relief. It was almost as though I'd had far too many cups of wine, though I hadn't had anything but a small cup of ale with my breakfast.

I nearly told her about how preoccupied, how distant Hywel had become over the years since we married. How I had felt him withdraw from me, like a waning moon. How he had become consumed by verse and scripture. How he spent hours each evening in the parlour, engaged in work I was not privy to. Writing letters.

Reading from his Bible. That in the weeks since the last loss, the distance had grown even greater. Before the words could leave me, I remembered myself. Held back.

'Perhaps it's something within me,' I finished, quietly. 'Perhaps I'm destined never to be a mother.' There it was. The truth of my feelings slipping free.

'Tell me, do you share a bed with your husband?'

I nodded, the heat of embarrassment licking like flames at my cheeks.

'We enjoy each other's company.'

The words sounded false even to my own ears.

Sara stood up and busied herself, scooping water from the pot over the fire. I took a moment to look around. On the sideboard I noticed a brass carving, showing a man, arms spread wide, a cloth wrapped about his lower body. It was a depiction of Iesu Grist. Jesus Christ. A bell turned on its side – it seemed to be missing its clapper. I wondered if it had been removed, or if it had simply worn down and broken away. I wondered if it meant anything at all. Besides them, a scattering of yellow petals, maybe tansy, was the only real colour in the cottage. Sara moved towards a barrel at the other side of the room, leaning against it to scrawl something on a piece of paper.

'This should work for you.' She handed me the paper, along with a sealed bottle, stoppered with beeswax. 'Hide the charm somewhere near your bed, then douse the bed linens in this water.'

'What's in it?'

'Water from my well. I've blessed it. It has an infusion of herbs and petals and some ground cyclamen root. It'll help.'

I examined the bottle, held it up to look at the clear liquid inside.

'Somewhere near the bed?' I asked. 'Like under the mattress?'

Without meaning to, I glanced towards the straw mound which made up her bed, pressed close to the wall, noting how uncomfortable it looked compared with my feather mattress and thick cotton coverlet.

She nodded.

'And it will work? I'll conceive? And the baby will survive?' I flinched at the desperation that had seeped into my own voice. The eagerness with which the words came.

She nodded again. That was when she made her promise: *'You will be with child before the frost thaws.'*

The Villagers

And so, it went like this – or so we heard. Sara Gwen at home in her *bwthyn*, below the rowan tree on the outskirts of the village, water hissing in a pot on the fire. An infusion of mint leaves and steam stinging the air. Perhaps she was scratching the devil's mark in her door. Perhaps she was rubbing a salve at her temples. The girl went to her then. A quiet tap at the door, like a robin pecking its entrance. Perhaps she knew the girl, the small face, the big eyes dark as a crow's, the upturned nose. Perhaps she recognised her as the gentlewoman whose husband owned Faen Maredudd and all its surrounding land. Perhaps she did not. Perhaps she asked *can I help you?* Some say the girl hesitated before crossing the threshold, and perhaps said *please, may I come in?* Perhaps she was nervous. Perhaps Sara had seen her at church, dressed in her finery and speaking with the minister after his sermons, though most say Sara doesn't attend church often, shunning the new ways, choosing to cloak herself in the past. Some say Sara prefers the freedom of pilgrimage, the wonder of visiting St Winifred's Well, the company of other villagers who, like her, grew up with the Catholic doctrine. Others say she worships the land, dancing bare amongst the trees each night, the chill wind biting her breasts.

November's cold was cruel. Bitter. Hywel was withdrawn – his words were comforting but his manner was as frosted as the ground outside, stiff as the ungiving grass and hardened moors. Despite his reassurances, his insistence that he too, longed for a baby as desperately as I did, we'd only been intimate once since the miscarriage.

Late one evening, as Hywel and I were lying in bed, the linens and coverlets piled around us in an attempt to keep warm, I reached over to him, running my hand along the length of his thigh.

He pushed it away.

'Doli, I'm studying my prayer book.' He spoke without looking at me.

In that moment, I saw his face as though it were new to me. The beginnings of faint lines running like lightning from the corners of his eyes, though he was not yet thirty. The way dark hair clung to his nostrils, as though spiders had made their home there.

'Hywel? Things have been ... strained between us lately,' I said, quietly.

'Hmm?' Again, he didn't look at me, his eyes still fixed on his scriptures. It was happening again, as it always did – each new loss dampened the spark between us, dragging him further away.

'Hywel?' I said, propped up on one elbow, pleading with him to look at me, to touch me as he used to, in the early years of our marriage.

'Not now, Doli. I need to pray. As should you.'

I rolled onto my side and stared at the drapes that hung around the bed until my eyes stung with tears.

Less than a week later it started to snow again. Hywel had ridden somewhere that evening – I wasn't even sure where – leaving me once again to my quiet sadness. He had been keeping a careful distance, often coming to bed long after the sun had set and the servants had settled in the hall for the night, so I was relieved when an old friend appeared at the door of Faen Maredudd.

'Rhys!' I said, when he was shown inside, interrupting Ruby and me. 'You are welcome, of course, but I'm afraid Hywel isn't here.'

'Not to worry,' he brushed some flakes from his shoulders. 'I was passing by when the snow started, I thought I'd best rest my horse. May I sit awhile?'

I dismissed Ruby and gestured for Rhys to join me. I didn't know whether or not Hywel had spoken to him about the most recent loss, and I couldn't bring myself to discuss it, not even with Rhys, who I'd known for almost as long as I'd known Hywel. A childhood friend of the Maredudd family, he and my husband were like brothers, and it showed in their easy manner with one another. If it weren't for their starkly different appearances, one might have thought the pair related. But where Hywel was tall and broad with dark hair and brown eyes, Rhys was much shorter, his hair light as a hay bale, his eyes pale blue. A smattering of freckles dusted his nose, even then, in deepest winter when the sun was loath to make an appearance.

Growing up, Rhys had always looked out for me, and took care to include me when he could. To this day he treated me as if I were an equal, with that comforting, caring warmth that often comes with old friendship. He was a welcome sight that evening. A distraction.

We sat in the parlour together talking as the snow fell outside, waiting for the weather to settle. I called for a jug of wine. Then another.

It was freeing, listening to Rhys talk about his travels and his trade, to think of something other than my baby, lost at the river's edge. That awful outpour of blood.

'Tell me, Doli. Have you come across the verses of Gwerful Mechain?' he asked, pulling a small book from his pocket. 'I've been recording them.'

The poems he read to me then were amongst some of the most astounding I'd ever heard. I fell in love with her words, instantly. *And the churchmen all, the radiant saints ... When they get the chance, have no restraints.*

The provocative verses left me flushing, furiously pink in the firelight. The way she wrote about the body and its pleasures, and also about Christ's passions, as though the two subjects were part of her, inseparable, was unlike anything I'd heard performed. Several times, I glanced towards the door, worried someone might overhear us.

We spoke for some time about the technical difficulty of it, the clever ways in which she often used her rhyme and her wit to imply more than one meaning.

'I wonder how she learned her craft?' I said. 'I've never heard of a woman writing with such structure and skill.'

'She was married,' Rhys said, looking at me, unblinking. 'But some of her poems imply she had a lover. A man by the name of Dafydd Llwyd. He was a poet too. I suspect he taught her. From what I can gather, she also spent much of her time around bards and performances. Here, listen to this.'

He read me a short poem then about a wet petticoat, about how it was drenched, 'wet and manky.'

In four lines Gwerful showed such astonishing mastery for rhyme and repeated letter sounds. The words left me giddy.

'You see how she adapts the strict form to her own advantage?' he said, marvelling at the page before him.

'Rhys,' I said, quietly.

'Yes?'

The heat of the flames, or perhaps it was the wine, was inching its way along my spine, teasing, stinging my neck.

'I have been writing poems of my own for some time now.' I spoke softly, feeling the thrill of the confession catch in my throat.

He looked at me, studying my face with intent, while I held myself still and steady, the fuzz of wine rounding the edges of my thoughts.

'That's extraordinary, Doli,' he beamed. 'What do you write about?'

I looked away, uncertain how much to tell him.

'I write about whatever strikes me,' I said, after a pause. 'Unlike the bards who perform their work, I don't have to sing for my supper, Rhys. I have the freedom to write about love and loss and desire and the beauty of the wind in the trees. The kites in the sky.'

I was giddy with the thought of it. Rhys laughed, then said, 'I wonder ... how does Hywel feel about this?'

Hywel. I chewed over his question, unsure how to answer. Hywel enjoyed listening to the bards, and wrote poetry of his own, and yet, I'd felt too shy to share my secret with him. I was worried he would laugh, or think my verses unsophisticated. He would tell me to stop, that writing wasn't a suitable pursuit for a woman.

'Perhaps I'll show him, one day.'

'Well, I think it's marvellous. Perhaps you would show me?'

I was hot, embarrassed.

'I did write something this morning,' I said. 'About the winter.' I took a deep breath, then recited my poem:

Chill wind whipping all around,
frost glistening on the frozen ground,
and what lies quiet, in deathly sleep...?
This stiffened, long forgotten sheep.

Afterwards, we sat in silence for a while, sipping from our cups and enjoying the snap and crackle of the fire, the comfortable quiet between us.

'I'm not sure the snow is going to stop any time soon,' I said, looking through the window at the swirling white flecks, trying to centre myself. 'Perhaps you should stay. I'll call Ruby to make up a bed for you.'

The Villagers

Some say the mistress struggles to keep children alive in the womb because the master's member is weak. Some say it's because she eats too much lamb. Drinks too much wine. Sits too often in stillness, reading poetry by candlelight. Why do you think the poor have more children? It's because they are seldom idle. Some say she copulates too often, and some say the problem is the act itself. That she defies nature. They say the master's seed cannot be sown because she sits atop his naked body as though he were a horse she set out to ride. They say she lets him know her from behind like a hound. It is unnatural. Wicked. Sinful. It's the way witches perform their dark acts with the devil.

November darkened into December and I found my mind still clouded with sadness and grief. The daylight was short, the nights black as coal and long as years. The chill in the air made even Faen Maredudd, with its many fires, thick stone walls and glass windows, bitingly cold, especially at night. The draughts whistling beneath the doorways were more bitter than usual, prompting the maids to stuff coverlets and linens in the empty spaces to stifle the sting of it.

It wasn't only the cold weather which ailed me. I found myself needing to lie down in the afternoons, with little energy to walk outside. I hadn't written a word of poetry in weeks, despite Rhys' encouragement. A strange and lingering sickness had settled in my stomach since the loss, and each time I peered into the looking glass above my bedroom chest, I found I'd grown more pale and drawn, my face thin as a skinned hare. My eyes like full moons. I didn't know whether it was the result of the loss, a long, tiresome winter sickness, or something else entirely. Perhaps, there was cause to hope … But I couldn't let my mind go there. Not yet.

Christmastide passed in a haze of cake, sweetmeats, mutton, veal, cheese, apples, freshly baked bread and good drink. Though the harvest had been poor this year, we were lucky – Hywel had friends across the country, and enough money to buy what we needed. There was Christmas cake flavoured with honey, ginger and pepper, which the kitchens had prepared weeks before, allowing the spices to mature as the ice set in outside.

Fires blazed in the hearth, and Faen Maredudd was suddenly filled with laughter and cheeks pinched pink as rose petals with merriment and ale. For some of the poorest of Llynidwen, hunkering at the side of our fire, spiced wine in their hands, would be their only solace this winter, and it cheered me to see them gathered there, enjoying the heat of the flames. *Croeso i chi gyd. You are all so welcome.*

And yet, I was unable to enjoy the celebrations as I usually would, dancing only half-heartedly to the fiddles and trumpets in the hall, the cut of boar's head churning in my stomach. I lurked at the edges of the festivities, wanting only to retire to my bedchamber, to pull the bedclothes over myself and embrace the darkness.

I thought obsessively of Sara's charm, and whether or not it would work. Whether maybe it had already. When I walked in the gardens, amongst the brittle branches and frozen thorns, or out on the icy cold moors, I looked at the shards of ice in the river, or at the hardened ground, and wondered when the frost might thaw.

I was working on my embroidery when Hywel reminded me we would be entertaining again that evening, in celebration of Twelfth Night. He'd invited Rhys, as well as several other guests, to dinner, and enlisted the services of a pair of bards.

'Our guests will be here near sundown,' he told me. 'Had you forgotten?' I hadn't – we hosted the bards often during the festive seasons. Hywel had even commissioned poems of his own in the years since we'd been married, once as an anniversary gift to me, once for his mother, in celebration of her birthday. Although I always enjoyed watching the performances, the thought of entertaining again this evening was unwelcome.

Still, I made an effort to smile at him, and placed my sewing to one side.

'Of course not, I'm just tired. Honestly Hywel, I'm not sure at the moment which day of the week it is from one day to the next. And I must admit, last year didn't give us much to celebrate. I'm glad to see it ended.'

Between the grief and the cold, November and December had felt sharp as daggers. In the week since Christmastide, I'd been exhausted, and Hywel had been away on business more times than I would have liked, leaving me to pace the house alone, feeling for all the world like an animal trapped inside by the vicious weather and howling winds.

Early in our marriage, I would find these frequent business trips difficult. Although I had Ruby for company, she was often needed in the kitchens, and I was accustomed to having Hywel's parents in the home during my first few years at Faen Maredudd, and to living with my own parents before that. Being by myself was another new skill I had to learn, as wife and mistress of the manor. By now, I was used to the time alone while my husband was away, but I longed for his company nonetheless.

Hywel strode across the parlour to me, frowning, and placed his hands at my temples.

'Then we are celebrating the beginning of a new year; a year of property, new acquisitions. Endless joy,' he said. 'Doli, are you quite well? You feel warm.' He adjusted his hands, feeling around my forehead and pressing his palms to my cheeks.

'I'm fine,' I told him, trying to smile. I was clammy. Nauseous. 'December was long and tiresome, and Christmastide was so busy. *Dyna'i gyd.*'

I longed for the frost to thaw. For the spring to blossom and bloom on the moors. I looked through the window at our gardens, dreaming of the sun's warmth on my skin, wondering when the first snowdrops might break through the soil.

I was so lost in thoughts of spring, that Hywel's voice startled me when he spoke again.

'Be ready soon, Doli *fach.*'

I turned away from the window and smiled up at him.

'Of course. Will the bards be joining us for supper?' I asked.

'Not this time my little mouse. They've sent word assuring me they will be well fed at Plas Mawr. They stayed last night with the Herberts. Still, I've asked the cook to keep a couple of her curlew pies aside. I'm sure they'll be in need of something after such a long journey here.'

'Yes,' I replied. 'What a good idea.'

As the sky began to darken, I went downstairs, smoothing my gown over my stomach as I walked, trying to flatten the creases. Approaching the hall I heard deep voices, carrying in quick, excited conversation.

Hywel and Rhys were standing in the centre of the hall, deep in discussion. Both turned to greet me as I entered.

'Doli.' Rhys stepped towards me, his arms extended. 'How do you fare?'

'I'm quite well, Rhys. I'm looking forward to the evening's celebrations.'

I turned to look around the hall, wondering who else Hywel had invited to supper. There was John Wynn, who had recently finished his tenure as sheriff of Meirioneth, accompanied by his eldest son, also John, a boy on the cusp of manhood. They were engaged in conversation with Hywel's parents, whom I hadn't seen in some time. His mother looked tired and tight-lipped. Perhaps the journey had left her feeling depleted – they would have travelled from the north, some forty miles on horseback. Then again, perhaps that was allowing her too much kindness – she often looked as though she'd been forced to shovel the stables herself. As I watched John Wynn and his son speaking with the same excited expression, the curve of their chins identical, I wondered what our child might have looked like. What would we have named a son, had I managed to reach childbed? I imagined Hywel would have been pleased for his son to bear his name.

My own parents were standing together at the far end of the room, examining the fireplace, where the Maredudd coat of arms was carved in sprawling detail. I made my way over to them, pleased to see that both their cheeks were plump and glowing in the firelight.

'Mam, Dadi,' I said, leaning forward to embrace first my mother, then my father. 'How are you both? You look well.'

My mother scowled.

'I fear the same cannot be said for you, Doli,' she replied, frowning. *Of course.* 'You look a little gaunt, not unlike a sparrow. Have you been eating enough? Do Hywel's servants not feed you well?' She glanced over at my husband, who was still deep in conversation with Rhys at the other side of the hall. A smile played about her lips but I was irritated by the comment nonetheless. She had been so keen for me to marry into the Maredudd family, but seemed determined to find fault whenever the opportunity presented itself.

'*Our* servants feed us perfectly well,' I said. 'In fact, Hywel hunts so well, we often have more than we can eat by ourselves.' Yes, the land had failed to yield as many radishes and parsnips as usual, given the intensely cold winter, but I would polish all the silver in the house myself before letting my mother know that. And it was true, Hywel had continued to provide enough meat to feed us plentifully. 'I've been a little out of sorts over the last few weeks, but it's nothing to worry about.'

'Well, it's very good to see you, Doli *fach*.' My father's eyes crinkled at the corners as he spoke. 'Very good indeed.' His hair had become thinner about his head, his beard more speckled with greys and whites. Had it really been that long since I'd seen him last?

'Are you waiting on any more guests to arrive?' my mother asked. She was still looking over towards Hywel. 'Your husband keeps looking towards the door.'

I turned, catching him just as he turned back towards Rhys. She was right – his eyes were flicking intermittently towards the doorway that led from the hall to the entryway.

'I don't know,' I replied, truthfully. 'I'm never sure who Hywel has invited to Faen Maredudd.' Perhaps I should have taken more interest, but I didn't have the same social aspirations as Hywel. He was always the most gracious host. Mam often said his generosity would be important in securing a higher position in society. Perhaps she was right. She usually was about these things.

My mother half shrugged, and turned back to the fireplace. She ran her fingers delicately along the carved shield, the eagle wings spread at the centre.

'Oh I've always adored the Maredudd crest,' she sighed. She said the same thing each time she looked at it.

My father rolled his eyes.

'You should consider panelling these walls, you know,' she continued, barely noticing my father. 'It's becoming more and more fashionable. I hear Catrin Parry has had it done.'

Mam and her preoccupation with appearances. Trends and fashions. Oyster tables. Tapestries. She'd always insisted on keeping abreast of the current styles, refusing to be outdone by any other family, if she could help it.

Not long after my grandfather had died, when my parents were negotiating my marriage to Hywel – and securing their own position in the Maredudd family, of course – Mam insisted on replacing every tallow candle in the house with wax, and serving only the best wine. Our log fires went unlit for several weeks afterwards.

Don't worry, Doli, she would say. *We have our name, and that is worth far more than money.*

When she had sauntered from the room, my father would mutter, *a name's not much use when those who possess it have frozen to death with a belly full of good wine.*

Mam was, of course, right about our name, though. Hywel's parents came to an easy agreement with my own, and I moved to Faen Maredudd not long afterwards.

The door to the hall opened wide, and in strode a handsome, bearded man. He looked to be about the same age as my father but he was dressed in finery, the ruff collar wide about his neck, his doublet gleaming silver grey like a winter moon.

Hywel cleared the hall in an instant, rushing to clasp his hand.

'Sir Thomas Mostyn,' he gushed, cheeks flushing pink. His voice was loud enough to carry across the hall to me. 'We, that is, myself and my wife —' here, he glanced at me, silently gesturing for me to go to him. 'Are honoured to host you. We were not sure you'd come, given how busy you seem to be.'

I took my place at his side and smiled sweetly. Always the docile mistress. *Such a pleasure to receive you, sir.*

'May I introduce my wife and lady of Faen Maredudd, my dearest Doli.'

'A pleasure,' the man replied, taking my hand in his and kissing the back of it. I was surprised by the smoothness of his lips against my skin, the sharp bristle of beard. Hywel had always been barefaced. The hair felt strange, unfamiliar. 'You are a sight for sore eyes, my dear.'

He was smiling, and yet ... There was something unnerving about him, something that left my tongue feeling dry in my mouth.

'Doli,' Hywel turned to me. 'This is Sir Thomas, our esteemed guest this evening.' Did I detect a small emphasis on the *sir?* I was startled, left momentarily speechless that a man of his nobility would choose to spend Twelfth Night with us, with Hywel and Rhys discussing land and trade, and my mother pining over wall panelling.

'It is truly my honour to be here,' he said smoothly. 'Please, accept my apologies for not having confirmed my attendance in advance – I have been, as you say, particularly busy. Happily, it happens that I was passing through Llynidwen on my way back to Gloddaith from the south. An evening in fine company with some bardic entertainment will serve me very well indeed. I don't believe I've seen the bards perform since I was a boy!'

Hywel beamed, and clapped his hands together. The sound echoed around the hall. I felt it in my teeth.

'Excellent!' he said. 'Well, now that we're all here, let's eat!'

Over supper, snippets of conversation and gossip reached me from around the table – the Mansels were planning to purchase another disused abbey; Roger ap Llwyd's son was away in London, studying the law. Again, I couldn't help but close my eyes and think of the son I might have borne. I pictured Hywel, handsome and strong. Myself rounding at his side. Then, eventually, a son with Hywel's dark hair. Would he, too, have travelled across the border? Gone to London for a season or two? Of course, he would have inherited our land, eventually.

From what I could hear from the conversation between my

mother and Hywel's, the Queen was unhappy with a member of her privy council, for disobeying orders and leaving the coast undefended. John Wynn was deep in quiet, almost whispered, conversation with Sir Thomas, much to Hywel's annoyance, and my father was regaling Hywel's father with an intense tale about hunting rabbits.

I returned my attention to Hywel, who was sitting to my side at the head of the table, and Rhys, perched on a bench directly opposite me. We talked of what changes we hoped the year might bring, each of us wishing for better fortune than we'd seen over the last.

'A number of sheep lost without trace and three cows dead of frost. That's all I have to show for the year,' Rhys said, shaking his head. 'And it's not only me who suffers. All across the county, crops are failing. The cold is too harsh. Nothing is thriving.' He sighed heavily, before catching my eye. 'It's enough to drive one to seek out a sorceress.' I felt the sharp intake of breath. Did he know? How could he? There was a twinkle in his eyes, however, and the hint of a smile twitched across his lip. *It was in jest, Doli, that's all.*

Hywel spluttered, almost choking on a mouthful of mutton pie. He took a long draught of wine to regain himself.

'Forgive me, but Rhys, whatever do you mean?' he said, once he'd recovered himself.

Rhys winked at me, and I allowed myself a small smile in return. *He doesn't know. You're safe.*

'Be calm Hywel,' he said flippantly, spearing a chunk of pink meat with his dagger. 'I'm speaking only in jest. Have you no fun about you this evening, man?'

'Of course,' Hywel flashed a tight smile. 'I only meant, well, surely even joking about such affairs is not wise, not at the moment.' He glanced nervously over towards Sir Thomas. 'You must have heard of the arrests made in Denbighshire? A woman was hanged.'

'Hanged?' I was emboldened by my third cup of wine, its heat rising in my chest. 'Whatever for?'

'Murder by witchcraft.' Hywel aimed a pointed stare in his friend's direction, but Rhys barely seemed to notice.

'And you, Hywel, must have heard of the way these so-called wise women carry on in these parts? But they are harmless, really – Catholics, most of them, as well as those that go to them for their...' he trailed off, pushing meat around his plate as though searching for the correct words in amongst the wet pastry. 'Services,' he said finally. 'Perhaps they should not be spoken of so flippantly. Still, we can't pretend they don't exist.'

Hywel remained quiet. The silence was heavy, hanging in the air like a veil.

'I'm sorry about your cows, Rhys.' I took another sip of wine, feeling the warmth of it in my throat. 'But please, I'm curious. Murder by witchcraft seems such a strange charge. What happened?'

Rhys glanced at Hywel, as though looking for permission to speak.

'You'd have to ask Sir Thomas,' he said. At this, Hywel's face reddened. I looked to where Sir Thomas was sitting, but he was still deep in conversation and didn't appear to have heard us speaking about him.

'I'm really not sure it's worth troubling yourself with the details, Doli my dear. It will only serve to frighten you.'

I felt my cheeks flush, hot with the sting of wine and Hywel's words. He was only a few years my senior, yet his constant dismissals never failed to make me feel like a child. Admittedly, I couldn't understand his world of business, trading and property – how could I, when I did little more than sit at home busying myself with embroidery, or walking the moors. How could I know anything of the world beyond the bounds of Faen Maredudd when my husband insisted on shielding me from anything of interest? Not for the first time I found myself lamenting that he wouldn't share his experiences of business with me over the dinner table, or in bed at night, when the house was still and quiet, and the servants asleep in the hall.

42

'I'm not at all frightened,' I assured him, striving to keep my voice level. Light. 'Merely curious.'

He rolled his eyes again and shared a knowing glance with Rhys.

'Always so curious, Doli. Very well – a woman was accused when a charm was found in Gloddaith.' *Sir Thomas' home.* He lowered his voice before going on. 'In fact, Sir Thomas had quarrelled with a friend of his – Mistress Jane Conwy, of Marle, I believe – not too long before. It's said, Mistress Conwy went to the *witsh* and asked her to lay a curse on him.'

'But he's not dead?' I said, glancing at him again. He was merrily enjoying his wine, laughing heartily at whatever story John Wynn was sharing with him. Clearly not cursed.

Rhys laughed, and settled down his spoon and dagger.

'*He's* not dead, no.'

'Then why —'

Rhys interrupted before I could finish.

'Another man died. A man the *witsh* had treated for sickness in the weeks before the curse was found in Gloddaith. They say she broke a woman's arm, and caused the madness of a child.'

'That's frightful, if it's true. But, did she do it?' I asked. 'How can they be certain she killed the man if he was sick anyway?'

Hywel and Rhys exchanged another glance, which irritated me. Hywel shrugged.

'Many people spoke against her before the assizes. It seems she'd acquired a rather poor reputation over the years.'

'What for?' I pressed, though I could see Hywel no longer wanted to entertain the conversation.

This time Rhys replied, smirking.

'For cursing.' He waved his dagger vaguely at the air, before continuing. 'Threatening, and so on. Some even said they'd seen her cavorting with the devil at night. She kept a cat, too. Fed it with her own blood, apparently. So it was decided, the woman was guilty. She was hanged some months ago, at the end of October I believe, at the centre of the town. A large crowd gathered to watch, so I'm told. Nasty business. Clearly, Sir Thomas was determined she would be punished for her sins.' He glanced again in Sir Thomas' direction. Until that moment, there'd been a lightness to his manner; but as he looked down the table to Sir Thomas, his face became set with an expression I couldn't quite read. Was it disdain, or respect?

'What was her name?' I asked, looking from Rhys to my husband.

Hywel shrugged, as Rhys continued to look at Sir Thomas with that unreadable expression on his face.

'Rhys?' I pressed.

Rhys blinked at me, his eyes slightly unfocussed as he returned his attention to the room.

'Gwen, I think,' he replied absently, before reaching again for his wine. The conversation was clearly over.

A servant stepped into the room, carrying a basin for our hands. His clattering broke the silence that had fallen over my husband, Rhys and me. *Good.* I watched as the servant moved about the table pouring water over so many pairs of hands, then offering the towel draped over his arm. Before leaving, he came back towards us, and bent to whisper something in Hywel's ear. My husband nodded, drained his wine, and stood up from his chair at the head of the table.

'And now, my dear guests,' Hywel announced, smiling widely and clapping his freshly washed hands together. 'I do believe the bards have arrived!'

Although I was weary, I had to admit that the bards would be a welcome source of entertainment. I recognised both men from our wedding celebration five years ago, enough time had passed since then that it felt like another life. Siôn Tudur and Lewis ap Edward had been in a group of six or seven, then. It was the first time I had heard such obscenities spoken in public, and so freely. The day had been long and tiring and beautiful, with playful mocking, flowing wine, and raucous laughter in equal abundance. It was hearing them recite their words while strumming their harps that gave me the confidence to begin writing my own verses, which I kept hidden in a small box beneath our bed.

Once the table and benches had been cleared to make space, they gave their performance up on the dais, skilfully plucking their harp strings and reciting their pieces. They sang about the yuletide and Twelfth Night, about travel, and to my delight, even a poem about Hywel and me, which I suspected Hywel had instructed. In truth, it was mostly about Hywel and his business affairs, his generosity and patronage as a landowner and man of the church, but to their credit they did also mention his lady with *gwallt melyn mân*. Wisping blonde hair. They called me *Doli, mor fach â Doli dwt*. As small as a poppet.

The way they strummed their harps to their strict metre, the complexities of the rhymes mid-line, left me feeling dizzy. I hoped to one day master the form as they had. I couldn't help but glance across at Rhys while they sang, thinking again about the night we'd shared together, the secret poetry we held between us. I hadn't felt able to write anything of my own for some time, but hearing Gwerful Mechain's verses had reignited a desire in me, and I longed to scratch lines of verse into the margins of my prayer book again. Perhaps, even, to share them with Rhys.

When the bards had given their performance, we rose from the bench, each of us clapping and cheering. Hywel nodded at me, a small jerk of his chin, then moved from my side to speak with one of the bards, leaving me to stride across the hall to greet the other.

'Your performance was excellent, as always,' I said, though I worried my smile didn't quite reach my eyes. I had enjoyed the poetry and music, of course, but my stomach had been cramping and I had begun to feel queasy as they sang. I wondered vaguely if I had drunk too much wine at dinner, and tried to steady myself by fixing my gaze on the bard's ruddy face.

'Thank you Mistress,' he replied. 'You're most kind.'

Rhys appeared at my side, a cup of wine still clasped in his hand.

'Siôn, another wonderful performance!' he said. 'Your mastery of *cynhangedd* is remarkable. You're well, I hope?'

'Well enough.' He looked tired, his kind eyes framed with reddish rings.

'How has business been?' Rhys pressed. 'Where are you on your circuits?'

Siôn sighed.

'In truth,' he said, eventually, 'things have been quiet lately. People don't seem to want our services as much as they used to.'

'I can't understand why that might be,' I said. 'Your performances are so wonderful.'

'The trouble, Mistress, is that the gentlemen and ladies who used to employ us are disappearing one by one.'

'Disappearing?' It sounded ominous. As though they'd been swallowed up by the river, or wandered into the woods and not returned. I dreamed of one day standing on the dais with the bards, performing my own pieces. With his words, the possibility was growing ever more distant.

'One family I used to visit every Easter has moved to London, and another to Chester. It seems that once their children are sent to school, they pack up their homes and move across the border looking for better trade. More opportunity, so I'm told.' He shook his head.

'Oh.' I looked to Rhys who was nodding thoughtfully at my side. 'That's a shame.' I wasn't sure what else to say. I was out of my depth, trying to hold a conversation about trade.

'Yes. Last week we attended Lleweni – John Salusbury's home. Are you familiar with it?'

Rhys nodded again.

'We've been once or twice,' I said. I found I couldn't speak much. My stomach was still cramping, my mouth filling with spit.

'Then you'll know, the Salusburys have always been generous hosts. There's always plenty to eat, endless pitchers of ale. But —' he lowered his voice then, and looked around conspiratorially, as though ensuring there was no one listening in. Of course, everyone in the hall was engaged in their own conversation. The hum of it washed over us, as though the room was filled by a swarm of bees. 'I fear the Salusburys are becoming increasingly *Sais*.' He whispered the last word. *Englished.*

'Oh?' I said. Again, I had nothing more useful to contribute. The heat from the fire in the hearth felt suddenly very warm on my cheeks, and I tried to take a subtle step backwards, away from the flames.

'I'm sure you're aware, Sir John married an English woman. He spends most of his time in London these days.'

I glanced over at Hywel, wondering if he was listening, but he was deep in conversation with the other bard. Sir Thomas had joined him and was clapping him on the shoulder now and then, between laughs and deep glugs of wine. Hywel, too, spent a lot of time in London on business. Was that such a bad thing? Maybe there were things I didn't understand.

'There's talk that he's a friend of Shakespeare, the playwright causing a stir in those parts. Perhaps you've heard of him? I'm told he even dabbles in poetry of his own, written in *Saesneg*.'

I glanced at Hywel again. Like Rhys, who wrote *englynion* regularly, my husband sometimes experimented with verse, though most often in English. It was something he strived to keep mostly private. His words returned to me now: *English is the way forward, Doli. We must speak it if we want to keep ahead. If we want to thrive.*

'Hywel's grandfather went to school in Caernarvon, to learn English.' I was only trying to contribute something to the conversation, but I regretted the words as soon as I'd said them. The bard looked irritated.

'I see,' he said shortly.

The heat from the fire was suffocating. A wave of nausea overtook me. My eyes were drawn to the oil painting hanging above the mantel, where Hywel's face, and my own, stared back in angry defiance. The hall became dark and grainy, as though I was looking at it through heavy rainfall.

Then I heard two faint voices at once, one saying *Mistress?* and the other *Doli?*

Before I could be sure what was happening, I was engulfed by darkness.

When I woke, I was lying in my own bed. The curtains were drawn tight, a fire roaring in the hearth. Hywel was at my bedside, his brow furrowed, his mouth twisted.

'Hywel?' I said, tentatively. My voice was thin, my throat hoarse, as I asked him what had happened.

'Doli!' He bent to kiss my forehead, and wrapped his arms awkwardly around my shoulders, lifting me slightly from the mattress. He told me I had collapsed. 'But,' he said. 'The physician has been. He says there's nothing to worry about. How are you feeling?'

There was concern, Hywel explained, that I might have developed a fever. My neck was checked for signs of swelling. But none were found, so I was carried to bed while the celebrations continued.

'In front of esteemed guests no less,' said Hywel. Was there a small hint of venom in his tone, or had I imagined it?

Sir Thomas.

I looked up at him then, searching his face for traces of anger. Irritation. But he was smiling, and I closed my eyes and leant back on the pillow, relieved. In truth I was enjoying the comfort and warmth of my own bed. The room was calm, the crackle of the fire soothing over the din of hurried voices and music that carried up from downstairs.

I told him then that I had not felt right for several days. Weeks even. I looked down at my hands and wondered; perhaps it was time to tell him the truth. But the words stuck in my throat.

'There was a suggestion of exhaustion. Or troubled nerves, perhaps?'

'I'm not exhausted, Hywel. At least, not from overexertion, or nerves. I'm not the one who rides to Bristol and London on business twice a month,' I reminded him. 'My days are slow and long. There is nothing to exhaust me.'

Hywel nodded and smiled and simpered and shushed.

'Yes, I told him as much. I also told him about the tale Rhys was spouting at the dinner table,' he said. I blinked, trying to bring his face into better focus. Surely, he didn't think that the news of the witch hanged in Denbigh had caused me to faint.

'You don't believe that the conversation over supper had anything to do with —'

'Well it can't be coincidence, Doli.'

I had to blink again, this time to stop myself from rolling my eyes. A habit he despised. *Unbecoming in a gentlewoman,* he liked to remind me.

'Sometimes, Hywel,' I told him. 'Things simply are coincidence.'

It was time to tell him. I knew it was time.

Without warning, the tapestry on the wall was a sudden blur of deep bloody reds and rich golds. I took a slow, steadying breath as the room around me lurched sideways. Then a tingling, hot sensation took hold of me, a sickness settling into my stomach and lunging up, and up, and —

'Quick – the basin,' I said, my voice sharper than I had intended, nodding at the bowl that sat on the oyster table across the room. I snatched the bowl from him a moment before bringing up the contents of my supper. My stomach cramped again. My face flushed with heat. Hywel looked horrified, his eyes flitting between the bowl and my face.

'It'll wash,' I said. He knew I despised that bowl, an ornate, porcelain thing. A wedding gift from his mother. Handed down from her mother. But he couldn't say I'd tarnished it on purpose. Still, I couldn't pretend it wasn't satisfying seeing the strings of strangled meat and lumps of undigested apple swilling in it.

I had no choice now. *Tell him.* I wiped my hand across my lips and looked up at my husband, before taking his hand in mine, placing it on my soft belly. His eyes met mine.

'The physician did not suggest ... didn't mention ... And we've scarcely been near each other. Not since...'

He searched my face, his brown eyes large and round. Did I imagine the hope brewing in them? The firelight glinted from his skin, sharpening the angles of his nose, his chin.

I clutched his palm in mine, pressed it more firmly to the small curve of my middle.

'It's early,' I told him. 'But yes, there's hope.'

I didn't tell him about the charm.

The Villagers

The rains beat down, relentless and heavy. The ground swelled. Sodden. Heaving. Wet. The sheep's hooves rotting in the earth where they stood. Our horses fell ill, their throats blistered and bleeding. Our cows weakened, heifers lay dead in the fields. Miserable sheep stood sodden, their hooves sinking in the marshland. Pigs ailed. Then our children grew sick. They would not sleep. Cried relentlessly. And then – crops did not sprout, vegetables rotted, though we took every care to store them properly. Ale went bad in our barrels. Crows swarmed. Babies slipped stiff from their mothers. Men broke their legs at farm work. We grew frail. There had to be a cause for so much misfortune. A *witsh* in our midst.

As the snowdrops began to nudge their way to the surface, I grew more and more certain: two hearts were beating inside of me – one in my chest, and another, deep in my belly. I imagined the steady rhythm of it. Pictured the babe curled snug as a dormouse in the darkness.

I thought, for what seemed to be the hundredth time, of Sara Gwen's words – *you will be with child before the frost thaws.*

I had taken the items from her, the paper charm and the vial of water, surprised at how steady my hands had appeared despite being sure they were trembling. My face had been hot and flushed from the flames that burned at the centre of the small house.

I shuddered at the thought of anyone ever learning the unnatural truth about the pregnancy. A baby should be a gift from God, created within the sanctity of a marriage, but this child would always be different … An infant conceived by not two, but three people. *A man. A woman. A witsh.*

Fertility charms weren't considered witchcraft until the Queen was crowned, and the Church turned once again against the Catholics. I thought of the trinkets I had seen in Sara Gwen's house – the brass carving of Jesus Christ, the bell without its clapper – and felt an unpleasant gnawing at my stomach. It didn't matter what it had been called in the past, it only mattered what it was considered now, and who learned of it.

One afternoon late in February, I was sitting beside Ruby in the parlour, carefully stitching a leaping deer into the corner of my embroidery. A storm had blown in, dragging with it charcoal skies and hammering rain. The windowpanes misted at the edges. As I tied off a thread, Hywel's voice cut through the heavy thrum of rain, startling me so that I pricked my thumb on the needle. A small bead of blood formed at my fingertip.

'Do you know,' he said. 'Sir Thomas always sets an extra place at the table. He calls it "the King's seat."'

'What for?' I wondered if it was some strange sort of rebellion, a refusal to acknowledge that we had a Queen on the throne, rather than a King. Some men found it hard to accept that a woman sat in the palace, closer to God than any living man. It didn't matter that few could remember living under a King's rule. It wouldn't have surprised me to learn Sir Thomas was one of them.

'Over a hundred years ago,' Hywel said, 'Sir Thomas' ancestors helped King Henry escape from Richard III's men as he was passing through from Pembrokeshire, gathering men to his cause. The king's men had been increasing their patrols after learning of Henry's plans for the throne, and went in search of him when he was staying with the Mostyns.' Here, he raised his eyebrows, paused. I think he expected me to be impressed that his new acquaintance had links to the crown, despite a full century having passed by. 'When the officer barged his way in,' he continued, 'demanding to know why there was an extra place set, they lied and said it was always set in case of an unexpected guest, and offered the meal to him!' He chuckled at this, shaking his head as if he'd been there to witness this quick thinking himself. 'They still set that extra place to this day – men of tradition, the Mostyns.'

'I see,' I said, though I wasn't sure I did. I couldn't help but think of the servants pulling out the silverware, polishing it, then clearing it away again, unused. It seemed like such a waste. I could feel Ruby bristling beside me and imagined she must be thinking something similar.

'Won't it be wonderful when we form family traditions of our own?' Hywel said. 'People will say the same about us – the Maredudds are men of propriety. Men of tradition.'

He smiled, lost in thoughts of the future, of our family. Unsure what to say, I turned back to my stitching, but it wasn't long before a huge clap of thunder startled me into pricking my finger again. Only, it wasn't thunder. It was the sound of the parlour door being thrown open. The maid who hurtled into the room was young, barely past childhood. She was almost breathless, her chest heaving beneath her smock.

53

'Master,' she panted. 'Mistress. Hurry! You must see what I found while I was dusting.'

For an awful moment, I thought she had found my scribbled verses, my poems – but it wasn't that.

She held a scrap of paper in a shaking hand, and my heart leapt into my throat before plummeting to the pit of my stomach like a stone. The charm.

'What is it, Margiad?' Hywel rose from his armchair, reaching out his hand towards the maid.

'It looks like an old piece of paper to me,' I said quickly, sucking the beading blood from my finger before bringing my eyes back to my embroidery, concentrating on the white tip of the deer's tail. Ruby stiffened beside me. I feared if I caught her eye, she might understand, might know what I had done, despite her warnings. Would that be better? Would it be worse?

Up until now, I had almost forced myself to forget the thing existed. To convince myself that this baby was mine and Hywel's alone.

'Margiad, pass it here,' Hywel said, extending his arm for it. 'Quickly now.'

Heat rose from my chest, colouring my cheeks. I kept my head down, trying to remain calm, as I heard the low rustling of Hywel unwrapping the paper.

One beat. Two.

When he spoke, his words were quick, clipped. Dangerous.

'What is the meaning of this?' His previous exuberance had vanished, and in its place, a small, barely-detectable quiver – I might have missed it, had I not been so intimately attuned to his changeable nature. After all, I knew better than anyone, except perhaps Rhys, the nature of his sullen moods when things didn't go to plan. I knew his temperament, quick to anger whenever he felt embarrassed or ashamed or beaten, the childlike joy that shone from him when he hunted on the moors, drawing back his bow and aiming it skywards at the curlews. But, to my dread, I couldn't identify what this shift in his tone meant. Was it anger, fear, or another emotion entirely?

'I reckon it's a curse, sir,' Margiad said, almost gleeful. 'I found it when I was dusting up in your bedchamber. I was just setting about flipping the mattress, and there it was, folded up small and tucked underneath.'

I glanced up at the maid, then risked looking at Ruby. Her lips were parted slightly, her cheeks flushed, but her face remained unreadable. What was she thinking? I thought, then, of a time, several years earlier, when she had learned one of our servants had been pilfering milk from the pantry – she'd been so keen to tell us all about it, skulking into the parlour one evening after supper, smirking. The servant had been promptly dismissed, of course. This young maid reminded me of the way Ruby was when we were younger. Eager to please. Perhaps she had the same need for excitement where there was none to be found. Like an itch that had to be scratched. I needed to rid her of the notion this was anything sinister, or she'd spread the gossip easily as butter.

'What makes you think it's a curse, Margiad?' I asked from my seat at the window, still clutching my embroidery. A shield of fabric and French knots.

'It looks like one,' she replied, a knowing note to her voice.

Beside me, Ruby remained unnaturally still, her knee pressing into mine. It was as though she was willing me to remember our conversation in the garden, while I was willing her, with everything in my being, to say nothing.

The young maid went on. She seemed to be warming to her performance now she had a captive audience.

'Women cursing their enemies, leaving the curses in door frames and hidden in fireplaces.' She spoke quickly. 'My mother's landlord was cursed only last week. He found a scrap of paper just like this, rolled up and tucked into a bottle in his barn. Up high in the rafters it was, up over the cows.' She was getting a small thrill out of this, out of knowing more than us.

'Thank you, Margiad,' I cut across her, trying to sound firm. 'I'm sure it's only an old recipe, or something like that. Besides,' I added, glancing at Hywel. 'We have no enemies.' My voice held stronger than I thought it would. I waited while my husband examined the paper, his eyes darting back and forth, a frown settling on his brow. 'Hywel?'

'This is no recipe, Doli. The words mean nothing to me, but the letters are written backwards. And these strange symbols ... Like a wheel...' His face paled. 'Besides, that bed was a wedding gift from my parents – no one else has ever used it. So unless you have hidden a recipe under the mattress, what could this be but a curse?'

Should I admit to it? I shut my eyes, took a deep breath, thinking of the witch hanged in Denbigh. It occurred to me, suddenly, how strange it was that the woman responsible for writing the curse was convicted, while the woman who asked for it, who hid it in Gloddaith, was not. If I told the truth now, the only consequence for me would be facing Hywel's anger. But I couldn't say the same for Sara Gwen.

'Hywel, be reasonable. Who would want to curse us, darling?'

My husband only looked at me in response, his eyes reflecting the storm that still raged outside. A muscle jumped in his jaw.

'Leave us,' Hywel barked at Margiad, keeping his gaze fixed on me. The maid scurried from the room, her eyes still glistening with excitement, no doubt heading straight for the servants' hall to share her story. Ruby slipped out as well, pulling the door shut behind her. My husband and I were left alone, with only the sound of the rain and Ruby's retreating footsteps cutting through the silence. I felt her absence straight away, the loss of protection she afforded me by her very presence.

Hywel started towards me, the paper scrunched tight in his fist. Standing, he was a head taller than I was. Maybe more. Sitting, he towered above me, and I found myself leaning backwards against the damp window.

He spoke quietly.

'What could be the meaning of this?'

I set down my embroidery, placed my hands on my lap, forcing myself to look straight at him.

'I don't know. Are you sure it's not something innocent?'

'What could it be but a curse?' He snapped at me, before regaining his composure and taking a deep breath. 'We need to destroy it.'

As he piled logs high, one on top of another in the hearth, the sun broke through the clouds, beaming in through the windows.

'Hywel, please. There's no need —' I wanted to plead with him, to snatch the charm from him before he destroyed it. Destroyed the magic. Destroyed our baby.

Hywel stayed silent as he fumbled for a flint, sparking it with a shaking hand. Once the fire was lit, he paced the room, waiting for the flames to lick higher. I watched them curl and climb along the logs, up towards the mantle. Sweat beading at the back of my neck as the sun's steady glare lit the room. The heat was unbearable.

I was furious with myself for not hiding the charm more thoroughly — why hadn't I sewn it into the canopy above the bed? It would only have taken a moment. Margiad would never have found it if I'd taken the time. And Ruby had been sitting beside me when it was discovered... she had surely guessed at my secret now.

Still pacing, Hywel murmured about cursing and spells and servants and unruly women, barely taking any notice of me, still perched by the window, clinging once again to my embroidery.

'Calm down. Please.' It was no use. Hywel only ever calmed down when he was ready to do so. It was the way he had always been, try as I might to settle his temper.

He stopped then, jolted, as though he had forgotten I was in the room with him at all, and turned to look at me.

'Calm down? Someone in this home plots to harm me and I intend to find out who it is.'

'To harm *you*?' I was irritated, but unsurprised by the assumption. 'Why not to harm me, or both of us? And why someone in *this* home? If you truly believe that bit of paper is cursed, it could be anyone's doing.'

His next words surprised me.

'Oh, I know exactly what this is Doli, and it hardly concerns you.' He took a step towards me, and I felt my heartbeat quicken. 'No. No ... This is about revenge.'

'Revenge?'

'Who can get into our bedchamber? Who might have a reason to lay a curse on me, on this household?'

I stared at him, uncertain, rummaging through my mind for anyone that might have crossed our threshold and given Hywel cause to believe they would want to harm him. Could he believe it had something to do with the bards that came at Twelfth Night, or with the villagers that were here over Christmastide? Surely not. We had hardly welcomed any guests in recent months. We'd offered dinner and a bed to an old family friend who was travelling by on his way from the north of the country. There might have been a meal or two for the village poor – the remainder of our suppers – but surely Hywel would not believe that a guest we had treated with kindness would want to do us any harm.

'The servants, Doli, the servants. It was one of the servants.' There was an urgency in his voice. 'Yes, that must be it. Only last week, I denied them a rise in wages.'

'Oh?' It was the first I had heard of the matter. Though I wasn't surprised that Hywel hadn't discussed it with me, I was somewhat surprised that Ruby hadn't mentioned it. Perhaps there were things she kept from me, after all.

'They had the audacity to ask for half a shilling a week on top of their current salaries. As though we have coins in abundance. Money to spare for their frivolities. Anyway, of course I told them no. And now, not a week later, this curse appears in our chamber? Of course it was the servants.'

'Hywel —' I wanted to defend them, Ruby, the cook, the gardener, the boy who tended the horses, and all the others, but I wasn't sure what to say. I couldn't find the right words to tell him that it was me who laid the paper beneath our bed. Each time I tried to speak, to tell him the truth, I saw a woman's neck snapping against a rope, a pair of feet grappling for a surface, dancing, relentless, until they came to a deathly stop. A baying crowd silencing. Bowed heads.

I turned to look through the window at the rain soaked moors. Kites and crows circled over the grasslands, sweeping and gliding towards the trees. I wondered at the half a shilling more the servants had asked for. Was it really all that much? Didn't we have enough to allow them that? In truth, I wasn't sure.

Hywel started to pace again, crunching the paper in his fist.

'The cook. It was her that led the charge. Yes. It all makes sense now, the way she's forever gathering herbs and spices in the garden, crushing lavender and grinding pepper into salves.' He stopped, muttered something to himself, then looked at me, eyes wide. 'I've seen her. I left her to it, thinking that little herb garden of hers was fit for no more than ingredients for pastries and puddings, but clearly I've been a fool. The ungrateful wretch.'

He stepped towards the fire, tearing the paper as he strode forward.

No.

'No need to worry, Doli. *Paid â becso.*' His face softened as he turned to me, his voice low, soothing. 'I will put an end to this.'

And with that, he tossed the torn pieces of paper into the fire. The fragments fell like rose petals at the end of a bloom, blazing red for a short instant before crumbling into ash. What would happen to our baby, now that the charm was destroyed?

I stared hopelessly at the ash in the grate, my hand half-raised as if I could somehow stop Hywel from destroying the certainty of our future. Our baby. His face was triumphant, gleaming. As I lowered my hand, I felt a blow strike, deep in my stomach, hot as lightning. My vision began to swim in and out of focus, and Hywel's face, that odd expression, danced before me.

'Yes.' His voice seemed to be so far away, fading with my darkening vision. 'Yes, I will put an end to this. Let there be no doubt.'

Thinking about Margiad and the charm kept me awake that night. The rain was still lashing against the windows, the memory of that brief hint of sunshine long since forgotten. If anything, the storm had worsened, raindrops falling upon the hall like gunstones. Hywel was snoring beside me, the barrel of his chest rising and falling in a steady rhythm. The dying light of the fire lit one side of his face, forming deep shadows in the small frown that creased his brow, and I wondered what he might be dreaming about.

I rolled over and, burying my head into the pillow, tried to smother the sound of the storm outside. I couldn't get comfortable. I couldn't rest. Despite Hywel's warmth next to me, I shivered. My bones felt like ice.

Weary, I sat up and slowly, so as not to wake my husband, I swung my legs over the side of the bed. I padded across to the doorway of the bedchamber. As I opened the door I closed my eyes as though that would somehow stop the wood from creaking. Again, I saw it: Hywel's fist brandishing the paper. The secret to our child's conception. I remembered the embroidered deer clutched tight in my own fist, the pain I had felt in my stomach at the very same moment the fragments of paper were swallowed by flames.

Downstairs, I sat on the settle against the window and looked out into the dark night. The moon was a thin, silver thread sewn into the fabric of the sky, its light kissing the moors below. The cows hadn't long been moved back to the fields since being brought in for winter, and yet the grass was so waterlogged and heavy with rainfall it was barely fit for grazing. I could almost smell the sodden earth and that warm dampness that rises from wet animal hide from my perch behind the windowpane, glass Ruby liked to remind me we were fortunate to have. Most didn't have such protection from the elements.

When I first came to Faen Maredudd, I'd been shocked at the

number of windows here, the many chimneys and fireplaces. Though my family home had two storeys, a bier and plenty of land, Hywel's family had seemed unimaginably wealthy by comparison.

I was only fourteen summers old when my father and Hywel's had spent an evening negotiating our marriage over wine and pigeon meat.

I'd listened from the parlour as their voices grew louder with each freshly poured drink sloshing from the jug. Though he was only a few years my senior at seventeen, Hywel had seemed so wise. So experienced. Even then, he had already seen so much of the world. He spoke of plays with nymphs and pixies and Greek deities, of market towns and guest houses, of ships that docked loaded with crates of marble and exotic fruits in unimaginable colours.

Before we were married, I was sent to Faen Maredudd, on my father's wishes, to be educated and instructed on household management by Hywel's mother.

I hadn't expected to learn anything I hadn't already learned from my own mother, but things were done differently at Faen Maredudd. I watched my mother-in-law confidently instructing the servants in a way my mother was never inclined to do, and taking charge when they failed to meet her expectations. She scolded the cook in a way I was certain I would never be comfortable with, particularly coming into the home as an outsider. The cook had worked with Hywel's family since before I was a babe in arms. Despite my rank, I didn't feel I'd ever have the right to make demands of her.

I learned from Hywel's mother how to make preserves and cordials, by sugaring berries, primroses and violets. These were some of Hywel's favourite foods, though I'd long harboured a suspicion he preferred his mother's to mine. She brought a twine-wrapped package of them each time she visited, and I had to tell myself I was only imagining the satisfied smirk that settled about her lips each time she watched Hywel bite into one. She'd also taught me to make almond butter and marzipan, comfits and wafers, but I didn't engage in that sort of cooking often these days, finding more joy in walking, writing, and sewing.

I pressed my cheek to the cold glass, looking out into the moorland through bleary eyes. All was quiet. Still. My eyes began to drift shut as the rain finally began to soothe my restless mind. Until something strange caught my eye: a cloaked figure creeping along the bog, lurking behind knots of grass and stray rocks, sweeping along as though it were not touching the ground. I squinted, sure I must have mistaken a wild hog for a person, but the figure had gone, as quickly as it had appeared.

What was it? An omen? A malevolent spirit? I focussed on my breath, trying to steady the rising panic in my chest, trying to assure myself I'd imagined it. I'd been half-asleep. I must have dreamt it. But no, I knew what I'd seen was real, and the timing of the thing's appearance was too troubling to ignore. What could it be other than a sign of good magic gone bad, destroyed in a rush of fear and flames?

I fell into a restless, anxious sleep and woke sometime later with a stiffness in my neck and a sharp pain in my shoulder. The rain had finally stopped, and the sun was beginning to crown on the horizon, casting an amber glow on the watery moors. There was no sign of the strange, cloaked figure. I held my breath, listening for sounds of life in the house, the rustling of Ruby dressing upstairs, or of the servants bustling about the kitchen preparing breakfast, but couldn't hear anything. It was too early.

Relieved, I crept as quietly as I could, ghost-like, back up the stairs. Hywel was exactly as I had left him, unmoving as I slipped into bed beside him, folding my body beneath the linens. As I began to drift asleep, my stomach cramped again, and I saw my husband tearing the paper over and over, throwing the tiny scraps of it to the fire, watched them curdling like bad milk. In my dreams, he threw our child to the flames too. I watched in horror as the tiny, helpless body burned.

Daylight flooded the bedchamber when I woke again. The sun streamed through the glass, warming the length of one side of my body – it warmed my cheek, and my arm where it was flung outside the coverlet. Tired from my restless night, I had slept later than I should have. Hywel must have already dressed and made his way downstairs. I made my way down to the hall, but there was no sign of him.

Groggy, I took a seat at the table and waited for someone to bring me some cold meat, bread and ale for breakfast. The house was quiet and still. Light streamed through the windows into the hall, and I could hear birds calling to each other. I thought, then, of running through the grass as a child, chasing magpies from tree branch to tree branch. Watching their blue-black wings dancing.

As I was chewing on a crust of bread, Ruby swayed into the room carrying a few linen-wrapped parcels and a large book.

'*Bore da,* Ruby. What have you got?' I asked her, looking at the thick, mahogany-coloured book.

She set it on the table with a thud and shrugged.

'Another Bible. It was brought to the door this morning.'

'Why would Hywel want another Bible?' I wondered aloud, pulling the book towards me. Admittedly, the binding was beautiful. Four golden acorns decorated each corner, branches sprawling between them.

'It's a new edition, I think,' Ruby said.

I peeled open the front cover, careful not to smudge grease from my fingers over its pages, and read the inscription: *Y Beibl cyssegr-lan sef Yr Hen Destament, a'r Newydd.* A translation by William Morgan.

A Welsh Bible, then.

I handed it back to Ruby, who tucked the book under her arm, where it looked even bigger than it had first appeared. It was the first Welsh Bible I'd seen of its size.

'Hywel must have ordered it to donate to the Church,' I said.

I imagined he wanted the villagers to hear the scriptures in their own language. A language he had recently, inexplicably, begun to describe as *the wild tongue.* Most couldn't speak English, so didn't understand what was being read to them at church. Lately, Hywel seemed to think it was his duty to correct that … *They need to hear God's teachings as they are written.*

As I turned back to my breakfast, there was a short, sharp, familiar pain in my stomach. I dropped the cold meat to my plate, feeling suddenly sick. No blood had come. Not yet.

Still, yesterday's events lingered in my mind and I needed to be outside, to feel the vast openness of the skies.

'Ruby,' I called as she was walking away. 'Will you accompany me on a walk through the moors later? Please? I want to be out in the fresh air today. And it looks as though the rain has finally eased.'

At last, the skies appeared clearer, the grasslands less sodden than they were last night. Last night … I batted the memory of the strange, shadowy figure from my mind. The scorched paper.

Later, wrapped in cloaks and bracing ourselves, we ventured out and set off through the gardens towards the moors. It felt good to be outside, where magpies and jackdaws called each other overhead. The smell of roots and peat moss hit me, mud rising from the river to the north.

We trudged through the grass, still swollen with rainwater, avoiding the most boggy areas. Here and there, sheep moved idly about, their cloven hooves sinking into the ground. Once the house was out of sight, and only the river and the blackbirds surrounded us, I spoke, keeping my eyes fixed firmly ahead.

'Ruby?' I did my best to keep my voice level. 'The charm Margiad found in our bedchamber last night…'

'What about it?' Ruby attempted to sound bored, disinterested, but a hitch in her breath betrayed her. My tongue was stiff in my mouth, the words catching at my lips. But I could trust Ruby. This wasn't trivial gossip – I knew she wouldn't take it to the alehouse to share with other servants, or pass it on to her sisters. The stakes were far too great. If the justices heard of this, our name would be worth no more than the dirt we walked on.

'The master seemed convinced that what was written on that paper was a curse. He thinks it was placed there to hurt us. And, well, Margiad seemed certain it was something ungodly too. Has she said anything about it? To you? To the other servants?'

The dread was like a dead thing rotting in my stomach as I waited for her answer. But I had to ask her. I knew the servants were in the habit of coming together in the evening for their *swper bychan,* despite the church's teachings. Ruby had told me about it herself. They *must* have discussed it last night.

'Course she has! She was very pleased with herself, as it happens. Couldn't believe her luck, finding that charm in your bedchamber. She thinks she saved the master's life.' Ruby rolled her eyes at this, but I didn't find it as trivial as she did. 'She kept saying to us, *I might not be able to read, but I know enough about penmanship to have seen that those letters were written backwards.* She thinks she might get a few more coins in her next pay packet, actually.'

It was just as I had feared. They all knew of it. I pictured the servants then: the frantic chopping of carrots, the plucking of feathers, the grinding of herbs, and the story rising like steam from the pots.

'But, Ruby ... Margiad is wrong, isn't she? Writing something backwards doesn't mean that it's a curse. Does it?'

I felt my breath catch in my lungs as I spoke, suddenly struck cold. Could the charm that had helped me to conceive and keep hold of my baby have held more power still? Did Sara mean us harm? But why would she? It didn't make any sense.

'In truth, I don't know. I've heard that writing backwards can be an ill omen. Sometimes. But then again, it mightn't be anything sinister at all. It depends where the paper came from.'

She looked at me then, inviting me to confide in her, but I remained silent. I longed to be able to speak more freely with her, like we did when we were girls. But being mistress of a manor like Faen Maredudd carried a cost. I had to be aware of that. We reached a patch of land that was so saturated with water that our boots would be sodden if we were to venture any further. As we turned, Ruby spoke again.

'Well, Margiad has been saying that the curse must have been put there by someone who wanted to hurt the master. Or maybe even to hurt you.' Her voice dropped as she glanced sideways at me, despite the echoing emptiness of the moorland. 'A curse that's appeared from nowhere, that's been tucked away under your mattress so it wouldn't be found...? It doesn't look good.'

I felt the warmth seep into my cheeks at her words, but Ruby didn't seem to notice. Her eyes were cast upwards towards the jackdaws flitting overhead.

I sighed. I didn't know how to respond. I would so dearly have loved to tell Ruby everything – to tell her how the air in Sara's cottage was thick and hot with smoke from the fire and boundless hope, how it smelled of ash and crushed lavender, and damp earth. And perhaps, it was true, of magic.

But how could I, when she had warned me so assuredly not to go? She would be furious. Worse, she'd think me a fool. And if she did have too much wine one evening, if her lips did loosen...

Instead, I asked only, 'What do you suggest? What should I do now?'

She blanched, taken aback that I was asking her advice. Pleased, nonetheless.

'Well, if you really don't know where that paper came from, I could take it to my cousin, and ask her if she knows what it could be. She might recognise the words, or the symbols.'

'Your cousin?' Ruby didn't speak of her family often, and the mention of her cousin surprised me.

'Yes, Agnes. She has a...' Ruby hesitated. 'A certain amount of knowledge, about these things. I'm sure she'll be able to tell you if it's a curse or not.'

'It's not possible. Hywel burned the paper, Ruby. After you left the room.'

'Well then I'm not sure there's much you can do. Is it troubling you?'

'I'm worried that —' I stopped, closing my eyes momentarily, concentrating on the darkness behind my eyelids. What was I worried about? That the charm actually was a curse, after all? That the charm had worked but burning it might reverse its magic? It was too much to try to explain. Instead, I asked only – 'Your cousin. Is she a healer too?'

'Yes, of sorts.' By now, Ruby sounded bored, but I knew her well enough to know it was feigned indifference. 'She helps women in childbed. At the moment she's employed as a maid at a farmstead near Presteigne. She's acquainted with Sara Gwen.'

She gave me another searching look. A look that said: *I know. I know it was you who hid the charm.*

Again I pictured Margiad and the other servants, speaking about Faen Maredudd. Imagined them whispering about the curse found hidden in the master and mistress' chamber; the shouting that had followed; the sweat that cooled on the master's temples; the palpable fear that now clung to the walls. The villagers would talk. They would tell their stories to one another. The stories would evolve. Tongues would wag. Fingers would be pointed.

I had to tell Ruby the truth. I couldn't hold the words any longer. I needed someone who might understand.

I stopped walking.

'Ruby —' I paused, and took a breath. Suddenly it all flowed out, unstoppable. 'It was me. I hid the paper. I got it from Sara Gwen. But it was a charm, not a curse! I swear it.'

Ruby stopped and stared at me, her face slackening.

'I hoped ... But I didn't ... How could you do something like that? Do you know that the master has been accusing the servants of putting it there?'

A pang of guilt struck me at her words. I reassured her that I wouldn't let Hywel blame her, or any of the other servants.

'I'll find a way to make it right, Ruby. I promise.'

She chewed her bottom lip for a moment, while I braced myself for the words she was clearly mulling over.

'But Doli, I don't understand. Why would you? After I warned you not to meddle in magic? I warned you what was being said about Sara Gwen. Women with power like she has … It's not safe. Not at the moment. It's against the Lord's teachings.'

'But even the minister can give blessings,' I said.

'It's not the same thing.'

Something in the way she spoke, her voice quick, urgent, surprised me. Was she really so worried? I looked to the sky, and took a deep breath.

'I was desperate, Ruby.'

'But I warned you about the talk in the village, of witches and cursing, of Sara Gwen. If she's more than a wise woman … If she's … It's too dangerous to be involved in any of it. If she comes to the attention of the magistrates, you could be made to testify against her.'

'I had no choice. I had to do it, for the sake of my family.' She kept looking at me, judgement stark on her face, so I said, 'You wouldn't understand.'

I had only meant that there was no expectation on her to produce a healthy heir, no husband to answer to, no villagers holding her in high regard and the scrutiny that came with that position. I often felt the weight of my responsibility bound as tightly as a bodice about me, a feeling Ruby would never experience herself. Still, she looked at me as though I'd pushed her into the wet grass.

'Ruby, I —'

'Oh don't worry,' she said, terse.

'I only meant —'

'No. You're right. I *wouldn't* understand.'

She turned and walked away, leaving me standing by myself beside a large tree, its branches sprouting new leaves. I watched her figure becoming smaller and smaller, watched as she strode back towards the house. Waited for its shadow to swallow her whole.

The Villagers

We all heard of it, one way or another. Some folk whispered of it in the alehouse. Some told their husbands over the dinner table, spat out the story like a wishbone. The story was this: the young maid found a curse hidden in the bedchamber up at the big house. There was panic written on the poor master's face. They say the mistress stayed calm, quiet, and we wondered, did she know more than the rest of them? Did she write that curse herself? Things are tense there now, so they say. The servants are afraid to speak out of turn. Their wages already made smaller in punishment. The master is determined to find the wicked one. *Pwy â'm witshodd?* Every day he asks it, *who has witshed me?* The mistress says nothing in return.

The day had been long and tiresome, and I was troubled by my conversation with Ruby. Worried that something had been set in motion I was helpless to prevent. Hywel had been silent for most of the evening, sulking around the house, stalking through it as dark as a storm cloud.

Later that night, when we were getting ready for bed, he turned to me, hands poised at the buttons of his doublet.

'Tell me, what do you know of Sara Gwen?'

I froze, my nightdress clutched like a talisman in my fist. He couldn't know.

'I'm afraid I don't quite understand you,' I replied, playing for time. Hywel ran his eyes up and down the length of my body, snagging on each stitch of my dress.

'Sara Gwen,' he repeated, after a moment. 'She's a local woman. A *healer*, they say, as though there are such benevolent uses for witchcraft as healing.'

'Witchcraft?' I didn't mean to repeat him, but the word sounded so strange in the confines of our bedchamber. It was the first time I'd heard him using the term so offhandedly, so casually, as though it were a profession as simple as a cook or a maid or even a dressmaker.

He nodded but said nothing.

'I know of her.' Again, the memory surfaced of the white stone cottage, standing apart from the others, caught in the shadow of that big rowan tree. The red kites that circled above. 'From what I've heard, she spends most of her time alone. She prefers her own company.' *So you won't find anyone who knows anything.*

He searched me again, and I felt almost as though he was trying to draw the words from me, his eyes boring into my body. Looking for answers.

'Of course. An outsider. Go on,' he pressed. His voice was all the more menacing for its quietness, barely audible over the crackle of the fire in the hearth.

'I'm not sure what you want me to tell you, Hywel. I don't speak with many people in the village.'

That much was true. I rarely went into the village, and when I did it was usually on an errand to collect materials or baking supplies from the market. Hywel knew that I would walk out on the moors on occasion, sometimes with Ruby, more often alone. He also knew that there was no one to talk to out on the grasslands but the birds. No one to listen but the trees and the reeds.

Anything I did know about the villagers came from Ruby. I thought about telling Hywel this, but quickly reconsidered. I didn't want him to press her on the matter.

'You must know more, Doli. Surely you've heard whisperings, as I have? I expect she's old and haggard? Goatish and ugly?'

Of course, Sara was none of those things. In fact, I'd thought her quite beautiful, strange, like a carving. I felt ensnared, a fox caught in a trap. If he had heard whisperings, as he said, why did he need me to tell him what I knew? I looked to the window, at the low light of the moon pressing in like a reel of ribbon and illuminating a stretch of the coverlet. I tugged my nightdress over my head before turning back to my husband.

'Where do you expect me to have heard these "whisperings" Hywel? At church while everyone is gathered in close-shouldered silence? Or perhaps at the alehouse while I'm drinking with my companions?' I shouldn't have continued, shouldn't have been so bold, but I couldn't help myself. The rage rushed inside of me. Hywel knew I barely left the house, except to walk the moors. And he knew that when I did, as his wife, my conversations were limited, careful, considered. 'Perhaps you think I've indulged in gossip whilst gallivanting on horseback and hunting deer? Or maybe on one of my overnight business trips?'

I stared at him, willing him to understand my meaning.

'Of course not,' Hywel said, flushing. I wasn't sure whether the redness inching along his neck and cheeks was the result of anger at my brazenness, or embarrassment at his own assumptions. He knew how lonely I felt, all too often. Perhaps it had not occurred to him how different our lives were. 'You keep close companionship with Ruby. I thought maybe she might have said something of interest.'

I sighed, calming myself as much as I could. Trying to steady my trembling fingers.

'I know very little about Sara Gwen. She's a healer, I believe. She lives alone. That's all I know. Please, let's not talk of her any longer. I want to go to bed.'

Hywel smirked.

'Yes, she lives alone. But did you know, she's been married? Twice over, the old *witsh* has been widowed, I am told.'

'Oh.' There had been no hint of a man's presence in the cottage at all. 'How unfortunate,' I said. What sort of reaction was he expecting from me?

'Unfortunate?' he said. 'I hardly think so. Isn't it obvious what became of her husbands? No? They could be the very rats dwelling in our stables now.'

I would have laughed, but could see from the hard set of his face that he was entirely serious. I thought then, of the rat I'd seen skulking around Sara's cottage, its tail trailing thick and heavy along the ground. The bloodied paw.

Hywel stepped towards me, wrapping his hands around my shoulders, and almost shook me as he continued.

'Listen,' he said. 'I've been making enquiries. I've spoken with —' he paused, his tongue tracing the inside of his lips, 'The right people. I believe Sara Gwen could be the one responsible for cursing us.'

My eyes darted towards the bed, where the paper was found. I was of course relieved that he was no longer accusing the poor servants, but I wondered who he had been speaking with to come to these conclusions only a day after the event. I forced myself to meet his eyes, to breathe deeply.

'Hywel, I —'

He put his hand up to my face, stopping me from speaking.

'No need to go on, Doli. My sources are trustworthy people. Sara Gwen has a certain ... reputation.' He twirled the word about his tongue, as though it was vulgar, shameful and thrilling all at once.

'Hywel, think about what you're suggesting.' I put my hands to his chest, felt the strong, rapid beat of his heart, the thudding of his belief. I took a breath, hoping that my voice was level. That it didn't betray the way my heart pounded like a bird caged in my chest, or the churning in my stomach. 'How could she have come into the house to place the paper there? How would she have got into our bedchamber?'

He practically flung his hands into the air and stepped away from me, clearly exasperated, his doublet now half undone and hanging loose from one shoulder. 'Witchcraft, Doli. Witchcraft! Aren't you listening to me?'

'I am listening, Hywel. But I'm merely —'

'Witches sneak through keyholes at night, Doli. They slip in, silent as bats, and wreak havoc on the home as easily as if they were delivering butter.'

He spoke with such conviction, such certainty, as though he knew beyond a doubt that these things were true. I tried not to let the words in, but I couldn't help it. I remembered the strange shadowy figure I'd seen out on the moors, the way it vanished like a ghost. Then I began to imagine a slick, bat-like shadow unfurling through the keyhole of our bedchamber door. The thought left me feeling cold as ice.

'They can shape-shift into animal forms too, you know. Hares and cats, most often I believe, but I hear any animal is possible. It would have been easy, would it not, to miss a stray cat prowling around the kitchen?'

I thought of the cook and her large broom, intolerant of any stray creature, swatting away at the mice in the pantry, but didn't say anything. I could see by the hard set of Hywel's face that he wasn't going to be challenged on this. Who had he been speaking with?

'Hywel, darling. What reason would she have? What reason would anyone have, to want to hurt us?'

He glowered at me, his chest rising and falling. Rising. Falling. I tried again.

'Don't you think that it may have only been an old recipe, after all? Or some sort of prayer, perhaps? Something long forgotten?'

'*Iesu*, Doli!' It burst out of him, his voice raised, and I worried the servants might hear. 'Why do you refuse to see what is so plainly before you? These lands are rife with witches. Sir Thomas says...' Here, he stopped, looking at me 'Well, it doesn't matter. But we must do all we can to protect ourselves. To protect our tenants. The villagers are at risk too.'

'Hywel, I —'

'Do not oppose me, Doli.' His voice was cold. I took a step backwards, almost tripping over my nightdress.

He stepped towards me.

'Listen.' His eyes bored into mine, burning with a fire ready to destroy. 'I have always been tolerant of your whims and fancies, your strange wanderings across the moors, but don't forget – you are my *wife*. It's your duty to support me. Without question. If I am telling you something is true, it's because it's true. And this most certainly is true.' He stopped, sighed, extending an arm as though he was going to touch me, then letting it drop back to his side. 'I only want to protect you, Doli.' He looked at my rounding belly, half exposed beneath my nightdress. 'I love you, little mouse. Both of you. Do you understand?'

His face was a canvas stained with fear and fury. I held his gaze, held my fraying nerve, and nodded.

I do.

The Villagers

The mistress must think she's subtle, hiding the way her stomach rounds and blooms beneath her dress, but we've all seen it: the way she sweats in the congregation as the minister speaks. The way she walks with a hand pressed to her lower back. The dark shadows circling her eyes the way crows circle dead things. And there she goes, marching about the moors, unaccompanied. We heard the baby was conceived in the woods, a child of the moon and stars.

One morning in March, Hywel announced that Rhys would be joining us for supper. They would be spending the day hunting on the moors, now that the weather was more favourable. Winter's stubborn frost had relented, and though a constant drizzle mired the moors, and dampness lingered, the air was becoming warmer, daffodils peering up from the ground.

I couldn't do anything other than nod my head. I could scarcely bring myself to speak with Hywel, to meet his eye, without fearing he would somehow know my thoughts and learn my secrets. I couldn't forget how he'd looked at me that awful night, the cold intensity of his belief. It would be wonderful to spend the evening with Rhys, whose company I always enjoyed, but by now, the pregnancy had progressed further than any of the others, and I was more exhausted than I had ever been.

I wavered between feeling the fatigue must be a good sign – a baby growing well – and conviction that it was a bad omen. I had no one to ask who might know the answers, no one to confide in, unless ... but no, I couldn't risk it. My only comfort was in the knowledge that we would employ a midwife soon.

I pictured the baby curled inside me, slowly leeching away my energy, leaving me confused, tired as a hound after a hunt. I thought of asking advice from my mother, who had been in childbed several times. Or perhaps my sister, who had three children of her own already, but the idea of riding to visit either of them was enough to make me want to lie down and sleep for a week.

Of course, I could have written a letter. Hywel's father had taught me to write when I first came to Faen Maredudd. I had relished spending time at the table with him, pouring over the Bible by candlelight, copying the contours of each letter in dripping black ink. Learning to trace the letters of my own name, and Hywel's, Rhys' and Ruby's. But that was no use now – despite having been gifted a hornbook as a child, my sister couldn't read. Neither could my poor mother. Both preferred to spend their time rolling pastry, and perfecting their embroidery. *The Bible is read aloud at church,* Mam always said. *There's no need to read it at home.*

The thought of my sister's husband, or even my own father, reading my letter aloud to them, and having to transcribe a reply, caused an itching heat to travel up my neck. A woman's growing belly, the changes that came with carrying a child, were not for a man's ears. I couldn't bring myself to do it.

The weather was mild despite the damp, so I spent the afternoon walking on the moors. Though our gardens were usually beautiful in the springtime, with the daffodils and eyebright in bloom, I preferred to move beyond the confines of Faen Maredudd when I could. I wanted to be out in the open moors, where the grass grew wild and free as the birds, and the river gushed and gurgled. Damp seeped into my underskirts as they dragged along the sodden grasses, muddying my dress.

Coming to a stop at the riverbank, I knelt down slowly amongst the ragwort, then pressed my hands to the cool, damp earth. Although spring was unfurling, the ground was still heavy with mud after so much rainfall, especially with the buttery sun so mild and meek. I closed my eyes and tipped my face up, trying to feel the sun's warmth, listening to the crows calling and thinking about where Hywel and Rhys might be now. They were likely deep in the forest, a doe in their sights, or perhaps closing in on a hare, their horses tied with rope to nearby tree trunks. Stomping the ground.

There at the riverbank, my eyes scrunched tight, was where I first felt it. A fluttering, deep in my belly, like a tadpole growing its back legs – the baby, quickening.

When I opened my eyes again, I noticed a thin reel of red appearing in the water. It began like a narrow piece of thread beneath the surface, thickening as it swirled like a ribbon caught in the current. Then it grew again, until it looked like a pool of blood pulsating on the surface. Deep crimson. From where I sat, I could smell it, like a satchel of coins.

I looked around, frantic, expecting to see an injured animal at the riverbank – a deer or a rabbit – but there was nothing there. In the distance, three crows darted towards the grass then lifted back upwards towards the sky, a red kite swooping behind them. When I looked back to the river, the red swirl had gone as quickly as it had appeared. It took a long time for my heartbeat to steady. Perhaps it was simply unsettled mud, maybe fish or small frogs disturbing the riverbed. It might even have been my imagination. It must have been. And yet, I was so close to the place where I'd bled back in the winter, the place where I had lost my baby. The bloody water had to be more than a trick of the light ... it felt like a sign, an ill omen.

I closed my eyes, trying to steady my breathing and thought again of the strange, slippery shadow out on the moors, the charm shrivelling on the fire. I felt sick, my stomach frothing in time with the river.

I continued watching the water running for a while, finding its way over immovable rocks and algae, but I felt uneasy, as though someone was watching me, so I gathered up my damp skirts and headed towards home.

When I got back, a nauseating smell was seeping from the kitchen, of raw meat and uncooked fish. There was the lingering of some herbs I couldn't quite recognise – parsley, perhaps. I hurried up the stairs, avoiding the servants, and shut the bedchamber door firmly behind me.

As I lay on the bed, staring up at the ceiling, I kept myself very still, hoping to feel the baby moving again, but nothing happened. With little to do but await Hywel and Rhys' return, I let my eyes drift shut and dozed for most of the afternoon. When they finally arrived home, their voices carrying from the parlour up the stairs I heard another familiar voice. They were accompanied by a third person.

Groaning, I pulled myself out of bed and prepared to rub my teeth with a rosemary cloth, and comb my hair, before making my way downstairs, forcing a smile.

The men were in a good humour over supper. Their hunt was a success and the hares had been given to the kitchen staff to skin and prepare for our evening meal. Hywel explained to me that they had come across the third man – an old acquaintance – whilst hunting, and invited him back to Faen Maredudd to join us for food.

There was something about the man, whom Hywel introduced as Jacob Lloyd, that struck me as odd. Unsettling. I couldn't be sure what it was exactly. Maybe it was his sharp chin, or the way his eyes were pitch black, ratlike, stark against his pale skin. He was dressed very simply in a light cotton shirt and black jerkin. According to Rhys, Hywel and Jacob had met some years ago listening to debates at the Inns of Court in London, where Jacob had since settled.

'What brings you to Llynidwen?' I asked him, though in truth I wasn't particularly interested in his answer.

'I am here to spread the word of our Lord,' he said. It was then that I noticed the round brooch pinned to his jerkin and recognised him from that strange church service.

He was quieter, more reserved than either Hywel or Rhys, who laughed together, Hywel's eyes crinkling at the corners, catching the light as he speared his meat with his dagger. Tired as I was, I was perfectly happy sitting quietly, listening to them talk jovially of land acquisition and travel, of trade and hunting.

'We almost had a buck,' Rhys said. 'Until my old friend here let it go!'

'Come now Rhys, it was you that stepped on that branch and startled it!'

Both men seemed merry and it wasn't long before Hywel summoned a servant to bring more wine.

The servant sipped it himself first – *no poison, then* – then replenished our drinks. All but Jacob's, who placed his hand firmly above his cup, declining any more.

In the meantime, conversation had moved on.

'And what of your family life, Rhys? Are you still yet to meet your match on your travels?' Hywel asked.

'You know I'm yet to meet anyone I could happily call a wife, Hywel,' Rhys replied, a light smile dancing about his lips. 'Besides, the finest woman across all the border counties is already happily married.' He winked across the table at me, and I felt myself blush. I swiped at my cheeks, as though I could sweep the heat from them.

'I see your busy day hasn't dampened your charm,' I replied.

'Perhaps,' he went on, breaking his gaze to look down into his wine, 'I'm not destined to marry. Besides, I'm far too busy to take a wife.'

I opened my mouth but Hywel spoke first.

'Don't be absurd, Rhys! Of course you will marry. After all, how could you willingly forgo the opportunity to pass on your legacy? Your family name?'

He smiled at me for the first time that evening, looking fondly at my rounding stomach, where Rhys' eyes had also come to settle. I shifted on the bench, uncomfortable, as my bodice pinched against my ribs. I would need a seamstress to let my dresses out before long.

'Hywel,' I said, gently. 'Perhaps it's not that simple for everyone.' Heaven knows it had not been simple for us, either.

Jacob Lloyd remained silent, looking steadily between each of us in turn.

'Nonsense! Every man should have a son and heir!' Hywel smiled widely, taking another deep sip of wine.

'Perhaps,' I said, smiling myself. 'But all this talk of sons ... this baby could be a daughter. Have you even considered that possibility?'

He put a hand to his chin, making a show of considering the idea, then looked me square in the eye and said, 'I will love her all the same. Just as I love you, my little doll.'

I tried to smile. I wanted to be pleased, of course, but then I remembered the look that had overtaken him as he spoke of witchcraft. The fire crackled at the far end of the hall, and there it was again – the memory of the paper shrivelling in the flames.

As though in response, I felt a sudden jab a few inches below my midriff. It caught me unaware, and I touched my hand to the spot where I had felt the movement. I saw Rhys' eyes follow the movement in my periphery, as I took a slow, steadying breath. This baby had to be born alive and well. I wanted nothing more than to see it cradled against Hywel's broad chest. If I lost this child, after coming this far, it would break me.

I was desperate to confide in Hywel. Truly. Everything in my being tugged and pulled with the desire to tell him the truth – about the charm, about my fears – to have him strip the worry away from me as he always had in the past. But I couldn't do it. Something warned me not to. Something I couldn't ignore.

For weeks, I'd been trying to find the words to tell him about the charm, but each time I thought of it, I felt sick to the pit of my stomach. Hywel didn't forgive easily. I'd sought help from a woman people were calling a *witsh*. A woman whose name could soon be wagging on the tongues of magistrates and sheriffs. A woman whose home bloomed with tansy and spilled bloodied rats. I only hoped that, if he ever learned of it, he would believe my intentions were good. That I'd done it for us. For our child.

As though he had read my thoughts as clearly as the letters he kept piled on his desk, Hywel turned to Rhys and asked, 'did you hear about the stillbirth in Radnorshire?'

At this, Jacob's head whipped up.

Babies born stiff, arriving before they were ready, happened often, but it seemed a little tactless of Hywel to speak of it in almost the same breath as our own baby. Perhaps the news from Radnorshire had shaken him? Before I could wonder about how Hywel had even come to know about an event nearly twenty miles away, Rhys answered him.

'I did, as it happens. Terrible business.'

'Despicable.' Jacob practically spat the word.

Hywel chewed a mouthful of food thoughtfully before going on. 'Has she been arraigned yet?'

The wine caught in my throat and I coughed before asking, 'Arraigned? For losing her child?'

'No.' An impatient glance from Hywel. 'Not the mother. The woman who caused the death.'

'What do you mean?' I asked. My hands itched to clutch my belly, to hold my own baby safe and close.

Hywel sighed softly, irritated with my questions. But I was equally irritated – he should have known better than to carry on his conversations at the dinner table if he didn't plan to include everyone.

To my gratitude, Rhys answered me.

'A midwife attended the birth. Things seemed to be well enough, aside from the babe arriving several weeks sooner than expected. But when it was born, the infant failed to breathe.'

I pictured the scene: a woman red in the face and soaked with sweat, linens sticking to her dampened skin. A baby thudding stiff from her thighs. Had the baby been a boy or a girl? I wanted to ask, but thought better of it. Unlikely he would know anyway.

'That's terrible,' I said, trying to keep my voice steady. 'But not uncommon. How can anyone be blamed for an act of God?'

Hywel scoffed.

'An act of God? Perhaps you should curb your curiosity somewhat, Doli. It may well get you in trouble one day.'

He glanced at Jacob, who was smirking silently, as though in approval, and I felt myself flush. Furious. Hot. Rhys' eyes were still on me, however, looking at me intently, a small frown creasing his brow.

'There's talk of a woman named Kathryn Lewis. An old beggar woman, by all accounts. You know the sort.' I nodded, and Rhys continued. 'She was blamed for the stillbirth because there were witnesses to her crime – they saw her curse the woman's family.'

More talk of magic and curses. Amongst the poorer village folk, plenty were unashamed to crawl from door to door seeking charity, clattering their empty pots and pans. For those who gave in abundance, there would be stories and information, morsels of gossip. Those who refused were often met with thinly veiled threats. Perhaps this was something more...

'She had been to the farmhouse only months previous, begging milk and flour. The wife – Elizabeth Garrett – often obliged her, but this time it was the woman's husband who answered the door. Kathryn Lewis asked to speak to the wife – charity being a woman's area, of course – but the husband refused. He turned her away. He'd had enough of his wife giving away their hard-earned supplies, and with another child on the way, they had even less to spare. So, she dropped to her knees, raised her arms to the skies and laid a curse on the whole family, including the unborn infant.'

Without meaning to, I gasped, clasping a hand to my mouth.

'I hear she tore away her clothes to reveal her bare breasts while screaming the curse,' Jacob added, his voice level, matter-of-fact.

The image was almost comical. Like something from a play. Rhys, at least, seemed to find the idea funny.

'How could anyone do that? Wish harm on an infant?' I hated the quiver that had seeped into my own voice.

'People are desperate,' said Rhys. 'Starving. The rains poured without end all throughout the growing season last year. The soil around Llynidwen, all over Brecknockshire, has refused to yield more than a few sorry cauliflowers. Those who have their own corn and cheese have managed, but there hasn't been enough to sell on. The hunger is steering people towards madness. Kathryn Lewis wanders miles each day begging crumbs. She was far from home when she cursed the Garrett babe.'

I looked down at the food in front of us, guilt seeping into my stomach like a snake. We'd eaten well enough, I hadn't realised how difficult things had been for the poorer people over winter.

Hywel reached across his empty plate to clasp my hand in his.

'There are some terrible people in this world, Doli, especially amongst the poorer folk. Some can be truly savage.'

'They have nothing to lose, you see,' Jacob said, dismissive. 'They do not know the word of God. Especially in these parts.'

I felt the cold creep into my bones and pulled my hand from under Hywel's. I had already been doubtful of my ability to keep this baby safe, despite it being folded deep in my belly, as close to me as anyone or anything could ever be. The thought of yet more danger, something so beyond my control, left me feeling like one of Hywel's deer, caught before an arrow.

Perhaps Rhys saw the worry sitting like a mask across my face; he smiled, and spoke in much warmer tones.

'Have you appointed a midwife for your babe yet?'

I glanced at Hywel, trying to gather my thoughts. He looked calm, content with his wine, his belly full of good food. These men had spoken so readily of pregnancy, of stillbirth and loss, as though it were nothing. They had sipped their wine, nodded their heads, and talked of beggars and curses safe in the knowledge that they would never suffer the pain of carrying a child, only to lose it before hearing its cries. Watching it grow. It left my skin feeling nettle-pricked. Tingling. I turned back to Rhys, forcing myself to speak.

'Not yet.' I closed my eyes and thought of the midwife Hywel had appointed last time I had lost a child. A woman around my mother's age, with cold, rough hands and a lingering, faint scent of horse manure. I remembered the words she had said to me, as she examined me after the loss. *Some infants take a dislike to their mother's wombs. There is nothing to be done, if the child does not want to see life.* When I opened my eyes again, Rhys was still looking at me. Did he know there was more I wanted to say?

'Ruby knows of several midwives locally, but Hywel is keen for me to meet with the woman who attended his sister when she was in childbed.'

'Not only my sister,' Hywel chimed in. 'She also attended my mother – she saw my sisters and me into this world. Our baby will be in good, experienced hands under her care.'

Much later, long after the silverware had been cleared away and our guests had left, I heard voices raised within the parlour.

'Surely you realise the absurdity of your words, Jacob!'

The voice belonged to Rhys. Our guests hadn't left, after all. They must have retired to the parlour with Hywel.

'Merely an observation,' Jacob replied. 'A woman who fails to carry a child can only blame herself.'

'Herself, or witchcraft, in Kathryn Lewis' case?' Hywel's tone was jovial, his words coming quickly. I could picture the smile pulling at his lips.

'Why not both?' Jacob said. His voice was quieter than the other two, and I had to press myself closer to the door to hear his words properly. 'The curse may not have worked if it had been cast against someone more...' Here, there was a small pause. 'Pure of heart.'

'Hywel, surely you don't agree with this?' Rhys sounded incredulous. Good. I waited for my husband to say something, but he didn't. Rhys continued. 'Hywel, you do understand that you are including your own wife in your reasoning? You cannot possibly believe that Doli —'

'Of course I don't believe that Doli has committed any sin,' Hywel cut in, coolly. 'That's a ridiculous suggestion.'

My heartbeat quickened as I closed my eyes, listening closely.

'And yet it is one that our friend Jacob here has made,' Rhys muttered darkly.

'Not at all,' Jacob said, his voice still low and calm. 'What I am trying to say is that carrying a child is a gift bestowed upon us by the good Lord. It is a good wife's duty. If it cannot be done, there must be a reason for it.'

'Such as?' Rhys pressed.

'In some cases, the woman's body is too riddled with sin to bear something as pure as a child. In others, it is a punishment from God himself.'

'How so?' I could hear the impatience in Rhys' tone, and I loved him for it.

I leant closer to the door, careful not to make a sound. As they spoke, I pictured my husband and Rhys standing opposite one another, cups in hand, cheeks flushed in the firelight. I pictured Jacob Lloyd, stern and steadfast in his declarations; brooch glinting in the flames.

'We are all wicked at heart, Rhys. We may strive for piety and purity, but we all carry sin at our core. The real trick is in accepting our sin, and repenting. Only then can we be truly close to God.'

I heard a scoff. When Jacob spoke again, his voice was cool. Clipped.

'If we say we have no sin, we deceive ourselves, and the truth is not in us.'

I recognised the words from the Bible.

'And you believe that women who lose their babes before birth have not repented, do you Jacob? Is that your insinuation?'

Rhys' voice dripped with contempt.

Though I was not surprised at what I was hearing from Jacob Lloyd, who clearly read his Bible more frequently than anyone, I couldn't understand why my own husband remained silent. He knew better than most the pain I had endured with each pregnancy, each loss. He had endured it too. He had seen the suffering afterwards, the tears, the sickness, the blood. He had suffered, too.

All were silent for a moment. I hoped that Hywel was recalling the anguish of last time. The animal sounds that had escaped me. The sweat. The exhaustion. I hoped he was thinking about how afterwards he had held my hand and smoothed my hair. How he'd kissed my brow and touched his forehead to mine. How he'd cried with me, quietly, when the doors were shut and the midwife gone, the servants safely in their beds.

It was Rhys who broke the uncomfortable silence.

'Hywel? Surely you don't believe this? Do you?'

I waited for him to answer, silently willing him to contradict Jacob. To defend me as a husband should. To ask Jacob, firmly, to leave our home. When he finally spoke, I felt my heart crack in my chest, my throat tightening.

'I believe I do, yes. It's unpleasant, but, admittedly, what Jacob says makes sense. If a child is a gift from God, a purity, *how* can it be nurtured in a body of sin?'

I could scarcely breathe.

The Villagers

Picture Kathryn Lewis dragging her boots across the earth. Maybe sweat drips from her temples. Maybe it gathers at the backs of her swollen knees. Picture the arthritic hands, the bulging knuckles that clasp tight to her pot. Picture her begging for a dish aslosh with creamy milk, a smattering of flour. Now picture a group of sows, their bellies swollen with piglets, charging about the farm, mad as crows. We ask you: *what happened?* Some say Elizabeth Garrett was not as generous as she claims. That the milk she gave was already thick and sour. A poor enough offering for the beggar to curse the woman's sows. Of course, Elizabeth asked Kathryn to set them right, but she refused. She had to, didn't she? To cure the sows would be to admit to cursing them. Now picture Elizabeth, left with only one option ... to counteract the curse, she would have to draw blood ... Is that why Kathryn cursed Elizabeth's poor, unborn babe?

After that first quickening at the river's edge, the baby became real to me. A living, squirming thing inside of me. An immortal soul. I had thought the quickening would bring relief, but instead, the trepidation that had settled within me since Hywel burned the charm only grew, the flames of the anxiety blown bigger by that strange, bloody water I'd seen in the river.

The dinner table talk of cursing and stillbirth had frightened me more than I'd let Hywel believe, and I couldn't escape the fear that burning the charm might lead to something awful. Last night, I went to my husband looking for comfort, for kind words, but found nothing other than hesitation in the way he touched me, as though he was disturbed by my changing body. While I longed for his forgiveness and understanding, longed to hear him say, 'don't worry Doli, our baby will be well,' I couldn't shake the memory of the conversation I'd heard between him and Jacob Lloyd. The words sat like a weight on my chest.

Only one person could give me the reassurance I needed now. Going to see her was a huge risk, but not going, living with the fear hovering over me like a crow, was unbearable.

I gathered my things and headed towards the village, following the river that led, eventually, to Sara's cottage. My rounding belly, heavy, more noticeable than it had been even a week ago. I had thought about asking Ruby to come with me, but she was already cross about the charm, I couldn't tell her I was going again, not after we'd last spoken. I pushed the guilt from my mind. Red kites spun circles in the sky above me, occasionally dipping low enough over the path for me to see the umber undersides of their bellies. All around, the land showed the impact of the winter frosts and the spring rains they had given way to. Rotten radishes and half-formed carrots spilled from the soil around the farmsteads on the way. Miserable, wet oxen stared with sullen eyes as I passed by.

Sara was busy tending to a cluster of primroses at her front door when I arrived. In amongst the unruly leaves and dying stems, soggy flower heads bobbed, heavy with rainfall. Still, the garden was alive, beautiful in a sprawling, wild sort of way, quite unlike our trimmed, neat gardens and hedgerows at Faen Maredudd. I stood behind her for a while, waiting as she hummed quietly to herself. I was about to cough, wanting to announce myself somehow, when she straightened and turned to face me with a cluster of broken sticks and trailing roots in her hand.

'Are you going to hover all day, or do you want to come in?'

There was something about her, about the way she moved, graceful, as though dancing to unheard music that made her seem like part of the land itself. A flower pruned and freed from its roots. *You are mistress of Faen Maredudd,* I told myself. *No need to be intimidated.*

'I'm sorry,' I said. 'I didn't want to interrupt. I didn't know how to —'

She gestured towards the front door.

'*Dere.* Come inside,' she said.

I stepped into the cottage – I'd forgotten how small it was. It took a moment for my eyes to adjust from the bright light of the April sun outside, to the gloomy cottage with its slatted windows. Even with the door left wide open, inviting in a cool breeze, the cottage was dark. The smell of damp earth and lavender hit me, just as it had last time, despite the change in season. Perhaps in weeks to come, when the heat had grown and the days lengthened, the floor of beaten earth would be dryer and warmer.

Sara looked pointedly at my middle.

'I see the charm worked. *Llongyfarchiadau*, mistress.'

Instinctively, my hand moved to my stomach. Why did I feel embarrassed? Exposed? I couldn't escape the sense that we were bound together now, bonded by the baby she had helped me to conceive.

'Yes. The baby has started to flutter inside me,' I said, wanting to smile but finding myself unable to. 'I worry...' I stopped, searching for the words. I needed to tell her the charm had been destroyed. After all, it was the reason I'd come. Instead, I said, 'The quickening ... There is so much that could yet go wrong.'

Sara nodded.

'Understandable,' she said. 'Carrying children is a difficult task. It requires strength of character and mind. Strength of body. Being in childbed is not unlike being on your deathbed. It's a woman's task, no doubt.'

She spoke as though she knew how it felt to be with child, and it occurred to me that I had never asked if she had children of her own. I remembered then, what Hywel had told me about the husbands that had disappeared. I looked around the cottage, as though I might see traces of them – a pair of boots at the door, or a cape hanging like animal hide. But the cottage showed no indication of a man's presence.

'How did you know?' I blurted, before I could stop myself.

Sara was quiet, thoughtful.

'Know what?' she asked, eventually.

'That the charm would work? You said I'd be with child before the frost thawed. How could you have known?'

She only looked at me, and smiled.

'What do you want me to do, Doli?' she asked.

I stayed quiet. I thought she would have an answer, a solution, something to reassure me. A new charm, maybe, to keep us safe. Standing there then, in the cool darkness of the cottage, I felt foolish. Perhaps I should not have come after all. I wanted to tell her about Hywel burning the charm, to ask if its destruction might harm the baby. I wanted to tell her everything about the last few months – the grief, the heartache, the surprise at being with child once again amidst the sadness and confusion of the last loss – but found I could barely speak at all.

'You are not the first woman to find herself in this predicament, Doli. And there will be many more that follow you. I can feel the baby for you, if you'd like? To ensure she's well?'

She.

'It's a girl?'

'Just a feeling,' she said, the creases at her eyes deepening.

'Are you a midwife as well, then?' I asked, momentarily distracted from the question that had been pressing at my mind for weeks.

She smiled again and replied, 'of sorts. My work is about caring for people. Sometimes that means helping women in childbed.' She gestured towards the pallet bed in the corner. 'Now lie here.'

I lay down, conscious of my growing stomach – was it too big? Too small?

Sara began prodding along my middle with her fingertips. While she worked, I stared up at the bunches of dried herbs and flowers, bound together and hanging from the rafters. Clusters of lavender crammed into every corner.

'The babe is well,' she said.

Relief flooded through me, warming me to my core. We were safe, for now.

'Thank you. Thank you so much,' I said, sitting up. 'Is there anything I can do to help the baby stay safe?'

'What do you mean?' she asked, frowning a little.

'Last time we...' I trailed off, thinking. 'The physician suggested it might have been my fault, that I should have taken my confinement, rested, taken better care of myself.'

Sara scoffed.

'Nonsense. Women with far busier lives than you have perfectly healthy babies, one after the other. Do you think they stop to rest? Of course they don't. They take a broom to their floors and churn their butter up until the moment they come to childbed. Then they do it all over again. Walking the moors and hosting dinners will not cause your baby any harm.'

I felt myself flush, embarrassed at the way she perceived my life. Though of course, she was right.

'Then perhaps I was too idle?' I said, tentative. *Please,* I wanted to say. *Help me.*

She raised a hand, her palm spread between us. The gesture was similar to the one she had made the first time I'd visited. It had bristled me then, to be silenced by a peasant woman. But this time I felt comforted by it. By her certainty.

'Mistress, stop worrying. You are not to blame.'

It was the first time anyone had said those words to me. The relief was like warm river water flooding my body as I dared to believe the losses may not have been my fault after all. I felt lighter.

'What about riding on horseback?' I asked her, remembering what Hywel had said about being careful.

'Keep doing what you've always done. If you're comfortable, your baby will be too. Here —' She thrust a bunch of chamomile into my hands. 'Steep these in boiled water to drink before bed. And be sure to pray while you do it. God will protect you. And the babe.' I nodded.

Despite my joy at knowing our baby was well, I couldn't let the relief bloom as I wanted to, not yet. I needed to address the root of the worry and strain that had been plaguing me.

'There's one more thing,' I said. 'The charm. The one you gave me. One of our maids found it, and well, it was destroyed. My husband threw it on the fire.'

She scowled, troubled.

'It won't harm the baby, will it?'

My breath came shallow as she chewed her lip, looking off into the dark corners of the cottage.

'It shouldn't,' she said. 'But these are forces beyond our control, mistress.'

My heart sank. It wasn't the answer I'd come here for. I would never have risked coming here again if I wasn't so frightened, so desperate to hear that the baby would be well – despite Hywel's actions.

Unsure how to respond, I nodded. Then in desperation, I said, 'I can pay you, of course.' I pulled a velvet pouch from my skirts, the coins inside jingling musically as I lifted it. 'How much —'

She shook her head and put her hands out in front of her before I could finish. 'I don't ask for payment in coin,' she said.

'Wine then?' I said. 'Or butter? We brew good ale at Faen Maredudd, I can have a cask sent to you. What are you in need of...?' I trailed off, spotting a large wooden barrel near the back door – she had enough ale, then.

She stayed quiet for a moment, studying me. She had a way of doing that, leaving you feeling exposed, as though she was seeing your very soul.

'I believe I will be in need of your help in the future,' she said. 'Hold your payment, until then.'

It seemed such a strange thing to say. What did she mean?

As she stared at me, I felt the mood in the room shift, as though a cloud had rolled in overhead. It was time to leave. When I re-emerged, blinking in the bright light, the dandelion yellow of the sun breaking through the clouds was a shock, and it took me a moment to readjust after the darkness of Sara's home.

As I was about to embark on the trail home, there was a rustling in the bushes at the other side of the river – likely a fox or a rabbit, or even a small bird picking its way through the roots and brambles. And yet ... the movement brought with it a creeping sensation, something prickled at my skin. Was someone watching me?

I rubbed my eyes with my fists, trying to get a clearer view, but there was nothing unusual to be seen, and the leaves had already settled to a stillness amongst the dense tree trunks.

The Villagers

They say there have been hangings across the border. *Yn Lloegr*. In England, women have swung from the gallows, their feet dancing high above the crowds. In Scotland it is worse. King James has made sure of that. Women have burned on great biers, their bodies like tallow candles, melting, then stiffening. Blackened. Charred. Women branded witch – *witsh*. They say the smell of burning hair is rancid. They say it fills the air like mizzle.

Finally, the rain began to ease. As the weather improved, so too did my humour. The tiredness subsided a little and I began to walk out on the grasslands again, enjoying the faint sunlight on my skin. Often, I felt my daughter rolling like a fish when I walked near to the river, as though she was trying to slither free and jump into the water. The poetry had come back to me, and I often found myself lost in thoughts of new verses and rhymes, rushing home from my walks to scribble the words in my prayer book.

Hywel had been so busy preparing trade for the markets in Bristol and Chester that I'd barely seen him in weeks. Each time we encountered each other in the bedchamber, he seemed surprised by how much my body had changed, how my stomach had grown round and firm as an apple. He often seemed afraid to touch me now, treating me like a delicate doll, as though holding me too close might cause the baby to come barrelling out before her time. Once or twice, when he had placed his hands on me, the baby had kicked him, furious. He hadn't laughed with me.

I had been so sure that this pregnancy, this baby, would draw us closer together. That Hywel might begin, once again, to see me as he used to, to hold me. Love me. But if anything, it felt as though we had only grown further apart – my growing belly like a wall between us, pushing him further away with each passing week.

One morning, in early May, I woke to a soreness at the base of my spine. With each step I felt as though a crow was pecking at me, a small, sharp beak chipping its insistence at my back. There was an urgency to keep moving, to loosen my hips and legs and to be outside in the clean air. Though the fires hadn't been lit since the rains eased, the smoke clung to the rugs, the curtains, the coverlets, and I often felt I was choking on it.

Over breakfast, I squirmed on the hard wooden bench, readjusting and crossing my legs, trying to ease the pressure on my back.

'What's wrong?' Hywel asked, impatient despite the concern creasing his brow.

'Nothing,' I told him.

'If you're sure,' he said slowly. 'Rhys and I are expected in Shrewsbury today, on business. But if you would rather I stay...'

I interrupted him before he could finish his offer to stay at home.

'That won't be necessary.' I put down my crust of bread and tried to smile. 'You're always about some business or other. What is it today?'

He smiled back, almost indulgent. It was the way a father might smile at a child asking questions it wouldn't comprehend the answers to. It irritated me.

'Business that wouldn't interest you, Doli, my dear. Acquisitions, law, and the like. And what will you do today?'

I ignored his question.

'When will you be back?'

'Tonight,' he smiled. 'Or perhaps tomorrow, if someone can offer us shelter. There is, I believe, an inn near Shrewsbury in which we might stay.'

I nodded. There were scarcely any inns that offered more than a cup of ale and a weak stew in these parts, but whenever Hywel travelled across the marches towards England, he seemed to find a bed for the night without issue. He was always gone for longer than he said he would be.

I swallowed a mouthful of cold meat and cleared my throat.

'I thought I might go to the market with Ruby this afternoon. I'd like to buy some fabrics to make something for the baby. It's been such a terribly long, tiresome winter. Won't it be a relief to see trade come back to the village?'

'Of course!' Hywel replied, thoughtful. 'The market! I had quite forgotten trade was resuming for the season today. Although —' he scowled. 'You needn't go yourself. Ask Ruby to fetch whatever you need. Or one of the other servants.'

'I want to go. It's the first market of the season – I want to look around.'

He shrugged, finished his ale and moved back from the table, the bench scraping loudly against the floor.

'As you please.'

The village was bustling. Hordes of sheep nodded dully in their pens, their earthen scent blanketing the square. Angular cattle lowed and people called to each other across the crowds.

There were some stalls selling parcels of butter and cheese, but not as many as last year. With so much livestock lost over winter, the farmers didn't have enough to sell on.

I followed Ruby towards a stall selling sheep's wool, ducking away from a harassed looking woman tugging an infant by the sleeve of its dress with a baby clutched to her chest.

She greeted the young woman behind the stall warmly.

'Mistress,' she turned to me. 'This is my cousin Agnes.'

Agnes barely looked older than myself and Ruby, but there was a hardness about her eyes, a cool determination in the way she gazed out at the market. Her hair was the colour of autumn leaves, cascading down her back in ringlets. Beside her, I felt drab and small, suddenly aware of my own pale complexion, my light hair scraped back behind the ears and tucked under my cap.

'It's a pleasure to make your acquaintance,' I said. 'My name is Doli Maredudd, mistress of Faen Maredudd.' Involuntarily, I glanced behind me in the direction of the big house, half expecting to see its windows like eyes watching over me.

'I know who you are,' Agnes said, in an accent even thicker than Ruby's. 'We ate at your house over Christmastide. Rabbit stew. It was delicious.'

I blushed, pleased, though it was Hywel that had caught the rabbits, and I hadn't prepared any of the meal myself.

'I'm glad to hear it. My husband trapped the rabbits himself.'

Ruby looked pleased too.

'Agnes was working at the Garrett farm, near Presteigne, but she's recently found new employ with the Jones', just across the village,' she said, nodding in the direction of the nearby farmsteads. 'It's good to have you nearer to us again, Agnes.'

'I'm glad to see the Jones' trade wasn't too greatly diminished by the cold season,' I told her. 'I know many families suffered this year.'

'I've only been at the Jones' farm a few weeks,' she replied. 'But they seem to have managed well enough. Their holding is well sheltered, with enough space to bring the animals indoors for winter. The Garretts weren't quite so lucky.'

Garrett. The name struck me as familiar, somehow, like a lost thing found years after it has been forgotten.

'I'm sorry to hear that,' I said. 'Is that why you left?'

'The barley didn't grow well last year. Then we lost some sheep and a pig,' she replied simply. Then, glancing at Ruby slyly, 'Though they say that was all Kathryn Lewis' doing.'

Kathryn Lewis. That name again. Then it dawned on me why I recognised the name of the farm – Elizabeth Garrett was the woman that Hywel, Rhys and Jacob had been discussing over supper. The stillbirth.

I tried not to say anything. It certainly wasn't my place. But I couldn't hold the words back, not with my own baby bobbing pleasantly in my belly, reassuring me with each kick and roll. I didn't know Elizabeth Garrett, but I felt some sort of connection with her, given the circumstances.

'I was sorry to hear of the misfortune. The baby,' I said, bowing my head. 'How did your mistress seem, when you departed?'

Agnes shrugged.

'She ploughs ahead. The land must be tended and the other children cared for. The babe was not the first to be lost. It won't be the last.'

I was taken aback by the hard tone of her voice; my hand cupped my stomach.

I left Ruby to speak alone with her cousin and occupied myself wandering about the stalls. There was nothing of much significance to see, and nothing that we didn't produce for ourselves on our own land, but I was enjoying being away from the house with its long winding passages, its constant draughts. It was enough simply to see different faces, to hear different voices, listen to small snippets of conversation and feel the sun on my face.

When I found a woman selling lengths of linen, I chose a soft yellow fabric – the colour reminded me of some lemons Hywel had once brought back from a trip to London, a long time ago. My mouth watered at the memory as I asked for enough to stitch a gown for the baby, and selected some pretty wooden beads to use as buttons.

'She's bold,' I said to Ruby as we made our way home along the river. 'To wear her hair that way in public.'

'Agnes?'

'Yes, of course. Who else?'

Ruby smiled and shrugged one shoulder, careless.

'She's always been that way. *Defiant,* her father used to call it. She was lucky to find employ at the Jones' farm. The Garretts' too. She's been dismissed by a few employers, in the past.'

'She has? Because of her hair?'

Ruby glanced sideways at me, almost scowling.

'No. I forget what the problem was. Something unfounded, probably.'

'Was she dismissed from the Garretts' holding?' I asked, noting that Agnes hadn't really answered my question about her reason for leaving when I'd asked earlier.

Ruby looked at me and considered for a moment. The river burbled pleasantly as we walked.

'Yes. Resources became sparse. And with the babe dead there was less need for servants than they'd anticipated.'

I wondered if that was why Agnes' tone had seemed so cold, so dismissive, when she spoke of the loss. Did she resent the family? Did she blame the poor cursed infant for the sudden loss of her position?

'Agnes is the cousin you told me about?' I asked, finding myself somehow fascinated with her – her tumbling hair and her simple, abrupt nature.

Ruby nodded.

'The one who heals people sometimes? And helps women in childbed?'

Ruby nodded again, quiet.

'But she's not a midwife?'

'No. Well, she's not trained, in the traditional sense.'

'Then where did she learn her skills?' I asked. It interested me, the way poorer people relied on women with no medical training over midwives who'd studied their trade, made their oaths.

'Not everyone can afford licensed midwives,' Ruby replied simply, when I shared this thought with her. Of course. I felt my cheeks flush with embarrassment. Stupidity. 'Besides, women like Agnes learn from others, often their mothers, who learned from their own mothers. They're qualified by their experience, whether they've taken an oath or not.'

'I suppose so,' I said, thinking of the awful midwife Hywel had brought last time.

She shrugged. 'It's true.'

There was something gay and playful about her as we walked. Carefree. Perhaps spending time with her cousin had reminded her of her childhood. Or perhaps they slunk off to the alehouse while I was wandering about the market. That seemed more likely.

'Was she there? Did she help deliver the Garrett baby?' I asked, quieting my voice, though there was no one around to hear us. Besides, our voices wouldn't have carried over the rush of the river and the gentle hum of the wind through the trees above us.

She did, Ruby spoke curtly and it was clear she had no intention of elaborating on the story.

As we reached the pathway back to our gardens, just before the brow of the hill where the house would loom into sight, Ruby bent and scooped something up from the ground. As she straightened, I saw what she was cradling: a tiny bird's skull. The bone was dirty white, cracked along the temple. She pressed it to her ear.

'What on earth are you doing, Ruby? That looks filthy.'

'I'm listening,' she replied. 'For birdsong.'

She pressed the thing to my ear.

'Listen, can you hear it? Isn't it beautiful.'

Standing sometime later in the gardens, I listened to the evening sky settling, birds chirruping all around, bats squeaking overhead. All day, the sun had been pleasant and promising, as though heralding in the beginning of a newer, brighter season, but now suddenly the clouds began to gather and roll, and it felt as though thunder may clap and lightning strike at any moment. Perhaps summer warmth was not as close as I had hoped.

Earlier that evening, I'd managed to press Ruby a little more about Agnes. The curse, the Radnorshire stillbirth, the grief that followed. The fear. How Agnes had left the home in a sorry state of rotting barley and sadness.

She'd warned me then, her eyes searching and serious, not to tell anyone about my visit to Sara Gwen.

'Talk is getting louder. Whispers are carrying like the wind through the trees.' She stopped, looking around. Lowered her voice. 'Sara Gwen is already being watched.'

'Watched?' I remembered the strange feeling I'd had when leaving the cottage. 'Watched by whom? What for?'

'The justice will have given the orders, but everyone knows the master has his ear. As do many noblemen across the county. Who wants her watched is anyone's guess, really.'

'But what exactly is it they're watching for?'

Ruby shrugged.

'Signs of witchcraft. Malice. Fraternising with the devil. Shows of Catholic worship, maybe.'

I scoffed.

'They'd have to arrest half the village of Llynidwen, half the county, if they were going to arrest people for holding the old faith.'

Ruby shrugged again. She knew I was right.

The Villagers

Witshes are old, lame, blear-eyed, pale, foul and full of wrinkles. Lean. Deformed. They are poor, sullen, superstitious and Papist: women who know no religion. They can make themselves invisible, and deprive men of their most private parts. They can bring souls from the grave, tear snakes to pieces with words alone. Their looks can stun lambs. In the witshes' drowsy minds, the devil has a fine seat.

One evening late in May, I sat across the table from Hywel, roast pheasant and plates of vegetables between us, but he was unusually quiet. He drank several cups of Gascony wine in quick succession, pausing only to chew his food hurriedly.

Afterwards, I scooped up the lemon yellow fabric and went to find him in the parlour, where he was reclined comfortably on the settle, another cup of wine in his hand. I was intending to show him the fabric, hoping it would lift his spirits, but his face was so sombre that I thought better of it.

'Hywel?' I said. 'Is something wrong?'

He rubbed his temples, his brow furrowed and tight, before looking at me.

I waited for him to reply. Outside, the sun was setting, casting a warm, amber glow across the red and gold rug. Finally, he spoke.

'Is something wrong? you ask.' His voice was quiet. 'Perhaps you should sit down, Doli.'

He opened his arms to me, inviting me to sit on his lap.

'Hywel, I —'

'Sit,' he said again, more firmly this time. I crossed the room and perched on his lap, wincing at a sudden kick to my ribcage, as though the baby was responding to my discomfort. I used to sit in his lap like this when we were younger, when I first moved to Faen Maredudd. We'd steal moments in the buttery or in the stables behind his mother's back, in the years before his parents moved away, leaving the home to us. The warmth of his body against mine was the same, now, but something felt wrong.

'Please,' I said, turning my head so that I could look at his face. 'Tell me. What's upset you?'

Without warning, he laughed. A deep, barking laugh like a clap of thunder. At my sudden flinch, he laughed all the more.

'What could possibly have upset me? Let me think. Could it be that my wife has been seen leaving the home of a woman people all across the county are calling a *witsh*?'

My heart dropped. There it was again, that feeling, like a spider crawling along my spine. I knew I was being watched. I tried to stand, but Hywel had his hands on my thighs, holding me in place.

'Hywel, you don't understand.'

'Then please, help me to understand.'

'She's not like you said, Hywel. She's a charmer. A soothsayer. They say she can heal the sick, cure animals, protect the home. Even tell the future.'

I waited for him to respond but he stayed silent and continued staring at me coolly, so I went on. I couldn't keep it from him any longer.

'I asked her for a charm, something to help us, to help me, to carry a child. Hywel, you know how difficult it's been, how painful each time.' I paused again, searching his face for signs of understanding. Compassion. Anything. 'I couldn't bear it any longer. I couldn't stand seeing the hurt, the disappointment on your face each time the bleeding started. I couldn't handle the pain, the exhaustion, the heartbreak of losing another baby. The certainty it was my fault, somehow. I was desperate.'

'Yes. It's been difficult. To say the least,' he uttered quietly, his gaze flicking towards the window which overlooked the garden and our rosebush. 'But that's no excuse to turn to witchcraft. Tell me, what did Sara Gwen do for you?'

'She gave me a charm. I tucked it under our mattress. That's what Margiad found. It wasn't the servants trying to curse us. Or an old recipe. It was me. It was supposed to help, it was supposed to make things better, to bring us a child at last. And, Hywel, it did.'

In that moment, I hoped he would look at me, at my growing belly, and see things as I did. See that I had to turn to magic because midwives and physicians and prayers had failed me. For years, they had failed me. But he rubbed his hand over his chin, then said simply, 'Doli.'

The anger had disappeared from his voice; he sounded only tired, defeated.

'I wanted to tell you. I've been wanting to tell you for so long, but I heard you talking with Rhys and Jacob, and well, how could I possibly have told you then? After what you said?'

'What I said?' His face softened then. 'Doli, I didn't mean ... I wasn't talking about you.'

Tears filled my eyes. I blinked them away furiously, determined not to cry.

'How could you not be? You said women lose their babies because of sin. That women who can't bear children must be to blame. You didn't even deny it when Rhys challenged you.'

He looked down at the rug, staring fixedly at one spot.

'Yes,' he said. 'I did, I suppose. But we are all born in sin, Doli. Every one of us. We must ask forgiveness from the Lord. Always.'

'I was scared. I was scared because you threw the charm on the fire, and if the magic was strong enough to work, I thought burning it might hurt the baby. So I went to see Sara again, for reassurance. That's all.'

Hywel's eyes grew wider, but he stayed silent, staring at my face. I looked away, unable to meet his gaze any longer.

'Say something, please.'

At last, he sighed, pushing me from his lap and standing up.

'That was foolish of you, Doli. Stupid. I can't understand why you'd meddle with such unknown, ungodly forces?'

'I told you why. Because —'

'Quiet.' He held his palm up to silence me. 'You're naïve, Doli. So very naïve. These people, these women, they don't want to help us. Why would they? They mean us harm. It's undoubtedly witchcraft. It's ungodly.'

'It's —'

'It's exactly like I told you. Soothsaying, fortune-telling, healing—' he waved his hands about. 'All a clever way to disguise what they are really up to. Devil's work, Doli. Things have been strange in this house since Margiad found that thing.' He crossed the room then, going to stand at the window, looking out into the gardens. 'Have you seen our crops recently? The herb garden? The cook has done well with what we have but surely you're aware seasoning has been sparse. The doves are unhappy, they're plucking each other to baldness. And the house itself? Some nights I can barely sleep more than an hour for all the racket.'

'Racket?' I asked.

'Noises...' he waved his hand vaguely about. 'At night. As though someone were running around the rooms, knocking the pots and pans about down in the kitchens. Doors rattling in their hinges, wind howling at the windows.'

'I haven't heard anything,' I said, though I was thinking of the strange, ghostly figure out on the moors, the pulsating blood on the river's surface as spring bloomed. I hadn't heard anything at night but it was undeniable something unnatural was underway.

He looked at me, frowning.

'I'm sorry, Hywel. I should have told you what it was when Margiad found it. I should never have let you burn it.'

'No. You shouldn't have brought it into this house in the first place. Besides, burning that piece of paper might have been a good thing, if she is indeed an advocate of the devil.'

'No, Hywel, I —'

He interrupted me again. 'Don't you see? It wasn't a charm, Doli, it was a curse.'

'I don't think it was, Hywel. It worked, didn't it?'

I pressed my hand to my stomach, willing him to look at me, at the bump rounding my middle, to remember that we had created something beautiful. That good came from my actions.

'Who's to say?' he spat. 'That infant may not be mine at all. It could be a child of the devil.'

I gasped, feeling for all the world as though my own husband had taken his dagger to my cheek.

'How could you say that?' I asked, my voice small, shaking. 'How can you even —'

'Quiet. Please. I'm thinking.'

I opened my mouth, wanting to argue, but closed it again when

107

the words failed to form. I had seen him this way before – determined to the point of recklessness. When Hywel had his mind set on something, there was no swaying him.

'When she's arrested, you'll have to testify about this. It's only more evidence to give at the assizes. We must inform the justices at once. I'll speak with Sir Thomas, ask for his advice. Jacob, too.'

'Arrested?'

I shuddered. Surely this wasn't cause for arrest, for assizes? Not here, in Llynidwen. Didn't the magistrates have more important things to think of than witchcraft and magic? There were thieves and criminals on the roads, conmen and pedlars who tricked widows and old maids. Women weren't dragged to the assizes. It simply didn't happen.

Looking at Hywel's face, his nostrils flaring with his breath, I knew he would see this through. If he had his way, Sara would be hanged. And it would be, at least in part, my fault.

I took a horse from the stables and set out for Allt-Goras at dawn, before the first light broke. It wasn't that I didn't want Hywel to see me, to ask where I was going – he would find out anyway no doubt. It was simply that I couldn't face him that morning, nor anyone else, for that matter. I didn't even tell Ruby my plans.

I worried Hywel might have tried to stop me riding my mare. He'd already made insinuations about me needing to rest, to move slowly, to be still. If he had his way, I wouldn't leave the confines of Faen Maredudd. The thought of being trapped indoors, moving idly from one settle to the next, was suffocating.

There was the promise of sunlight and warmth as I rode along the moors, though the early morning air was cold. We were heading towards summer, each day warmer than the last, and yet there was a constant chill in my bones, a stiffness I couldn't shake.

Riding on horseback had become less comfortable as my body had grown bigger. My thighs pulled and stung as I braced them over the horse's flanks, the outsides of my hips needling. Nevertheless, I managed the miles to Rhys' house without incident, arriving as the sun broke through the clouds, the horizon growing yellow as buttercups.

I was greeted by one of Rhys' servants, who showed me to the parlour. Rhys' home was larger than ours, his grounds sprawling and vast. *Old money*, Mam called it. With each visit, I found myself mesmerised at the grandiosity of his furniture, the intricacy of the carvings in the woodwork. While I waited, I stared up at the painting hanging over the fireplace, Rhys' likeness captured perfectly, right down to the last freckle.

'Doli! *Bore da*. To what do I owe the pleasure, *bore 'ma?*'

I turned to see Rhys entering the room. His surprise was well-hidden behind his smile, though I could see the traces of it on his brow.

'Please, sit.'

He gestured towards the settle and I took a seat, feeling small perched at its edge. He sat beside me.

When I didn't say anything, Rhys cleared his throat, and pulled a piece of paper from his pocket.

'I have something to share with you, actually. A new poem. Perhaps you will look at it when you get home.'

I took the paper from him, preoccupied with my thoughts, but unable to find the right words to tell him what I'd done.

Now that I was here, uncertainty nagged at me. I picked at a loose thread on my dress, wondering what to say. How to say it. It was true, Rhys did hold more influence over Hywel than I did – I wouldn't have come otherwise – but how much more I couldn't say. Besides, Hywel was a stubborn man. How often had I seen him do exactly the opposite of what was asked of him, merely as a matter of pride?

Rhys was looking at me expectantly, so I began.

'Rhys ... I need your help. I'm afraid I've done something I shouldn't have.'

Rhys sat back quietly, his eyes focussed on mine. Waiting.

Before I could go on, the servant was back, balancing a tray with two cups of ale. Rhys took both, handing one to me. I immediately took a big gulp, feeling my hands shake as I pressed the cup to my mouth.

I tried again to speak, but the words wouldn't come. I was aware of how my lips hung, slightly parted.

Rhys leaned forward, concern creasing his brow. His hand twitched in his lap, as though he wanted to reach out, but was held back by something.

'Doli? You're worrying me.'

'I've done something I shouldn't have done,' I said again.

'Oh?'

'I went to see a woman, a healer. Her name is Sara Gwen. You might have heard of her?'

I waited for Rhys to give some indication that he had, but he barely moved, so I carried on.

'She gave me a charm. A charm to —' Instead of finishing my sentence, I looked down, placing my hands over my stretched stomach.

Rhys nodded.

'I see. Go on.'

'I knew it was a risky thing to do, but Rhys, I had to do something. I'm expected to provide Hywel, to provide our family, with an heir, and, well...' I trailed off, embarrassed. 'I thought she might be able to help me keep...' I said quietly, feeling my skin prick pink with shame. 'It's been so many years. So many losses.'

Rhys was quiet for a moment. When he finally spoke, his voice was gentle, his words slow, as though he was approaching a wounded animal. He moved closer to me, and I looked into his eyes, letting their stillness calm me, just for a moment.

'Doli. Surely you don't believe your pregnancy is the result of some scribbled charm? Wise women might be able to soothe a fever or give tinctures for unsettled infants, but you're giving this woman more credit than she's due. She can't be responsible for something as sacred as the conception of a child. That's between you, Hywel, and God.'

He cleared his throat, then moved away from me. I took another slow sip of my ale, and considered his words.

'But Rhys, it can't be a coincidence, can it? My body has failed me so many times. And now...'

'Why not?' he asked, with a sad smile. 'A thing may be strange but that doesn't make it untrue.'

I chewed my lip for a moment, thinking. Could it be possible that Sara's charm had nothing to do with this pregnancy? That her magic was a mere coincidence of timing? However this baby came to be, the outcome was the same: Sara was being watched, branded a witch. Hywel was furious with me. And if there was any truth to it, if Sara was a witch, what did it mean for me, for my baby, now that the charm had been destroyed?

'Why are you telling me about this, Doli?' Rhys asked quietly, reminding me why I had come. 'You know what people are saying about wise women lately. It isn't sensible, for a woman of your rank, to admit to consulting with one whose name is already known to certain officials.' So, he had heard of her then. 'Not in these parts of the land, at least.'

My heartbeat quickened. His words slipped through me as though I'd swallowed an eel, landing in my stomach like a cold dead thing.

'I don't mean, of course, that I would say anything to anyone. Only that you must be careful. The villagers are growing more suspicious, more fearful. Hywel has told me about talk he's heard ... from his tenants. And Jacob Lloyd is always in his ear.'

'I know.' I reached over, squeezed his hand gratefully, before remembering myself and pulling it back. I didn't add that he and Ruby were the only people I spoke to about anything aside from estate affairs beyond my own husband. 'I'm telling you because I need your help. I told Hywel about the charm. I had to – he knew I'd been to see Sara. I told him what I'd done and he was just as furious as I feared he would be. He wants Sara arrested and tried for witchcraft. I think he'd already made enquiries about her, even before I told him about this. He was suspicious of her ... of her skills.'

There was no need to say what we both already knew – that when Hywel wanted a thing to happen, it always did.

'But Doli – if Hywel truly believes that this woman, this Sara Gwen, helped you to conceive, why would he want to see her punished?'

'He says all witchcraft is evil, even when it doesn't appear to be. He even said this child could belong to the devil.' My voice cracked as I spoke. Coming from my own mouth, the words stung as much as they had when Hywel had said them. 'My husband believes everything comes with a price.'

Rhys' smile was terse. It did not reach his eyes.

'Ah, yes the words of a true man of business,' he said, his eyes fixed on the bulge of my dress.

'Rhys, I can't be responsible for the indictment of an innocent woman. Please, you must speak with him.'

'You have paid her a visit, Doli, no more than that.' His voice was calm, soft. 'You are therefore not responsible for whatever becomes of her. And as for her innocence ... well,' he shrugged. 'As things now stand she's either a *witsh* or a fraud, I'm afraid.'

'Rhys,' I tried again. 'Please.'

He sighed.

'You know as well as I do that your husband is a stubborn man.'

'But he listens to you, Rhys. You know he does.'

'At times, yes. But not always.' Rhys looked down at his lap. 'Has he ever told you about what I said to him, before your betrothal was formally arranged?'

I shook my head.

'Your family is well respected, of course, but there are always certain...' He paused here to sip his ale, before continuing. 'Nuances, to take into account when arranging a marriage. I'm sorry to say that I encouraged Hywel to consider a pairing with one of the Herbert girls. Please, don't take offence,' he said as I stiffened. 'It was nothing to do with you. The Herberts had been buying ecclesiastical properties all over Flintshire, their wealth was growing by the day. It would have been a particularly fortuitous match, that's all.'

'Did Hywel think so?' I asked, feeling the hurt wash over me at the thought of Hywel married to another woman. Of Rhys encouraging him.

'Of course,' Rhys said. He looked at me and sighed. 'But that didn't matter. Hywel wouldn't hear of it. By this point, he'd already been introduced to you, Doli. You charmed him. He was enamoured with you.'

I believed him. Hywel was always charming, always bringing freshly picked flowers for me and bread baked at Faen Maredudd for my mother. And there was something else that drew me to him, in the beginning. Something I had never told anyone, not even Hywel ... Years ago, when I was still a small child, I'd been playing outside my home with my sister, when a woman with cloudy eyes and a thin cloak of worsted draped about her shoulders approached me. She told me I would marry a man with hair and eyes dark as storm clouds. A man with rings of gold on his fingers and velvet in his voice. When I saw Hywel years later, I recognised him immediately as the man who would be my husband. I'd pictured him, clear as an oil painting, for years before we met. Like magic. I wanted to tell Rhys about this, but I worried about how it might sound to him. Would he think I was a *witsh*? It sounded like a child's bedtime story. And so I said nothing, waiting for Rhys to go on.

'And so you see. He doesn't always listen to me.'

I remained seated and still, stunned into silence by Rhys' story. I hadn't known there had been anyone else considered for a match with Hywel. Perhaps that was naïve of me.

'And just as well,' Rhys added. 'I still remember the way he looked at you when you first met. You were a great match, as he knew you would be.'

I wanted to tell him Hywel hadn't looked at me the way he used to for a long time. That each time we sat across the table from one another, I tried to meet his eyes, to find love there, or some hint of tenderness, but saw mostly agitation. That his head was always buried in some books, his ledger, his letters. His Bible seemed more important to him than I was, lately. I shook my head.

'Even so, you said yourself you don't believe Sara Gwen could be responsible for this pregnancy. That she can't truly be a *witsh*. So you must try.'

When Rhys sighed again, it was heavy, filled with the weight of something unspoken.

'For you Doli, I will speak with him. But I can't make any promises.'

The sun was high in the sky by the time I left Allt-Goras and I wagered it must have been nearing midday. The morning was so pleasant that I decided to extend my journey by travelling back through the village, passing by houses and farmsteads before reaching the river that would lead me back to Faen Maredudd.

The warm breeze carried the scents of cooking lard and lye, grease thickening the air around me. Men shouted and small children whined and laughed as my horse trotted along the road. Women sat in the doorways of their houses, darning gowns or soothing crying infants, enjoying the sun on their cheeks.

At the centre of the village, a cluster of children were playing in the dust. Two girls were spinning circles around a small child, who crouched in the mud, while a group of boys flicked marbles back and forth. The children looked ashen, thin, their gowns threadbare in places, and I remembered the yellow fabric I had bought for my own baby. I was no seamstress, but I was quick enough with a needle. I hoped that if I surprised Hywel with the gown once it was sewn, it might lift his spirits. I thought it might help us both, to be able to picture the child.

As I approached one of the last houses before reaching the curve

114

in the river that would take me towards home, I saw a gaggle of women huddled together. I heard a familiar voice, and recognised the tumble of red hair before I placed it – Agnes. The women turned at the sound of my horse's hooves, and lowered their voices, almost whispering. Some had their arms folded across their chests. I thought I heard them say something about Sara Gwen – at least it sounded as though they said her name, but I couldn't be certain.

I slowed my horse, intending to stop to greet them, then thought better of it. After all, without Ruby accompanying me, what business did I have speaking with farmhands and other village women? Instead, I lifted my hand in greeting as I passed by. Agnes smiled at me, but the women standing around her looked towards me distastefully, their faces scrunched as though they had swallowed soured milk. One, a woman whose dark hair spilled from her frilled cap, cradled a thin grey cat in her arms. She glowered at me, though I'd never seen her before and couldn't imagine what reason she would have to look at me in such a way.

Sighing, I dug my heels to the horses' flanks, until she quickened to a trot, and left the women behind me.

When I arrived home, the house was quiet and still. It seemed especially so, compared with the gay noises of the village. The entryway was dark and cool. Ruby rounded the corner, greeting me with her usual humour, but before she could take my riding cloak Hywel appeared from the parlour, gesturing for her to leave.

I assessed his face for signs of anger but it was unreadable.

'Where have you been?' he asked me coolly.

I thought about lying, and telling him I had been riding, but it would only delay the inevitable. He would find out soon enough.

'I couldn't sleep,' I told him. 'So I rose early and went to take the air. I rode as far as Allt-Goras and called on Rhys.'

Hywel looked at me, unblinking and silent.

'You rode all that way on your own?'

I nodded. Waiting.

'And you called on Rhys? Without me?'

I nodded again, then said simply, 'You know Rhys is like a brother to me, Hywel.'

He looked at me, his eyes moving up and down my body as though trying to find a hint of a lie snagged on my dress, or caught between my teeth.

'He showed me a new poem he's written – he must have been inspired by the bards at Twelfth Night,' I said. I handed Hywel the paper, which I'd already stopped to read on the way home. Hywel smiled at the words inked across the page; I longed to have him smile that way at something I'd written. I told myself that perhaps, one day, I would show him my verses, though I knew it was unlikely.

'Is Rhys well?' he asked as he handed the paper back.

'Quite well,' I replied, as I reached up to kiss his cheek.

He sighed.

'Doli, you are carrying our child. It isn't wise to ride for miles alone. Besides, people will begin to talk.'

'Talk? About what?'

He looked pointedly at my stomach, then rubbed his hands over his face. He looked tired, his eyes streaked with blood like red bolts of lightning, his forehead clammy. He hadn't been sleeping well since finding the charm, burning it. The worry was eating him, stripping the fat from his bones before my eyes.

'The midwife is here to see you. Had you forgotten?'

'No, of course not,' I lied, glancing around.

'She's waiting in the parlour. Come.'

Feeling like a scolded dog trailing its master, I followed him into the parlour, where a slight, elderly woman sat on the high-backed wooden chair. A tray of empty cups and pastry crumbs lay in front of her and I felt a pang of guilt at having kept her waiting.

When she heard us enter, she stood up, clasping her hands in front of her apron and dipping her capped head slightly. Despite her small stature, she seemed sturdy, her body strong and sinewy.

'My wife has returned at last,' Hywel said. His smile didn't reach his eyes. 'Doli, this is Mary Hughes, the midwife I've been telling you about.'

I smiled at her, and made an effort to meet her eyes, which were watery, and pale as the sky on an icy winter morning.

'Mary,' I said. 'It's wonderful to meet you. My husband speaks very highly of you.'

She touched a long, wrinkled hand to her chest. Her skin was so white and thin it made me think of Bible pages. Perhaps that was why Hywel liked her so much.

'That's very kind. I've known your husband for a very long time, of course,' she chuckled. 'Since the day he was born, in fact.'

'Mary is a marvellous midwife, as I've already told you, Doli. She delivered my sisters and me, and, more recently, my sister's own children.'

The midwife dipped her head again.

'Of course. How is the newest family member?' I asked. 'I hope Anne is well? We are yet to meet her baby.'

'She is very well indeed,' Mary replied. 'I hope I can be of service to you also, now that you are growing nearer to your time.'

I smiled at her again, but uncertainty unfurled within me. I found myself growing nervous each time I thought of the birth. Of the sweet, cloying smell of blood and sweat and fear. Of thick, trailing cords and bruised babies. I was readying myself, once again, to battle with death.

'We've employed other midwives in the past, of course,' I told her. 'But I'm afraid I didn't find any particularly...' I paused, searching for the right word. 'Agreeable. I hope that isn't unkind of me to say.'

'Local women,' Hywel added, by way of explanation. He coughed, before saying, 'None of our children have yet been born living, as you know.'

'Well,' Mary said. 'We will do our best to ensure this one is. That may mean bedrest. Perhaps less time spent on your horse.'

That familiar feeling again, as though I'd swallowed a jagged stone.

I turned to Hywel. He smiled at me – was it encouraging, or smug?

'I'll leave you both to discuss...' he trailed off, waving his hand in the air, before continuing. 'Whatever it is you need to discuss.'

Once he had gone, I sat opposite Mary, and she clasped her hands on her lap again. It occurred to me then how much like a rodent she looked, with her pinched little face and sharp cheekbones. Her pale, watchful eyes.

She asked how I was feeling, and we discussed ways to ease my discomfort – lavender to help with sleep, milk baths to soften the skin and ease the joints, chamomile brewed with boiled water to calm the nerves. Her methods didn't seem at all far removed from what a wise woman might suggest. I remembered the bunches of lavender hanging from the rafters in Sara's cottage. The endless sprigs of tansy.

'Now, Doli, I do have one more matter to discuss with you,' she said finally. 'The master has asked me to stay, until the baby is born.'

I was stunned into silence, sure I'd misheard her.

'I'm sorry? Hywel has asked you to —'

'To stay, yes.' She had the good grace to blush a little, a smudge of pink forming on her otherwise pallid complexion. 'Although, of course, no one can be blamed for your previous losses, the master would like me to stay here, at Faen Maredudd, so that I can keep watch over the situation.'

'The situation?' I asked, feeling the heat rise in my chest. The familiar sense of anxiety was like a little sparrow beating its wings against my ribs.

'I estimate the baby will arrive late in the summer. The master would like me to stay until then, to ensure everything goes smoothly.'

I was afraid to open my mouth, sure I might let out a shriek of indignation, so I kept my lips pressed firmly together and said nothing at all.

Later that evening, I gathered my strength, imagining my fury was an animal held tight at my hip, a wolf straining at its shackles.

I kept my voice slow and steady while the beast snarled at my side, desperate to be let loose.

'Hywel, I think there may have been a misunderstanding of some sort?'

He looked up from his papers, waiting for me to go on.

'The midwife claims she is to stay?'

'Yes?'

'Is that quite necessary?'

My heart thumped at my ribcage as he looked at me, considering. 'I believe so.'

'May I ask why?'

I was amazed at the calm, demure way in which I was able to put this question to him, as though I was merely trying to understand the depth of his genius. As though I was not silently seething.

He scratched his chin.

'I had a strange dream last night,' Hywel said. 'I believe, perhaps, it confirms my suspicions.'

Hywel wasn't usually one to discuss anything that had happened in the bedchamber, especially dreams, and I was momentarily waylaid by his words.

I waited for him to go on.

'I dreamt a huge black bird, a crow, I think, was following me around the house, from the parlour to the kitchens. It chased me about the hall, incessantly chirping, pecking at me until finally, finally, I grabbed the damned thing and broke its neck.'

Hywel's face was pale as he spoke, stark as moonlight. Sweat pricked at his brow. My anger was momentarily replaced with worry.

'*Cariad*, are you feeling unwell?' I asked him. 'You look feverish. Shall I ask the cook for some —'

He batted me away, irritated.

'I'm perfectly well. Listen. The bird, it lay dead on the floor, its neck wrung. But even the kitchen cat —' he paused and glanced around, as though looking for the cat. 'Even the damned cat wouldn't touch the foul beast.'

'Hywel, it was only a dream. And I don't see how —'

'No, Doli. There must be more to it. It's a sign. There's wickedness in our midst. Wickedness and malice. And so you ask me, why I feel it is necessary that Mary resides with us until the baby is born, and my answer to you is this: there is darkness all around us, Doli.' He paused to gesture around the parlour, as though he expected shadows to spill from the tapestries. 'Darkness we cannot control. We need all the help we can get.'

The Villagers

We scorched chairs and doorframes, seared the burns deep, scratched away at the ash with knives. Spoons. Our bare hands. We carved them into every dark corner, so that evil spirits could no longer lurk there. Because we knew about the *witshes*, hiding in the shadows. We broke apart old shoes, cut away the uppers and sliced the buckles and laces clean. We laid them carefully in the foundations. We gathered discarded horseshoes, knowing their iron would repel the witshes and sorcerers who had cursed this land. We hung them over our doorways or at our mantels, ready to impale any evildoers who might try to enter. We did what we had to do. We kept ourselves safe.

As the spring rain gave way to an oppressive summer heat, Mary watched me intently, insinuating herself into every facet of my life. She insisted I sit in bed as much as possible, while she sat on the stool beside me, usually occupying herself with sewing, or falling asleep with the loose skin of her chin and neck squashed against her chest. She even brought me a small brass bell to call for refreshment. She made me drinks of stewed chamomile and lavender. She accompanied me on walks through the gardens and helped me to prune the rosebush. I had to wait until night fell to write any of my poetry down, keeping the words in my mind until I could get to my prayer book.

> *I long for the day that we can meet,*
> *My baby born in summer heat.*

Whenever I tried to leave the house alone, she insisted on coming with me. It was stifling. Suffocating. Still, I knew she meant well and I felt guilty for thinking unkindly of her, at least until Ruby said something about her keeping such a close watch over me *on the master's orders*. When I complained to Hywel, he insisted it was in my best interest. 'It's for your own good, Doli. What sort of husband would I be if I allowed you unending freedom to roam about with no one to watch over you? Anything could happen.'

'I have Ruby,' I said, but he only rolled his eyes in response.

'You need to listen to him,' Ruby told me, one afternoon as we sat darning together. I opened my mouth to argue but she kept talking. 'Be dutiful. Compliant. Give Mary no reason to believe you want to go anywhere without her. She likes to keep busy. If she believes you're taking every opportunity to rest, she might watch you less closely. I could even distract her, if you want to go out.'

The hope of freedom, of being outside without the intensity of Mary's gaze, bloomed within me.

A week went by before an opportunity to sneak out presented itself. Hywel had ridden across the marches to Herefordshire on business, so I told Mary I was exhausted and would be staying in my bed for several more hours. Ruby feigned a sore head and asked her to help scatter grain for the doves and sweep the flagstones in the hall. Mary agreed readily – she wasn't accustomed to being idle. As soon as Ruby told me that she was occupied with helping the cook to pluck chickens in the kitchen, I slipped through the gardens and out onto the moors.

I was walking through the village without any particular purpose beyond being somewhere other than my home when it happened. Cramps, like the beginning of birthing pains, began without warning. My heartbeat quickened in my chest as my mouth flooded with spittle. It couldn't be that my time had come yet. It was too soon.

I crouched, catching myself on the cool stone wall, picturing the blood and sweat that was to come. This was it. The beginning of what I'd been dreading: the result of Hywel burning the charm. Another terrible loss. Worse this time – I'd come so close, let myself hope.

'Pardon me. Are you alright, mistress?'

I looked up to see a young girl in a tattered cap and smock staring at me. Her eyes darted to my rounded stomach, too big to conceal even beneath the layers of my dress, and her brows knitted together.

'Please, come and sit down for a moment.'

Before I could protest, she was pulling me towards the alehouse. Pain pinched at my middle and I braced myself.

The girl took my elbow and nudged me into the building, sitting me, almost pushing me, down at a sticky wooden table amongst some other women, before disappearing. Frantic, I looked around for her, but her body had been swallowed by a crowd of people.

It was the first time I had ever entered the premises, though it had sat in the village of Llynidwen for as long as I could remember. The room was small, crowded, with a sawdust floor and a pervasively sweet smell.

A moment later the girl returned, placing a cup of beer on the table in front of me.

'Here, take a sip of this,' she said, concern still etched over her face.

I thanked her as she took a seat opposite me, smiling uncertainly at her lap.

I was about to ask her name when another cramping pain seized my stomach, but it was milder than the last, and passed more quickly. She must have noticed me wincing, because she gestured at the cup of beer before me.

'Take a deep breath, then have some more to drink. The pain will pass,' she said.

I smiled, grateful, and thanked her again before swallowing another mouthful of beer.

'*Iesu*, Rebecca, d'you know who this is?'

The voice came from my right and I turned to see who had spoken. I had been so gripped by anxiety and discomfort as I'd stumbled in and sat down that I hadn't seen her. I hadn't noticed the autumnal tumble of hair that was now brushing my own shoulders.

'Agnes,' I said, relieved to see a familiar face.

'Are you well, mistress?' she asked, before turning to my rescuer. 'Becs, this is Doli Maredudd, mistress up at the big house over the moors.'

Rebecca's face paled, her mouth settling into a small 'o'.

'Oh, I'm so sorry, I shouldn't have —'

I raised a hand to stop her.

'Please, *paid*. Don't apologise. You helped me. I shouldn't have been wandering on my own.' It was a painful admission – Hywel had been right. As he so often was.

She smiled warmly at me then. It was pleasant to be in the company of other young women, despite the circumstances.

'Why were you wandering alone? I didn't think you were allowed out without Ruby or that midwife of yours to accompany you,' Agnes said, taking a large mouthful of her own beer.

I paused, taken aback at being spoken to so boldly, and wondered how many beers she had already had this morning.

'I am allowed to do as I please,' I replied, coolly, though it wasn't true. 'What I mean to say is, I don't answer to anyone. Certainly not to you.'

Rebecca blushed at my tone, but Agnes seemed remarkably unconcerned.

'Well, good for you, mistress. I meant no offence,' she shrugged.

'Ruby is helping with May Day preparations,' I told her. 'We'll be hosting a feast, as usual.'

At this, she raised her eyebrows and drained her beer.

'Good luck with that. If you've enough to host a feast, you might consider sharing your secrets. Most of us are going hungry.'

I flushed.

'There may be less than we've had in the past,' I said, remembering Hywel's remarks about the herbs and the lack of seasoning. Cook's plants withering and dying. 'But we've plenty of potatoes, and some birds have been brought in from the marches.'

'If you've got the money for it...' Agnes muttered.

Rebecca glared across the table at her, then asked me: 'Are you feeling better?' Her voice was warm, soft as honey.

'Yes, thank you,' I replied. 'Much better. I'm not sure what happened, but it's passed now.'

I rubbed my swollen stomach and felt my cheeks colouring.

'False labour,' Agnes said simply.

'Pardon?' I asked, embarrassed.

'It's not uncommon,' Rebecca smiled. 'It can happen as your time draws near. Happened to me often, with all three pregnancies.'

'You have three children?' I asked her, surprised. She looked young.

She smiled again – a smaller, sadder smile this time.

'Only one living,' she said.

Without meaning to, I clapped a hand to my stomach.

'I'm sorry,' I said, uselessly.

She shrugged with one shoulder.

'Thank you, mistress. That's appreciated.'

125

I dipped my head, and pushed myself back from the table, so that I could reach into my skirts.

'I should go home,' I said. 'But please, let me pay you for my beer.' I looked around the table, and clutched my satchel, then added – 'for all your beers.'

I opened the satchel and stared stupidly at the coins, realising I had no idea how many to offer.

Agnes reached in and took a few, tossing them to the centre of the table.

Rebecca frowned, and placed two of the coins back in my palm.

'*Diolch i chi*, mistress,' she said. Then Agnes sighed and drained her cup. 'Before you go home, we should make certain everything truly is well. *Dere*. Come with me.'

I thanked Rebecca again, then nodded at Agnes.

'This way.'

As I walked back through the alehouse, I wondered if I was being watched. Eyes peered from behind cups, heads turned away just enough to look inconspicuous. Whispers. Laughter.

'To spear any witches that try to pass through,' Agnes said, noticing me looking at the horse shoe that had been nailed above the door.

Outside we walked side-by-side and I took the opportunity to study her more closely. Though her hair was tousled and red, her face was much like Ruby's, small and cat-like. It occurred to me then for the first time how similar they were. They had the same green eyes, the same rounded noses and milk-pale skin. Agnes' fingernails were blackened and packed deep with dirt, but she smelled sweet, like rosewater. Walking beside her was like standing beside the rosebush in our gardens during the summer months when it was in full bloom.

We walked for a while past houses and farmsteads, eventually coming towards the river, then turning near the path that led to the lake. A kite circled overhead, unusually low, following the river just as we were.

'This is the way to Sara Gwen's house?' I asked, though of course I knew it was. By now, the grass was speckled yellow with bog asphodel.

Agnes nodded.

'You know her?'

She nodded again.

'Agnes,' I stopped walking and reached out to grab her hand. 'I can't go with you. You must have heard what people are saying about Sara?'

'What people are saying and what is true are very different things,' Agnes said, pulling her hand free and continuing along the path.

'No, Agnes, wait!' I couldn't follow her. Hywel would be furious if I went anywhere near the *bwthyn*.

But the cramps had left a dull ache in my back, and a nagging dread in my stomach. What if this wasn't only false labour? What if it was something more? I couldn't help but think of the charm, shrivelling on the fire. The dreams I'd had since. A baby burning to ash. The banging and rattling that had kept Hywel awake at night. Even Sara hadn't been sure of the implications of Hywel's actions on that horrible spring day.

'I have a midwife back at home,' I said, hastening to keep pace with Agnes. 'I can speak with her. I'm sure she'll be able to —'

'Do as you wish,' she said, without looking back. 'But Sara is the woman you need.'

My gut churned and my hands itched at the thought of Hywel's anger if he found out. It was too dangerous – he was already suspicious of Sara, already spitting accusations. Going there now could put her life at risk, maybe even Agnes' life too. But my stomach was still taut with the memory of the cramps, my body still threatening to expel my baby too early. I couldn't lose her. Not now. I was so near to my time.

I glanced around, looking back in the direction we'd come to make sure no one was following us before hurrying after Agnes, pushed forward by the weight that had lingered in my chest since the pains had taken hold.

When we reached the familiar cottage, she rapped once at the door, then swung it open and walked in, gesturing for me to follow.

'Sara?' she called, as we stepped into the house, our footsteps muffled by the beaten earth.

The air had been cool, damp, still charged with the threat of rain the last time I'd come. By now, it was much warmer, no fire burned in the hearth and I didn't find myself choking on thick smoke or the heady scent of herbs.

She appeared, as though forming from a shadow, in the corner of the room near the bed, a limp furry thing swinging from her fist.

'Agnes,' she said. 'I was about to make a pottage.'

The rabbit's neck was wrung at an obscene angle, blood matting its fur.

'I had it from John Boot, as a thank you,' she said. She looked at me then, her eyes narrowing. 'I see you brought Mistress Maredudd.'

I smiled back at her, but Agnes spoke for me.

'She had pains. False labour, I reckon it was. But I thought we'd best come here before sending her home.'

Sara studied me, her eyes travelling over my body, pausing briefly on my belly.

'Of course,' she smiled.

That's when they came. Before any of us could say another word, there was the sound of horses' hooves drawing nearer. *Clunk-clunk.* Men's voices carrying through the open slats in the stone.

We stayed quiet, listening, as the men came to a stop outside and dismounted their horses. They were loud, jovial, well-spoken.

I glanced sideways at Agnes. It would be of no consequence to her being seen here, but tongues would wag if I was caught here, in the company of two peasant women. Especially when one was the local *swynwraig*, publicly branded a *witsh*. Accused by my own husband, no less. I looked around, frantic. There was no way out that wouldn't expose me. I was trapped.

'Quick,' Sara said under her breath. 'You can hide in the pantry.'

She pointed to a door to our left, which Agnes and I darted through just as a loud steady rapping sounded at the front door.

Pressing my face to the narrow opening in the pantry door, I could see a slim portion of the room beyond, Sara's chest rising and falling before she swung the front door open.

'Gentlemen,' she said.

She didn't stand back to let her guests in.

When we first met, I had been struck by Sara's height, but the man standing before her in the doorway now was at least a foot taller than she was, and broad as an ox. His imposing figure blocked the sunlight from streaming through the open door, casting a shadow across the floor that reached almost as far as the pantry.

When he spoke, his voice was thunder, deep and rumbling.

'Sara, I trust you were expecting us. If your skill in soothsaying is indeed as great as your reputation suggests.'

His grin was wide but his eyes remained icy, his tone mocking.

'I'm afraid I'm busy, gentlemen,' Sara said, pressing her palms to the door frame either side of her and blocking the man from my view.

'Nonsense!' the man said, thrusting her arms out of his way and gesturing for his men to follow him inside.

'Leave the horses at the well,' he called over his shoulder as he stepped over the threshold and passed Sara. Two men followed, their faces obscured by Sara's back. One of them seemed to shove her with his shoulder as he passed, jostling her sideways. There was something familiar about him, something I recognised in the cut of his doublet, in the way he strode. Then I saw it – the round silver brooch pinned at his collar bone. *Jacob Lloyd.* The men disappeared completely from my line of vision as they stepped further into the cottage, and I wondered if this was how men of rank treated peasant women. I couldn't imagine Hywel behaving so rudely towards anyone, not even troublesome tenants.

I tried to keep my breath steady, slow. If I was found hiding in the pantry, squatting here beside Agnes ... *Did you hear about the woman who was hanged? A large crowd gathered to watch...*

The men were all out of sight now, but their voices reached us clear as a spring brook as they demanded ale. I looked over at Agnes, squashed at my side, but her face was still, unreadable in the darkness.

'I'm afraid I don't have any to spare,' Sara told them, her voice steady and cool.

'Come now, Sara. I'm sure that's not quite true, is it? It's a sin to tell untruths, after all. Now, bring us ale, *please*.'

Though I couldn't see the men fully, I pictured the speaker with a smirk playing over his lips. It conjured the image of two fat purple worms, and I wondered if this was how it was to be a soothsayer, to have images enter the mind, unbidden, fully formed as oil paintings.

Agnes' breathing was shallow beside me. We listened to the clinking of cups, the sloshing and guzzling of ale. They talked amongst themselves, then began to probe Sara, asking her to help find their missing cattle, and to reveal the names of their mistresses, trying to test her abilities. They laughed. They were like stallions cramped into a stable, kicking and bucking. Drunk.

Sara's voice cut over them, cool and crisp.

'Given that there is a perfectly good alehouse not a mile away, I can't imagine you're here solely to drink the contents of my cask?'

The silence that followed her words was as menacing as their drunken chatter had been. The bite began at my stomach again, coursing along my back and down my thighs. The sudden pain took my breath and I had to clamp my hand to my mouth to stop myself from crying out. Agnes glanced over at me, her brow furrowed.

Then came a low buzzing, loud and insistent at my ear. A large black fly careened about the pantry, butting frantically at the door.

'More ale,' the man with the ox-arms said, and his companions muttered their agreement. I looked to Agnes, but still her face gave nothing away.

For several minutes, there was more drinking and sloshing, gradually loudening voices. A commotion. Clattering. Banging. My heart beat so furiously in my chest I would have been worried about them hearing it, and discovering our hiding place, were they not so loud themselves.

Inside my belly, the baby squirmed and rolled uncomfortably, as though in response to the loud noises.

'Did you place that fly in the jug, woman? Are you trying to poison us?'

The man sounded irate, and I couldn't imagine Sara's response did much to calm him.

'Fly? I'm not sure a fly has ever poisoned anyone, *sir*.'

Then another voice came.

'It was no ordinary fly. It was huge, and hideous. Large as a bumble bee.'

'Large as a baby mouse,' said Jacob Lloyd.

'Where is this fly now?' Sara asked them.

'It would seem the culprit has gone. Disappeared before our very eyes.'

'Yes, it would seem so.'

'I would be willing to wager that fly was a familiar spirit,' Jacob Lloyd said. Beside me, I felt Agnes stiffen.

'Almost certainly,' came the cool reply. 'As a matter of fact, I would not be surprised were you to tell me that that fly was the devil himself.'

My palms were wet with sweat, my legs trembling. The thud of my heart insistent and loud. Agnes only scoffed. She was raising her eyebrows in a manner that reminded me very much of Ruby.

More rustling, and the men were back at the front door.

'Yes, good. *Ewch o 'ma.* And don't come back.'

Jacob and his companion left, but the first man turned to Sara and pointed at her.

'Mark my words, Sara Gwen, you'll be sorry to have crossed us.'

'Not as sorry as you'll be,' she muttered, as the door slammed shut.

The Villagers

Some say she knew the men were coming before they arrived. That she heard the *clunk clunk* of their horses' hooves ahead of time. Some say she was prepared, that she flung open the door to let them in before they could knock. Before they could demand entry. Some say she cursed the ale before they even sat at the table. Placed her familiar there on the golden drink in hopes it would choke the men until they lay dying. Dying. Dead.

As the weather continued to warm and the grasslands dried out, I waited for news of Sara Gwen's arrest, but none came. We drew closer to midsummer, and I began to hope that all would be forgotten amidst the celebrations and sunshine.

I spent so long outdoors, amongst the marigolds and the moors, that my skin began to darken, growing tanned as a nut under the sun. Hywel chided me – *don't darken your skin Doli, you'll look as though you toil all day outdoors* – but his comments were light hearted. He was relieved, I think, to see that the rosy flush had come back to my cheeks, my enjoyment for being outside returned, even with Mary following me, fussing over every twinge and cramp.

The sun's insistent warmth did its best to chase the worry away, to sweep it from my mind, but still, the fear lingered, casting a darkness over my otherwise free and easy days. Of course, I was relieved that my belly had continued to grow, the babe turning like a fledgling inside of me, but there was also the constant, unshakeable awareness that I would soon be in childbed. Thoughts of sweat and blood and faeces plagued my days, as did the terrible knowledge that we might not both survive the labour. I made sure not to stray too far from Faen Maredudd, and stayed close to Ruby whenever Mary was busy, in case anything should happen.

I tried to shake away the nerves, focussing on the summer celebrations that were to come. Before long, bonfires would dot the village, the smoke sweeping over crops and pigsties, cleansing the air. On the nights of the vigils, we would set out tables in front of Faen Maredudd, laid full with sweet bread and good drink, jugs overflowing with golden ale and endless cups of wine. Juicing meats that dampened the mouth at the very thought of them.

After a warm afternoon spent dipping my ankles into the cool river water to relieve their swollen, dull ache, I arrived home to see a beautiful wreath of green birch, long fennel, St John's Wort and orpine adorning the front door. Inside, a garland of white lilies was draped over the balustrade lining the staircase. I found Ruby in the hall, surrounded by cuttings – orange and yellows and reds, blazing like a sunset across the flagstone floor. I asked what she was doing.

'I'm making wreaths, to put around the horns of our cattle. Want to join me?'

I sat beside her, letting her show me how to stitch the flowers together, gathering and tucking their stems into a perfect circle, like small suns held in our own two hands.

'We might have enough to give some as gifts to the villagers,' she said.

I winced as I readjusted myself, the baby rolling sickeningly inside of me.

'Ruby? Do you think Sara will come to the feast tonight?' I asked.

'Do you want her to come?'

I shrugged, wondering whether to tell her what I was really thinking. Wondering *how* to tell her. I hadn't mentioned the visit to Sara yet or the false birthing pains.

I knew I could trust her, of course I could. She was practically a sister to me. But I also knew that she enjoyed the status she held above the other servants. Being able to feed crumbs of information to them. And of course, she'd warned me about Sara. She wouldn't be pleased that I'd been back there again.

'Ruby ... I'm worried about something I saw, not long ago...'

I trailed off, hesitant to say too much more, but she filled the silence.

'The bailiff and his companions?' She sighed. 'I thought as much.'

Of course she knew. Agnes must have told her we were there.

'They spoke of a fly,' I said, stupidly.

'Why did you go to see her again Doli? When I helped you to sneak away from Mary, it was so that you could have some space to breathe freely, not so you could go back to Sara's *bwthyn*. Are you trying to get yourself killed? The villagers know about it, you know. They're saying she has a familiar. The word is being whispered and hissed all over the streets. I've heard it in the ale house, the market, in passageways. I've even heard it in the darkest corners of this house.'

'What word?' I asked, though I could have guessed at it: *witsh*.

She whispered it, leaning in close as though afraid she might be overheard. It was a word that held power, malice, destruction. If enough people echoed it, it could mean Sara's ruin. I closed my eyes, breathed deeply.

'Agnes took me there,' I said, as though that would improve the situation.

She sighed, ran a hand along her jaw, exasperated.

'I know. But Agnes isn't always right about everything. Still, a fly isn't evidence of anything. The justices might be looking for anything they can use against Sara, but they aren't stupid enough to try to use a fly as evidence at the assizes. The jury would laugh.'

'They said she would be sorry for crossing them.'

'She may well be,' Ruby said, plucking a buttercup from the pile on the floor in front of her. 'But there's nothing you can do now.'

I wanted to ask Ruby if she thought Hywel might have sent them. The bailiff and his men. Jacob Lloyd. But I daren't. I wasn't sure I really wanted the answer. Instead, we plucked flowers in silence, threading stems and pruning leaves until finally, she spoke again.

'Doli. You must stay away from her, for the time being. Please.'

I hadn't spoken to Hywel all day. He'd been busy with preparations, instructing the servants to fetch more firewood, prepare more sweetmeats, pour more ale. I had tried to be present, to greet the guests, to smile, but I was so tired. The heat and smoke and noise were sickening. Every now and then, my stomach rolled and I had to stop, catch my breath. I longed to have Ruby at my side but she was needed in the kitchens. Each time I tried to speak with her, she would be bustled along by the cook or handed a platter by one of the other servants.

Late in the evening, I was standing near the bonfire, watching the smoke billowing across the moors, snaking its way towards the village, my cheeks burning in the heat of the flames.

'You don't look yourself.'

I jumped, startled by a voice. I hadn't seen her come to stand beside me, distracted as I was. Sara had walked straight into the celebrations as though there was not a black mark against her name. As though she was not at the centre of vicious rumours and whispers.

'Why are you here?' I kept my voice low. 'You must know how much talk there is? They're calling for your arrest. You should be hiding.' I looked around for Hywel but couldn't see him anywhere. He'd been largely absent all evening, leaving me to play hostess alone.

'It's kind of you to worry, but I've done no wrong. I won't convince them of my guilt by hiding.'

We watched the fire for a while, listening to the snap and crackle of the branches at its centre.

'I'm tired,' I said eventually. 'And heavy as a heifer.' The anxiety tugged at my insides and a strange sense of dread had settled within me.

Sara turned to me properly, taking my hands in hers, and frowned.

'Have you been sick?' she asked.

I shook my head.

'There's a weight, here,' I placed a hand on my lower stomach. 'I feel like she's pressing down, wanting to come out. I'm jittery. Nervous.'

Sara frowned again, and reached into her satchel. She handed me a small pouch, and told me to smell it. Lavender.

'It will help you to relax,' she said. 'Put it on your pillow tonight. And if anything should happen, you can send for me.'

Again, I looked around for Hywel. Mary was standing across the courtyard sipping from a cup, staring intensely at us.

'I can't send for you,' I hissed. 'We've employed a midwife.'

She nodded.

'Of course.'

'But Sara, I've only been with child a little under eight months. She won't be born for some weeks yet, will she? Mary said —'

Sara cut across me. 'Perhaps you should prepare your bedchamber, regardless.'

'You should go,' I told her. 'If my husband sees you...'

I didn't need to finish the sentence. Sara looked at me, for a long time, her eyes alive with the flames of the bonfire.

'I'm not too worried about that. Your husband seems to be preoccupied this evening. He's nowhere to be seen.'

Was it that obvious? If Hywel's absence was conspicuous enough for Sara to notice, who else might have noticed he wasn't here? Where was he? Who was he with?

'I don't know what you mean. Now go,' I said, before turning and walking away.

The festivities continued long past sunset. Exhausted and uncomfortable, I withdrew, and went to sit by myself in the hall. I kicked my feet against the dais, too worried and too tired to celebrate. Too tired even to speak.

A woman stumbled in, almost collapsing against a bench. She stared absently at the drape hanging from the wall, her eyes flitting between the falcons, dense branches and scurrying mice embroidered there.

'Can I help you?' I called over to her, though it was a great effort to say anything at all.

'Mistress!' she said, cheerfully. 'I didn't see you sitting there.' She began walking unsteadily towards me, landing beside me on the dais with a thud. 'I must thank you,' she said.

'It's our pleasure to host the festivities.' I tried to speak warmly, but I could think only of my bed. My soft, feather mattress. My cool coverlet.

'Oh, not for this.' She gestured about her, though there was no one in the hall but us and a couple of servants sweeping near the far wall. 'Though, of course, we've enjoyed ourselves! No, I wanted to thank you for your generosity, a while back now.'

I didn't know what she was referring to, so I stayed quiet, trying to place her in my memory.

'Your husband. He came to ours, back in the winter. Brought a few pies. Gave us a couple of weeks to gather the money for our rent, when Dad died.'

'Ah, yes,' I smiled at her. 'My husband is a good man.'

'Mam and I were most grateful. And my sister, too. We've got little 'uns, in the house, still. Dad had a lot of children, and not a lot of space to put them. Another on the way, too.' She laughed, almost tipping over. 'My sister said, he'd be wanting payment of a different sort, your husband.'

'Pardon me?' I was shocked at her insinuation. Had I misheard?

'You know what men are like, mistress. Nothing is free.' She laughed again, looking pointedly at my swollen stomach, then shut her eyes and started snoring, though she was still sitting upright.

I shook her shoulder, rather more aggressively than I might have needed to.

'What do you mean?' My voice cracked. I was tired. I was confused. I wanted this woman to leave. 'Wake up. You! Please.'

It was no use. I gave up. I let her sit beside me, snoring like an old dog, while I waited for Hywel to reappear. I sat for some time, until the singing outside quietened, and the light from the bonfire dimmed to a gentle orange glow, and a faint crackling.

I was half asleep myself when it happened.

It was gentle at first, the swell of it beginning, worsening, then fading away as though I might have imagined it. It was soft, subtle enough that I could ignore it, if I wanted to, but present enough to detect an undeniable rhythm to it, like water lapping a shoreline, ebbing and flowing.

I looked through the window for Mary, or for Sara, but couldn't see either. Most of the villagers had gone home now, singing and laughing drunkenly, staggering away like foals learning to walk.

I breathed deeply, like Agnes had shown me, and walked slowly up the stairs, leaving the girl slumped on the dais. I told myself it would be false labour again. It would pass. I would go to sleep, and it would pass.

That night, everything changed. The pain grew and I woke from my sleep to the steady intensity of it. Within scarcely any time at all, I was entirely transformed – no longer a young woman of high rank, lavender daubed at her ears and collarbone, but a sweating, heaving farm animal, grunting and writhing.

Where was Hywel?

The pains came in waves, rolling like great thrashing things that threatened to overwhelm me. The heat was unbearable and I tore at my clothes, peeling my nightdress from my body in a frenzy.

Just as I was squatting at the head of the bed, gripping the posts as though I was gripping a horse's reins, trying desperately not to be flung from its back, Ruby burst through the door. I was aware that my petticoat was cleaved to my waist, my hair undone and hanging loose about my shoulders, sweat beading at my temple and my lips, but I was beyond embarrassment. Besides, Ruby had helped me to dress, and to bathe, often enough since I was a girl. Worse, she had seen me in the throes of loss, blood running in rivers along my thighs.

'What is it?' she asked me, quietly. 'Has your time come? Mistress? Doli?'

'I think so,' I said, trying to focus my vision on a knot in the wooden bed frame. 'But, Ruby, it's too soon.'

I pressed my face to the crack in the headboard.

'Should I wake Mary?' she asked.

The pain came again, harder this time, and I thrust myself forward with the power of it, feeling as though something was clawing at me from the inside. When it relinquished its grip, I was able to reply.

'Yes. Quickly! And find Hywel.'

She turned, her nightdress swishing like water as she walked away.

I listened to her footsteps echoing along the passage, then descending the stairs in heavy thuds that reminded me of the way Margiad had careened into the parlour with the charm clenched tight in her fist all those months ago.

I felt a strange *pop* and all of a sudden the birth waters came running from me as though I was the mouth of a river. I closed my eyes and gripped the bedpost more firmly, muttering prayers beneath my breath like a child, feeling the bloodied water pooling at my knees, soaking the bed linen, seeping deep into the mattress.

I was alone with only the relentless waxing and waning birthing pains as company, growing stronger and more fierce with each surge. All the while, I was consumed by the awful knowledge that this baby would either live or die, and there was nothing I could do about it. It was too soon for her to come. I breathed in, and out, trying to keep myself calm and steady. But it was no good – the panic was rising within me and I knew, with more certainty than I had ever known anything in my life, that I couldn't do this. I didn't have the strength. I was not brave enough. I was going to die.

I was dying.

Finally, Ruby came careering back into the bedchamber just as I was attempting to lower myself onto the birthing stool. To my horror, she was alone.

'Doli. It's the midwife. She tripped on a broken branch as she was rushing to collect water from the well. She can't walk. Her ankle is swollen up like a cauliflower.'

I stared at her in disbelief, unable to form words. I couldn't understand what she was saying.

'I've sent the cook to attend to her. What should I do? I can't find the master anywhere.'

I groaned, a long, involuntary sound, like a cow. There was an immense pressure, and I knew without doubt that the baby would be with us soon. When the words left my mouth, it was as though they had come from some unknown place deep inside of me.

'Go and find Sara Gwen,' I told Ruby, in a haze between the pains. 'Go quickly. Take my horse from the stable.'

Ruby hovered near the threshold, uncertain, staring at me as I rocked back and forth like a branch snagged in the river. I was caught in a current of my own.

'Go. Now. Please!'

'But, I don't think —' she stammered.

'Ruby! For once, do as I say!'

The pain came again, fierce and hot. It buckled me, threatening to overwhelm me, to split me in two. '*Cer i mofyn Sara Gwen.* She'll know what to do.'

By the time Sara and Ruby returned, I was panting on all fours, lowing like a heifer, heat curling along my limbs. Sweat dripped from my temples. It collected in the creases of my elbows, the backs of my knees.

The pains were coming thick and fast, followed by powerful shudders that felt as though the earth was moving inside of me. My knees shook, my thighs close to giving way.

'Her time is close,' I heard Sara say from somewhere nearby. 'Ruby, fetch linens, salt, spiced wine, swaddling strips and a bowl for the afterbirth. And bring a pan of boiled water.'

I heard Ruby hurrying away, but didn't turn to look. I needed to rest my head, close my eyes before the next pain came. Would the next quake be the one to split me in two? To break me at last.

'Doli?' Sara's voice was gentle and lilting. 'I'm here with you. Take this.'

She pushed something small and cold into my palm.

'Doli?' she said again.

I made a small noise, to let her know I was listening. It was all I could manage.

'You're doing so well. When the next pain comes, take a long, deep breath, then blow it out quickly, as though you're trying to blow out your candle before bed.'

I scrunched my eyes shut tight and waited.

When the pain came, I did as she'd instructed. Breathed in and out, in and out, longing for it to pass.

'*Dyna ni,* Doli, that's it. Your baby will be with us soon.'

I tried to keep my mind focussed on the baby. Pictured apple-round cheeks, small arms outstretched like saplings. Imagined the poetry she would bring. But it was so difficult to think of anything but the pain. The fatigue. Exhaustion wrapped itself around me like a heavy cloak. Sleep threatened to take me each time the pain subsided. It was a cruel trick – my eyes would close long enough for dreams to dance in my mind, then the next familiar bite would take hold of me.

I looked to the window and saw the faint hint of dawn. Somewhere, I was aware of Ruby rushing back into the room, and throwing something in a heap on the rug, just as my body tried its best to push the child from me, bearing down in an intense spasm.

'Nearly there. Pass me a length of linen steeped in boiled water. As hot as you can bear Ruby.'

Suddenly, heat like I had never felt covered me below. I thought inanely of the women in Scotland burned on charges of witchcraft, flames licking their heels. The entirety of my lower body was fire and heat.

Then in one furious gush, I felt her slip from me. The pain eased instantly and I turned, desperate to see my little girl.

Sara held her firmly, but she was limp and silent. Grey as an eel. A slick of white froth covered her little body. I was reminded of the dead rabbit that hung from Sara's fist last time I'd been in her cottage.

'What is it? What's wrong?' I asked. 'Sara?'

I watched, helpless, as Sara turned the baby on to her front and thumped her back, muttering under her breath all the while. Ruby hovered near the door, watching, eyes wide, just as quiet and still as my child. I couldn't move, couldn't even think clearly. Panic and grief engulfed me. Another one lost. Sara wasn't licensed. Had she brought holy water? The baby would be damned without it. Buried with no baptism.

Sara parted the baby's small mouth with her fingers, and tried to breathe the life into her. Her tiny body was silent, unmoving. I couldn't look away, though the sight of my child, so perfectly formed but limp, lifeless, quiet, was the worst thing I'd ever had to see. In that moment, I knew – this was my fault. My actions had caused this, this lifeless thing that my body had expelled. If I'd only hidden the charm better, Hywel would never have burned it, and things wouldn't have been this way. My baby wouldn't be dead.

Tears stung my eyes as I watched. She looked like the children that had come before, perfectly formed fingers and toes, but deathly still. A doll. But this one was bigger, stronger as she kicked and rolled inside of me. This one should have lived.

Finally, a cry. Small at first, and meek as a kitten's, then louder until it became a wailing shriek, and we all laughed in utter relief. My own cries matched the pitch of the baby's as I let the weight of the night escape me. The pain and the grief and the terrible shock of it.

Sara swaddled her in linen and handed her to me gently. I was surprised at the weight of her in my arms, the solid, squirming, mass.

'Here she is,' she said. '*Merch fach.*'

My daughter. The first of my children to survive the birth, despite it happening a little too soon. She looked up at me with deep, black eyes, her stare so intense, I was sure she knew me.

Sara showed me how to put the baby to my breast and help her to suckle. I'd planned to hire a wet nurse, but with her being born sooner than expected I hadn't found anyone suitable yet. I was amazed now, at the sheer instinctive joy that rushed through me at the feeling of my baby pressed to my breast. My living, breathing baby.

'Keep nursing her yourself,' Sara said. 'Don't entrust her care to a wet nurse. It'll be so much better for her.'

'It will?'

144

Though I was loath to admit it, I was relieved when she said it. I wanted to keep this baby, my baby, close, pressed to me like this, forever. I couldn't bear the thought of handing her to somebody else.

Sara nodded.

Later, when the afterbirth had come and I was settled back on my bed, Sara told me the heat of the linen steeped in boiled water helped to ease a baby's transition from one life to the next.

'Where did you learn it?' I asked her, through a haze of exhaustion.

She smiled.

'Where does anyone learn anything?' she replied, busying herself with collecting blood-soaked linens and rags from around the bedchamber. It was a strange answer, but in my tiredness I accepted it.

I thanked her, immeasurably glad she had been with me.

Hywel would be furious, no doubt, that I had sent for Sara, but what choice did I have? I refused to even consider what might have happened if I'd been left to labour alone.

When she was gone, I ran a finger along the babe's cheek, smooth and soft as a petal, pinched pink and dewy. I watched, fascinated, as her cheeks filled while she nursed at my breast, her tiny eyelashes fluttering.

Was this beautiful creature really my child, grown in my belly as the seasons changed, squirming like a fish as the leaves fell from the trees? Maybe not the male heir for which Hywel had hoped, but we'd been blessed with a healthy child. How could my world be anything other than joy and love?

I was dozing with the baby on my chest when Hywel raced into the room, eyes wide. His cheeks were flushed pink, whether with excitement or from the heat of the scorching summer sun as he rode home, I couldn't say.

He rushed to my side and sat next to me at the edge of the bed, fixing his eyes immediately on our daughter.

'A girl?' he asked, quietly. 'Ruby says we have a little girl?'

'Where were you?' I spoke through gritted teeth.

'I'm sorry Doli. I'm so sorry.' He stroked my hair, kissed the top of my head. 'I was called away ... an opportunity for ... It doesn't matter. I'm here now.'

I did my best to let go of the anger. To embrace this moment. Though I could feel the hurt, the sense of abandonment, sitting deep within me.

'I bought this, a while ago, from a shop in Bristol.' He lifted his arm and I noticed for the first time that he was holding something.

'A hobby horse?' I said. 'It's wonderful, Hywel. But for a girl?'

'Why not?' he replied. 'She will learn to ride when she's grown. And she'll be good at it too, I imagine, if she's anything like her mother. She may as well begin now.'

He lifted the hobby horse and placed its chestnut muzzle near to the baby's face, making soft neighing sounds. I laughed.

'Maybe not too soon. I think we'd best wait until she can walk, at least.'

Things between Hywel and me had been so difficult, so strained. He had been more focussed on his prayers and his business affairs than I'd ever seen him, barely meeting me with any tenderness. I'd felt so much anger towards him, over the last few months, my resentment only growing as the summer sun yellowed the grass and dried the riverbed. But surely, none of it mattered now. Now, everything would be better.

Hywel laughed, and I saw that his eyes glistened with moisture. I loved him more in that moment than I ever had.

I closed my eyes and we were silent for some time, while I enjoyed the easy warmth of our daughter on my chest, the way her breath ebbed and flowed.

'What will we call her?' I asked Hywel.

There had been names, in the past. Girls' names discussed by the fire on cold winter evenings. Boys' names whispered into the darkness in the middle of the night, when one of us had woken from a dream.

But with each failed pregnancy, the exchanging of names grew to seem like a bad omen. This time, neither of us had said a word.

'Why don't you choose her name?' Hywel said, his eyes still boring into our daughter's face. 'She looks like you.'

'She looks like a baby,' I told him, smoothing the blood-mottled tuft of fair hair.

His answer surprised me – I'd thought he'd want to name her for his mother, or perhaps his sister, as he'd suggested in the past.

I paused, taking in my daughter's face – the pink cheeks, the long, fine eyelashes, the lips like rose petals.

'Then she will be Awen,' I said. 'Awen Margaret.'

Hywel considered for a moment.

'A Welsh name? Are you sure?'

I nodded.

'Of course.'

'Bardic inspiration ... I'll give it some thought,' he said, before kissing me on the forehead. 'She's perfect.'

I closed my eyes again, wondering idly when I might be able to bathe. I was increasingly aware of the sweat that covered my body, the blood drying to a crust on my thighs.

'What is this?' Hywel's voice cut the silence as I drifted away with my thoughts. His tone had lost its previous warmth and was cold. Hard. Urgent. I opened my eyes.

He was clutching a small, square piece of tin. I held out my hand for the mysterious object, wanting to examine it more closely.

As soon as he dropped it into my palm and I felt the cool touch of the metal, the weight of it, I recognised it as the object Sara had pressed into my hand during the birth, though I hadn't looked at it until now.

'Where did you find this?'

'Here, on the chest,' Hywel replied, his eyes not leaving mine. 'What is it Doroli?'

I peered at it more closely, unsure why Hywel was so upset. It looked a little like a coin, but there were symbols and letters engraved on its surface. I rubbed my thumb over the grooves, back and forth. Back and forth.

'I'm not sure,' I said. 'Sara Gwen —'

He interrupted before I could finish my sentence.

'She was here?'

It was as though I'd swallowed a stone. I had assumed Ruby had told him what had happened once he'd arrived home, but perhaps he'd bounded up to the bedchamber too quickly for that. Or perhaps she felt it wasn't her place. Perhaps she was scared of how he might respond.

But Sara helped me. She'd delivered our baby safely and brought about that first, glorious cry. Surely, Hywel couldn't be cross about that. Surely this would prompt him to drop his campaign against her. He would see reason, now, almost certainly.

So I told him. I told him about the midwife and her ankle, about being alone and afraid, about Sara and her reassuring words and whispered encouragement. I told him about the all-consuming fear when Awen slipped from me, rigid and deathly silent, and the way Sara shared her own breath with our baby, made her greyish-blue hue pink, then helped her to suckle at the breast. I told him everything. The feelings of fear, joy, relief, were so intense that I wanted to cry, but it was as though I had no tears left. Or maybe I was too exhausted to cry.

'I don't blame you, Doli. How could I? You are a mere gentry wife, no match for a servant of the devil. But surely you must see?'

I was tired, hot, confused.

'See what?'

'You think it mere coincidence that Mary's ankle was broken before the birth?'

'I think it's as Ruby says. She tripped.'

Hywel looked from me to Awen and back again.

'Sweet Doli. She has played you for a fool. I should have made more effort to have Sara Gwen arrested long ago, when you first told me about that dreaded curse.'

'It wasn't a curse,' I reminded him. 'It was a charm.'

'Still, I should have seen to it that she was spoken to by the magistrate.'

'On what grounds?' I asked, emboldened by the hate seething in his voice, and the memory of Sara's lips pressed to Awen's. 'She had done no wrong.'

'Perhaps you're right. Perhaps the justices wouldn't have acted then. They would have needed more substantial evidence, I suppose.' He spoke almost as though to himself. 'But they must act now. Surely.'

'Hywel, please. I know you have your suspicions, but Sara helped me. She helped to deliver our daughter safely. You can ask Ruby, if you want.'

'Is that so? Or did she use witchcraft to arrange a situation in which she might be present for the birth of our first child? Did she storm in and manipulate you with her cunning words and ways?'

'No,' I stuttered, confused. I was beginning to doubt my own recollection of events. 'To what end Hywel? Why would she want to do that?'

'Witches don't need just cause, Doli! Their goal is simply to spread misery and malice wherever they go. And where better, than in the most influential home of Llynidwen?'

'No, Hywel, she —'

'What of the afterbirth?' he said.

'What?'

'Where is the afterbirth?'

I thought of the placenta, and the pulsing cord thick as rope that had slipped from me shortly after Awen did. I remembered it, coiled like a dead snake in the china bowl.

'I don't know,' I began. 'I suppose she took it, to dispose of.'

'Yes. Yes. To dispose of. That's certainly what she would have you believe.'

'What else would she possibly want with it?' I thought again of the pool of crimson blood and the hot smell of iron, like a knot of rusted old keys. My stomach cramped at the memory of it.

'She'll use it in her sordid acts of witchcraft and sorcery, Doli.'

Before I could answer, he pressed his face into his hands, then turned and left our bedchamber.

Beside me, Awen stirred and began to cry.

It had been a week since the birth, and I was still sore, still bleeding. At Hywel's insistence, the physician had come the day after Awen had arrived, to look over us all. Awen, he said, was perfectly well, and a good size, for a child born so early. He insisted on examining me, in a way I found invasive and uncomfortable, his thick fingers nudging my sore flesh, sharp nails catching and taking my breath away. After the sudden and shocking way Awen had careened into the world, I didn't want to be touched by anyone but her.

Before leaving, he'd bound Mary's bruised and swollen ankle and given her a stick to help her walk. Hywel had given him more coins than seemed necessary, and sent him on his way with a pouch full of marzipan.

My husband's initial elation at Awen's birth was short-lived. Since learning of Sara's involvement, he had been overtaken by a strange mood. He'd been quiet, sombre, imploring me to consider an English name for Awen, insisting on calling her Ann, as though it were an affectionate shortened form of her name.

'Why don't you want to appoint a wet nurse?' he asked, on seeing me nursing Awen the morning after she was born. 'Won't you consider it?'

I shook my head.

'It's highly unusual, Doli. It's not as though we lack the finances. You're not some low born wife of a labourer forced to nurse an endless torrent of children.'

'An endless torrent of children,' I echoed, speaking slowly. I was thinking of all those we had lost, all that had come before Awen, that I was never able to put to my breast. 'No. But this one. This one I want to nurse myself.'

He stayed silent for a moment, considering me.

He'd asked the same question numerous times over that first week, and by now I was feeling anxious, as though something malign was lingering in the house with us. Hywel's temper thrown up against the walls like a dark shadow. Awen had become increasingly unsettled as the days wore on, crying for milk whenever I tried to hand her to Ruby or put her down. It was more difficult than I'd anticipated and I was beginning to worry Hywel might be right.

'She was born early, she craves closeness,' Ruby assured me, and so I persisted, pushed on by a stubborn determination and a pervading sense of guilt.

That evening, Rhys had arrived before supper, clutching a silver rattle for Awen. Thankfully, Hywel's agitation had subsided with his friend's appearance, and seemed to dissipate more and more with each cup of wine. He drank enough over supper to redden his eyes and slur his words. Now, he was sauntering around the parlour, jovial, proud.

'Isn't she beautiful, Rhys? Here, do you want to hold her?'

His voice cut across my thoughts as he snatched Awen from me, causing her to stir and let out an indignant shriek as she was thrust towards Rhys. He held her awkwardly, his face uncertain, as Hywel laughed.

'Haven't you ever seen a baby before!?'

I went to his side, and showed him how to support her head.

'She's perfect,' he said, looking down at her with fondness. The movement had disturbed her, and she whined, puckering her lips.

'She is,' I said. 'She makes me want to sing'

'I would love to hear you sing,' Rhys replied, laughing. 'I'm sure she has much inspiration to offer.'

'Oh! Yes, yes! A performance! What an excellent idea.' Hywel spoke excitedly, his voice too loud for the parlour. 'We must invite the bards again. We must celebrate!'

I laughed.

'I thought we *were* celebrating. You're certainly merry enough for it.'

Tired and sore as I was, I hadn't wanted to drink much over dinner myself, and found Hywel's high spirits that evening disconcerting.

'Cards!' he clapped his hands together. 'We shall play cards!'

He looked through the dressoir, found nothing, then cast about the room for a servant to fetch a deck of playing cards. It was only the three of us in the parlour, so he mumbled something about getting them himself, and left the room, his step hurried and eager.

The silence he left behind was distracting. Uncomfortable. I hadn't seen Rhys since my last visit to Allt-Goras, when I had told him about the charm and my involvement with Sara Gwen. Awen's hurried breathing between us seemed suddenly as loud as a brook rushing.

'Thank you for the rattle, Rhys,' I said, quietly. 'It's wonderful. Awen will be delighted.'

He'd had the rattle engraved with Awen's name, the letters spiralling beautifully along the handle. When shaken, it chimed with an otherworldly music.

Rhys didn't reply. He was staring intently down at Awen, still cradled in his arms, now twisting her head and smacking her lips. After a short while, he reached out and smoothed her hair with a gentle thumb, murmuring and hushing.

As I opened my mouth to speak, the door flung open, crashing into the armchair that was positioned beside it. Hywel bounded happily back into the room.

The Villagers

Some said the babe was prayed for and granted. A gift from God. A miracle. Some say the mistress hung mandrake above her bed. Some say the baby was fathered by the devil. We heard the baby was a poppet shaped with tallow wax and given to the mistress to swallow whole until it bloomed in her belly.

At church the following Sunday, tiredness racked my body, my eyes gritty as though someone had rubbed dirt in them. I struggled to stay awake as the minister droned on, his voice soft and soothing in the summer heat. My legs were heavy, my shoulders stiff from leaning against the stone wall.

Awen hadn't been resting well since her birth, waking through the night and hungry throughout the day; I was in danger of falling asleep, until the minister spoke of a young girl, Bess Evans. He told us she was laid at home with her parents, consumed by fever and asked us all to pray for her. I found myself clutching Awen all the more tightly to my chest, dizzy and breathless at the thought of the small, limp body that had slipped from me the night she was born.

Women and small children crowded around us as we left the church. They cooed at Awen's wrinkled nose. Some reached out a hand to put a finger to her cheek then clearly thought better of it. There was nothing like the sweat and blood and bile of childbirth, the afterpains and shivers, to unite women. To loosen the threads between ranks.

A woman in a lace cap and brown smock approached us, wanting to discuss an issue regarding her land with Hywel. It took me a moment, but when she spoke I recognised her as the woman who had sat snoring beside me on the dais at the midsummer celebrations. Now that the wine had worn off, she looked different – neatly dressed, hands clasped over her stomach, which was now a small bump I hadn't noticed at the midsummer festivities. Her words were well-pronounced, no longer slurred.

'You know I care a great deal for each of my tenants and their wellbeing, but I must insist we do not discuss these matters on the day of the Lord.' His tone seemed unnecessarily barbed, and I wondered if they'd had a previous disagreement.

'Of course, *master*.' She dipped her head and wandered away with the crowd pouring into the lane towards the market square and the village.

'Do you know her?' I asked Hywel, remembering his absence that

154

evening and her slurred words – *he'd be wanting payment of a different sort. You know what men are like, mistress* – but he shook his head.

'No more than I know the rest of our tenants.'

'You will visit her? During the week?' I asked Hywel, concerned that, although I suspected she was merely trying to catch a glimpse of Awen, there may be truth to her worries about the quality of her soil. If our tenants were unable to grow their own food, it would be our duty to provide for them.

'Of course,' Hywel said. 'I have several visits to make in the village, actually.' He glanced behind him, towards the church doors, where the minister was standing saying his goodbyes.

Ruby made her way through the congregation, heading towards us.

'Doli,' Hywel said. 'Would you mind walking home with Ruby today? I need to speak with the minister.'

'Of course.'

I dipped my head and allowed him to kiss my cheek before we parted ways.

'It's a shame,' I said to Ruby as we picked our way back home along the river. 'About the poor Evans girl. Elizabeth, is it?'

I wondered if that was what Hywel wanted to discuss with the minister. Perhaps he was arranging to help the family by appointing a physician.

'Bess?' Ruby replied, kicking dirt beneath her clogs. 'Yes, it is a shame. Especially for someone so young. But there's nothing much to be done about it. She'll recover, or she won't.'

'Perhaps.'

I stroked Awen's head absently as we walked, remembering her birth, and the knowledge that had consumed me as the birthing pains took hold. That she would either live, or die, and that it was beyond my will. Beyond anyone's will, other than God's … *and Sara Gwen's.*

That image again. Since Awen was delivered, it had entered my mind like a visitation each time my eyes had closed. The image of Sara, bent over her small, limp body, breathing the life into her tiny, parted lips.

'Well,' I said, decidedly. 'We must pray for her.'

Ruby nodded, then paused before speaking.

'I fear it may not help.'

'Why not? I know we cannot hope to change God's will, but we must do something.'

'There is talk amongst the villagers,' Ruby said quietly. 'About Yeoman Evans.'

'Talk? What sort of talk?'

'I've heard it said that he quarrelled, not too long ago, with Old Jane Clarke. I'm not sure what about. Though the yeoman has turned to drink. Everyone knows he's gambled away his business, his animals, his home. It's likely he lost to her at a game of cards and couldn't pay. They say Jane sought the help of a *witsh* to inflict her revenge.'

'Who told you this, Ruby?' I heard the quiver in my voice as I spoke, felt the cool dread in my chest as I pictured my own Awen, sick with fever at the will of a witch. I had found, in the week and a half since Awen was born, my heartbeat quickened more easily, my palms would suddenly slicken with sweat. Shadows made me flinch. I shook my head a little, trying to clear my mind of the darkness that crowded me, even on this hot summer day with the sun high and bright above us.

'I don't recall,' she said. I could tell she was lying. 'I've heard it from several people.'

'Well, that doesn't make it true.'

I didn't believe my own words. Doubt seeped through me like a cold brook.

'What better revenge,' said Ruby. 'Than to inflict ill on an enemy's child?'

She nodded at Awen, swaddled in my arms, and I knew what she said was true. I would die before seeing any ill inflicted on her.

'And who do they say is the *witsh* that did this, Ruby? Who do they believe has enough evil in her heart to curse an innocent child?'

Her answer, when it came, didn't surprise me. She had already been accused of cursing the Garrett family, already been hounded by frightened village people and questioned by yeomen.

'It was Kathryn Lewis.'

As we walked, Ruby told me that many of the villagers had begun to carve protective marks into their front doors, and were even buying amulets from pedlars and whitesmiths.

'Are people really so frightened?' I asked her.

She nodded. 'They seem to be, mistress. I know of several millers and yeomen who have wrapped cats and placed them in their chimney breasts. To ward off witches.'

'Do you think she is a *witsh*? Kathryn Lewis?'

Ruby shrugged.

'Who can say,' she said. 'If she's not, she's done a good job of convincing everyone that she is.'

'Why would she want to do that?' I asked, confused.

'I don't know. Protection. Charity. Fear. She's a strange woman. Perhaps it serves her well to be considered a *witsh*.'

'Perhaps,' I said, quietly. 'But won't it get her in trouble, if she's not careful?'

Ruby looked at me sideways, clicking her tongue.

'It might. But only if she crosses the wrong people. The Garretts and the Evanses don't have the power to bring any trouble upon her.'

'No,' I said. *But the Maredudds do.*

Over supper that evening, a meal of salt sturgeon, scallops and sweet puddings, I asked Hywel about Bess Evans.

'Should we send food? Maybe some meat pies or pastries?'

'Perhaps,' he said, looking thoughtfully at his plate. 'Though I'm not sure pastries will help the poor girl.'

I was reminded of Ruby's words, and wondered if Hywel had also heard the rumours about Kathryn Lewis. There was not much local gossip that escaped Hywel's knowledge.

'Why not? Surely the family would appreciate some hearty food? It might serve to ease their burden, if only a little.'

Hywel chewed slowly, then placed his dagger on his plate.

'Doli, I have it on good authority that Sara Gwen was there last night, helping to treat little Bess Evans.'

He spoke as though helping to treat a sick child was a sinful thing.

It occurred to me then that Sara hadn't been in church that morning. Perhaps she had sat the night with the family, and had gone home to sleep. Perhaps she was still there at the Evans' home now. I pictured her murmuring her charms and her prayers, sweeping salves over the child's forehead. Drawing her fingers from temple to shoulder and back again in imitation of the cross.

Then again, it was not unusual not to see Sara at church. After all, Ruby had told me, all those months ago, that she was a church papist.

'Oh.' We'd stepped into a more precarious conversation than I'd anticipated. 'Well, Sara is well-versed in healing. I'm sure she will do everything she can to help the poor child. You know she saved Awen's life.' I looked down at our baby, held in one arm as I attempted to eat with the other.

Hywel scoffed, and I felt a heavy weight in my chest. I stopped chewing.

'Stop saying that, Doli. You were exhausted, in pain, hysterical. You must have imagined it.'

I stared at him, desperate to argue but cowed by his expression.

'Perhaps they can't afford a physician,' I said, instead.

'There is talk. Little Bess Evans was cursed by Kathryn Lewis. Do you know who has been seen out walking at night, in the company of Kathryn Lewis? Who has been keeping company with the wretched woman the whole county is calling a *witsh*? Your benevolent friend, Sara Gwen.'

I couldn't speak. There was nothing to say.

'Today,' he said. 'Her fever has worsened. She convulses. Her eyes roll in her head. She froths at the mouth. Mark my words Doli – the girl will be dead by morning.'

Hywel was right. Bess Evans succumbed to her fever in the dead of night.

I learned of it the following afternoon, when Awen had finally settled into a restless sleep after a long morning of crying and nursing. This was her pattern, a routine that played out through the day and night. Her sleep was short and disturbed, as though she was dreaming of horrors only known to her. I tried to push the memory of the charm burning on the fire away, tried to assure myself this was simply what babies were like, but I couldn't shift the thought that something was wrong. Something brought about by dark magic.

I was passing by the kitchen when I heard Hywel's voice from within. He sounded agitated, his words clipped and cool.

'It is not for you to decide,' he said.

The reply, when it came, was quiet, almost muffled.

'No, of course not.'

'You should have gone straight to Doroli. She is mistress of this household.'

'Of course, it was my mistake. I hadn't wanted to disturb her, with the baby being so small.'

'Indeed. Nevertheless, Ruby is not mistress, despite what she may think, and you most certainly are not mistress.'

'Of course not,' came the reply. I recognised the voice now as belonging to the cook. Then there was a deep sigh, and a rustle, followed by the quick-paced tapping of shoes on the flagstone.

Hywel appeared, framed in the kitchen doorway, his cheeks pink.

'Is everything alright?' I asked, cautiously. I worried something had transpired between Ruby and the cook, or that Ruby had said something out of turn, as she was wont to do. Something had clearly upset my husband.

Hywel's face softened when he looked at me, but it was strained, his jaw tense.

'Everything is fine. There's nothing to concern yourself with.'

He looked tired. I wished, not for the first time, that he wouldn't keep things from me, as though our household affairs didn't concern me too. Sometimes, I feared he forgot I was not still the child I was when we first met. That we had both grown, both come of age.

'Are you certain?' I pressed. 'I heard Ruby's name, and mine.'

He sighed, and gestured for me to follow him towards the parlour. I fell into step beside him.

'The Evans girl has died,' he said. 'As I predicted she would.'

The sadness that overcame me was intense and unexpected, given I had never even met the poor girl, the tears at my eyes forcing Hywel to take pity on me and wrap his arms around my shoulders. Perhaps it was because I imagined Awen in all children now. I saw her rosebud pink lips in other infants; saw the thistle-down softness of her hair on other children's heads; imagined her growing to be like the children I saw playing marbles in their smocks and breeches in the village. Perhaps it was that I had scarcely slept in two weeks.

Hywel said nothing as he pushed the parlour door, keeping his arm back to hold it open for me.

He closed it quietly behind us before speaking again.

'Her grandmother came here this morning, begging. Brandishing an empty pot at our doorstep by all accounts.'

I couldn't understand why this plea for aid would have upset Hywel, who was always so quick to assist those that needed it.

'Well, that's understandable, Hywel. Besides, we spoke only last night about sending food to the Evans'.'

'Yes, of course. Giving alms is not the issue.'

He rubbed his temples and I took a step towards him. Pressed a palm to his chest.

'Then what is?'

'It seems that the cook took it upon herself to fill the pot with milk.'

160

I stared at him, wondering why a small amount of milk had caused him so much distress.

'I expect deference from our servants, Doli. As mistress of Faen Maredudd, it is *your* place to either grant or deny charity.'

So that's what this was about. I wasn't sure what to say.

'It's your place,' he repeated. 'And yours alone.'

I pressed myself into his chest, feeling the rise and fall of it against my cheek. He was tense, but he didn't pull away. Though I couldn't understand his anger, I appreciated that he was defending me as mistress. That he felt I should be treated with respect.

'I would have sent her home with much more than a pot full of milk,' I said, my words mumbled into his doublet.

'Precisely.' He sighed. 'It doesn't bode well to have only offered a small amount of milk. It will seem uncharitable. People will talk, they will say we are not gracious.'

'Don't worry, darling,' I said, pulling back as his breathing steadied. 'I will go there myself tomorrow, with more offerings. No one will have cause to say we aren't tender-hearted. All will be well.'

The Villagers

Some say Sara learned to write when she was only a child. That she had an unnatural talent for it. Some say she learned to do it with the help of a crystal stone. Some say she learned to write her own name so she could mark it in the devil's ledger. *Afiach*. Let's say Sara is a woman of ill fame, long suspected of being given over to sorcery. Let's say she is often called *witsh* to her face, and seems not to mind. Some say she is a nightwalker, rising from her cot and wandering the darkened countryside for nefarious purposes, her fetid gown snagging on brambles.

The following morning, I left the house carrying a basket filled with sweet buns and pastries, as well as a small bowl of milk pottage. It was warm outside, Awen was bound to my chest with thick woollen blankets, making my journey slow and laborious.

'Tell them they may keep the basket and the bowl, as a gift,' Hywel had said before I left him standing in the entry hall. 'That ought to please them.'

I picked my way along the river towards town, grateful that Awen was sleeping soundly at my chest. By now, I was accustomed to her waking at the smallest noise, the slightest movement. And each time she woke, she cried, thrashing her head and pounding her little fists as though my chest was a drum. Sleep felt to me now like a distant memory. Something that happened only in another life.

I followed the path as Ruby had directed, over the moors where rabbits spilled from hedgerows, darting in front of me and cross-stitching their little bodies across the grass. I went through the village, then into a dark wooded area, enjoying the cool shade cast by the branches.

As I was making my way through the copse of trees, everything around me darkened. It was as though the sun had been swallowed up, and everything else with it – no birds chirruped from the brambles, no insects hummed. In a panic, I turned, spinning a circle looking for any trace of daylight. A voice in my ear hissed – *Doroli* – and I jumped back, tripping over a tree root, clutching my hand to Awen to keep her safely bound to me. I pressed my hands to the ground to push myself back up and felt it move beneath me. The roots had come alive, like writhing snakes with tree bark skin knotting themselves across the earth.

I screamed, ran, emerging among heaped mounds of earth and dung that had been shaped crudely into homesteads. I took a moment to regain myself, my breath coming fast and heavy, my hands shaking. Somehow, I still had hold of the basket which contained the pottage.

I looked around, worried I was in the wrong place. These were certainly not the sort of homes I would have expected to find a yeoman and his family inhabiting, but I remembered what Ruby had told me about the man's debts.

A small girl ran past, carrying a loaf of bread in one arm and a poppet in the other.

'Excuse me?' I said, my voice trembling, and she whipped around, clutching the loaf to her chest reflexively, as though I was about to reach out and steal it.

'I'm sorry to have startled you,' I said to the girl, and her face relaxed, her shoulders dropping a little. 'Do you know which of these homes belongs to the Evans family?'

The girl silently pointed towards one of the houses. I thanked her before heading towards it. There was no path between these cylindrical huts, only a blanket of cracked dry earth. Here and there, there was the hardened imprint of a horse's hoof, and the occasional trace of a boot. I imagined in winter the ground here must be sodden and swollen with mud. I was glad of the warm, dry weather.

I hovered at the door for a moment, listening for signs that the family was home, but all was quiet within. I knocked, suddenly hoping they weren't here. What words of comfort could be offered to a mother hovering at the cusp of grief? Maybe I could leave the basket of food at their door to be discovered later. That would be better than having to find the right thing to say.

Before I could turn and retreat to the comfort of my own gardens, the door swung open, and I was greeted by a stout, round woman. Her face was lined with worried pleats, her hair wisping in grey strands from beneath her cap. She looked startled, her eyes passing over me, taking in the basket in my hands then coming to rest on Awen, who was still sleeping contentedly at my chest beneath the blanket, despite the strange disturbance in the trees.

Over her shoulder, I could see inside the home. I had thought Sara's cottage was simple, but the Evans' home was no more than a single room, a cot at one of its curved walls, straw strewn across the ground. The smell of urine was like a thick fog, warm and stale in the summer heat. I breathed through my mouth in an attempt to avoid it.

'Yes?' There was a note of impatience in the woman's voice. A small child emerged from the darkness to appear at her side, clutching her skirts and peering up at me curiously.

'Good day,' I said, trying to smile.

'Can I help you, mistress?' the woman asked, curt, pressing her hand to the child's head.

'Forgive me,' I replied. 'I – My name is Doli Maredudd. I am mistress at Faen Maredudd, up at the other end of Llynidwen.'

She nodded.

'Yes,' she said. 'I assumed as much.'

I blushed, suddenly aware of my velvet dress, the thickness of the blanket that bound Awen to me, considerably softer than the sack dress the child before me was wearing.

'I've brought you some food,' I held the basket out to her. 'Forgive us, a member of your family came to our home yesterday in search of charity and was given far less than we could spare. I hope this will make amends.'

'There's not much as can make amends for the loss of a child,' she smiled sadly, looking again at Awen.

'Of course not.' I felt hot. Itchy. 'You have our condolences. Your daughter is at peace with our Lord now, I'm sure. You'll be kept in our prayers.'

She blinked, taking the basket from me silently.

'Thank you, mistress.'

I bowed my head, and turned to leave, before a thought struck, quick as lightning, turning me back to her again.

'I'm sorry,' I said, pressing a hand instinctively to the back of Awen's head. 'I wondered —' I stopped, unsure how to ask what I needed to know, without causing offence. 'What happened ... to your daughter? Only, I heard Sara Gwen had been here, and...' I trailed off, uncertain, silenced by the grave look on her face. The resignation.

'Aye. Sara Gwen was here. She did what she could for our Bess, but she was beyond saving. When the Lord has decided it's our time, there's little anyone can do.'

I nodded.

As I made my way home over the moors, I thought of her words. Was there some comfort in the knowledge that God's will was carried out no matter what humans might do to intervene? What about women hanged on charges of witchcraft, or thieves left to rot in gaol? Was that also God's will? I was almost certain Hywel would claim it was – after all, he believed the justices were doing God's work. And what of the people, children amongst them, that were killed and maimed by the witches? Elizabeth Garrett's baby. Where did they fall, I wondered, in God's plan? Did they join him in heaven after death, or did the witches send them straight to hell, to keep company with the devil?

I couldn't bear the thought of going home through that copse of trees, so I walked along the outskirts of the village, taking the narrow path past Sara Gwen's cottage, dust clouds gathering at my feet with each step.

Not long after I reached the riverbank, Awen stirred and began to whine at my chest. I made shushing noises to soothe her, but she was restless, her arms and legs writhing against the shawl that held her to me, her back arching, head pushing back searching for milk. She was strong, for a creature so small.

Last night, before she packed her bags and left Faen Maredudd, I asked Mary for her counsel – the exhaustion was like a living thing in my body, leaving me uneasy and jumpy. Her parting guidance was to swaddle Awen. *She'll calm down eventually, dear. Don't you worry.* She didn't seem to understand that Awen's crying was inconsolable. That the sound of it churned my stomach like the sound of someone scraping the bottom of a rusted bucket. How I longed for her to sleep peacefully and contentedly, as I always imagined babies did. How she was only ever settled when she was at suck. She would fall asleep, her lips still wrapped around my nipple, then wake and search for more milk the moment I tried to move, pinning me once more to my rocking chair.

I wouldn't have minded terribly – I was tired, and had nothing more to do than to rest and cradle Awen – but the pain was another matter. As her suck grew stronger, I began to find nursing uncomfortable and sore. Each time she drew her head back and reattached herself to me, the pain was so sharp I would curl my toes and wince as the breath was stripped from me, feeling sick to my stomach.

If Sara was home, perhaps she could offer some guidance on Awen's fitful sleep, or even a balm that might help her to rest more easily. I shook my head free of the thought – it was an impossibility, far too dangerous to even consider.

As I rounded the corner, bringing the little cottage into view, I saw two men on horseback coming towards me along the path. Without thinking, I slipped behind a tree. I couldn't risk being seen this close to the house. They might say something to Hywel. As though she felt it too, Awen quietened at my chest, and I continued to tap her back to soothe her, silently muttering a prayer that she would stay still and quiet. *Don't give us away, Awen fach.*

From my hiding spot, I watched the men tether their horses to the big rowan tree beside the cottage. One man was large, thickset and dark. The other was like a weasel at his side, carrying a leather folio and wearing gloves, despite the warm weather. From high above, a large kite perched on one of the tree's branches, watching them intently. Silent. They entered through the front door, but still I felt rooted amongst the trees, reluctant to leave. Something wasn't right. I was certain of it.

I kept watch from the shadows. Waiting. Every now and then, the horses scraped their hooves on the ground. The kite didn't move, not even to stretch its wings or turn its head. It kept its eyes fixed on the cottage door, watching.

Eventually, the men re-emerged, the smaller man tucking his

book under his arm. Sara was with them, escorted unwillingly by the larger man, who jostled her through her frontage and towards the horses, a length of rope trailing from her wrists. She kept her chin pointed towards the clear sky above, almost as though in prayer. I thought I could see her lips moving, muttering something hurried while she walked.

She looked over towards the river, towards the shelter of trees I was lurking in. Towards me. Her eyes were golden, impossibly vibrant and clear despite the space between us. I felt suddenly as though we were much nearer, as though I was standing with her and could see into her eyes, and she into mine. I drew back, shielding my body with the thick tree trunk, hoping she couldn't see me. I patted Awen again. By some miracle, she'd gone back to sleep, *diolch i Dduw.*

There was an awful, deafening hissing at my ear. I whipped around, horrified to see a huge snake uncoiling from the trees, its jaw wide open, its soulless black eyes staring straight at me. Instinctively, I turned away, wrapping both arms tightly around Awen, eyes scrunched shut. I waited for the beast to strike at my head.

When nothing happened, I turned back, tentative. It was only a branch. A dense, gnarled branch jutting towards me, withered and long as a snake. The tip even had a knot in the wood that looked like an eye. My heart was thundering.

I looked back to where the men and Sara were gathered, and saw the larger man shove Sara's back, roughly. She mounted his horse before he did, struggling up onto its back with both her hands bound. Where were they taking her?

The horses tore off in the direction they first came from, and I watched as the speck of the convoy grew smaller and smaller, the sound of the horses' hooves fading. I waited until they were fully out of sight to start back on the path towards home. Even though Sara and the men were gone, I kept to the shadow of the trees as I walked.

I tried to calm myself, but my heart echoed with the beat of the horses' hooves. I listened to the river, keeping my eyes on the mottled branches, trying to search for blackberry blossoms blooming from the shrubbery, but it was no use. I was shaking. I hadn't gone far when Awen woke again and began to cry and I felt the pitch of it in the swell of my breasts. I would have to feed her soon. I quickened my step, hastening to reach the quiet solace of my home.

Once I'd nursed Awen, I went to find Ruby, and told her about the snakes.

'It happened twice?' she asked, chewing her lip.

'Yes. Once in the trees before I went to the Evans' house, and then again on my way back. And Ruby...' I paused, wondering how much to tell her. 'When it happened the second time, it was as Sara Gwen was being arrested.'

Ruby only looked at me with a hard, unreadable stare, and said nothing.

'What do you think it means?' I asked. She took a while to reply, looking to the window and back to me before speaking.

'Doli, I don't know. It could mean anything. It could mean that you're lacking sleep, as most new mothers are. You look exhausted. Or, it could mean that Sara knew you were there.'

'You think she did it? Why would —'

'She knows Hywel wanted her arrested. Maybe she thinks you should have stopped him. Maybe it was a message.'

'Stopped him? I've tried to tell him what happened when Awen was born. He doesn't want to hear it. There's nothing I can say to...' I trailed off. 'Besides, it's not as though Hywel arrested her himself.'

'I'm not accusing you. I'm only telling you what it could mean. Maybe you should speak with the master.'

I thrust Awen into her arms and went to find Hywel. He was sitting by himself in the parlour, hunched over his ledger.

He looked up as I entered.

'Ah Doli. How were the wretched family? Did they like the pottage?'

'They were as expected, Hywel. They've lost a child. Pottage can only go so far.'

His smile dropped as I approached. He nodded.

'Yes, of course.'

I hesitated, rethinking the conversation. I didn't want him to know I'd been near Sara's house, but I had to ask him about the arrest.

'I had to pass Sara Gwen's *bwthyn*, on the way home. There was a fallen tree that made it impossible to get home without going that way,' I hastened to add, before he grew suspicious.

He glared at me for a moment, seeming to consider whether or not I was telling the truth. The moment his frown softened, I pressed him.

'Two men. They went into Sara Gwen's home and came out some time later with her. Her hands were bound. Hywel, I think they may have been arresting her. Do you know anything about this?'

'Ah, yes. That will have been the bishop and his clerk, I imagine. I had received word that she would be examined soon. I'm glad they didn't dawdle.'

'Examined? What do you mean?'

'Witchcraft is a crime against the Church, Doli. As is murder. It's reasonable that the bishop should want to take the old hag's sworn testimony, is it not?'

'Witchcraft? Murder?'

'Murder by witchcraft, yes.'

I said nothing, waiting for him to go on. I knew Hywel believed Sara had cursed us, that she'd broken Mary's leg and taken the afterbirth, but he hadn't spoken of murder until today.

'Do you deny that Bess Evans is dead? You went to the Evans' home yourself. You spoke with her grieving mother?'

'No, but Hywel, I —'

I found myself lost for words, unable to form a coherent sentence. I tried again.

171

'Sara Gwen tried to help Bess Evans. She brought Awen safely into this world. That's something no other midwife has managed. She saved our baby's life, Hywel.'

He spluttered.

'This, again!? And you call her a midwife? She is no midwife. She's a sorceress who maimed our midwife, broke her leg, infiltrated our home and came to you at your most vulnerable hour. That's exactly how these vile women operate.' He practically spat the words. 'And now, you seem convinced that she somehow resurrected our daughter. Brought her back from the dead! If there was any intervention in her birth, it was God that did it.'

'But Awen —'

Before I could decide what I wanted to say, I heard Awen's cries, growing louder and angrier. Ruby entered the hall, carrying our baby in her arms.

'I'm sorry, mistress,' she said. Her tone was always more formal when Hywel was present. 'I've tried to comfort her but she won't stop crying. She's searching for milk again.'

My heart dropped. *Of course.* No amount of nursing could settle her for long.

I took a deep breath, steadying myself, before extending my arms for Ruby to pass her to me.

Hywel scowled.

'This is why wet nurses are recommended,' he said.

'I'm her mother,' I told him, sharply.

I clutched Awen near my chest as she cried, clawing at the fabrics of my dress. Her scrunched little fist pounded me, as though she were trying to pummel the milk from me. Furious in her hunger.

'Perhaps we should discuss this later,' I said, turning away.

He snorted.

'Doli, there is nothing to discuss. These are not your decisions to make. They are barely even my decisions to make.'

I turned back to him, hot and angry but determined to keep my voice steady.

'That's not true. You have influence in Llynidwen. You have the bishop's ear, and the magistrate's. You could stop this.'

Awen found her fingers and started sucking on them, a greedy, bird-like *caw* coming from her mouth.

'Perhaps you misunderstand,' he said, his voice cold. 'I don't want to stop it, Doli. Now please, take that child elsewhere and feed her. She's giving me a sore head.'

I turned from him once more, fleeing the room before he could see the tears brimming in my eyes, threatening to spill. I was a river about to burst its banks.

As we approached July's end, Awen yellowed then paled. She cried incessantly. Nothing comforted her. I spent my days rocking, singing, swaddling, nursing and worrying. All useless ways to pass the time which ultimately offered her no relief. When I put her to my breast she writhed and flailed, her arms and legs pushing against me as though she was cross, or pained.

Two different physicians came, and neither were concerned. Both insisted Awen seemed well, and would settle in time. They even applauded her good appetite, laughing at her greed.

Only weeks ago, I'd been so filled with joy to have finally brought a healthy child into the world, but now I was failing more than ever. I shushed her and I hummed. I paced with her pressed to my chest or my shoulder, I showed her the light trickling through the windows in the quiet, early hours, but nothing silenced her relentless crying. When she slept, I placed her, gentle as though she were a dried petal, in her cradle, but immediately she would sense my withdrawal, wake and begin to cry again.

Oftentimes, I cried with her.

I'm ashamed to say I shouted at her on more than one occasion.

'I'm not sure I'm well suited to motherhood after all,' I told Ruby one evening, my eyes stinging, my voice wavering. 'I can't ever seem to settle Awen. I see women in the village with six or more children running happily about their ankles and babies strapped to their backs as though they were no more than pheasants in game bags. Why can't I do what they do? I'm useless.'

'Nonsense,' said Ruby. 'All women are suited to motherhood.'

'Well, not me.' I felt tears pricking my eyes and was afraid to go on, lest they spill over. 'Perhaps Awen doesn't like me. Perhaps she wishes for a better mother.'

My voice cracked. I turned my face away, ashamed.

'Things are difficult for many mothers, at first. It will get easier,' she said, her voice treacle soft.

'How can you be certain?'

She touched a hand to my arm.

'Because you're not the first woman to have a child, nor the first to find it challenging.'

I looked down at Awen, swaddled in my arms.

'I worry,' I said. 'That she's sick. Her skin is yellow and sallow. She's never content.'

Ruby scowled, casting her own eyes over my daughter, whose eyelids flickered in sleep, thin as paper.

'I don't think that's unusual,' she said.

'She's lost the fleshiness she had at birth.' My throat was tight as I spoke the words I'd been holding in, the reality I'd been trying to deny. 'Something's wrong, Ruby.'

'If you're concerned, you could speak with a physician again?'

'The physicians haven't been able to help. I know what this is Ruby. This is because Hywel burned the fertility charm.'

Ruby looked at me, then at Awen. She scrunched her lips together, as though holding in whatever she wanted to say. I knew I was right about this. Why else would my perfect baby be so unsettled? So unhappy?

Later that day, there was a knock at the bedroom door. A servant came to find me to tell me there was a beggar at the house. The staff had clearly paid heed to Hywel's recent rebuke about tending to visitors themselves. I left Awen with Ruby and went to the front door, where I found an elderly woman holding out an empty pot.

Her dress was threadbare, her shoes tattered. I wondered if she had come from the same small gathering of earthen mounds that I visited when I took the parcel of food to the Evans' home. Perhaps she'd heard of our generosity and come here in search of more. Or perhaps this was the grandmother who first visited and was turned away without enough.

I greeted her before instructing a passing servant to fetch a pie from the kitchen. While we waited for him to return, I examined the poor woman. Her hair was bedraggled beneath her cap, spilling out in thin grey wisps. She was missing most of her teeth, and one of her eyes veered unnervingly to the side. While her left eye stared straight at me, the right looked steadily towards our gardens.

Though it wasn't a cold day, I noticed she was shivering, her angular shoulders juddering beneath her worsted shawl. Perhaps I should have invited her in, but in truth I worried that would open the doors to many more beggars seeking food and shelter. In Llynidwen, word travelled more quickly than the darting sparrows through the hedgerows.

'You look cold,' I said instead, a little helplessly. The way one of her eyes roamed freely while the other remained fixed in place frightened me. She smelled of grease and urine – the stench turned my stomach, though it felt unkind to think it. I listened for the sound of footsteps on stone. Where was that pie?

'Aye,' she said. 'I am indeed. Cold in the chill air, and cold in my heart since becoming a widow all those years hence. And, mistress —' Suddenly, both eyes fixed themselves on me and I wondered if she had mastery of the roaming eye, or if it was coincidence that it had come to rest on my face now. 'I am colder still, now that my dear friend Sara has been arrested, dragged off to Tretower, where she will surely perish.'

'You know Sara?'

Was that why she was here? Did she hope to plead for mercy on

Sara's behalf? I'm ashamed to admit that I'd been so preoccupied trying to care for Awen, trying to settle her temper and soothe her constant crying, that I had scarce considered poor Sara.

'I do,' she said. My name is Kathryn Lewis – I'm very fond of Sara.'

So, this was her then. The witch, roaming the county muttering her curses. It was easy to see how her reputation had formed.

'Yes,' I said, cautious. 'I was sorry to hear of Sara's fate. But you need not despair. If she's innocent of any wrongdoing, she will soon be freed.' I heard the echo of Hywel in my words and hated it.

The woman cackled.

'No one is freed once the bishop puts a case to the assize judges. No.' Her right eye wandered again, searching the facade of the house. 'Sara used to bring me pottage and sit with me through the cold nights. Who will care for me now? I will surely perish too, now that she is gone. And then there'll be two corpses on your soul.'

I flinched at her words. I was unaccustomed to the village poor speaking to me so freely, and with such little deference. I wondered if she would have the gall to speak to Hywel this way. Was she so wretched, so poor, that she had nothing to lose?

'I'll go and enquire about your pie,' I said, desperate to get away from her. 'It's taking such a long time to be brought.' As I turned away from her, a creeping cold sensation crawled along my spine, as though a spider were crawling up my back. I felt as though I was wearing her damp, thin, ragged clothes and useless shoes myself.

She reached her hand out to stop me leaving, and said, 'Sara Gwen is a good woman.' When she touched me, I felt a crackle, like the spark of a flame, or a small flea, jump from her hand to mine. Suddenly, my vision lurched and I felt sick to my stomach. I was both hot and cold all at once. I tugged my hand away, with urgency. Her grip was much fiercer than her spindling, half-starved frame would suggest.

'Please, don't touch me.' My voice was cool. I had to fight the urge to close the door, leaving her shivering and hungry on the other side.

'As you wish,' she said with a smile that wasn't reflected in her eyes. 'But you'll do well to remember that you're no better than the rest of us. Sitting here in your grand house working away at your pastry crusts and your embroidery.' She smiled all the wider, before continuing, suddenly gleeful. 'You piss and shit and bleed like the rest of us do.' She cackled at this, then spat at the floor. A rumbling thunder cracked across the horizon. Warm rain began to stream from above, dripping from the doorway and plashing on the stone step below.

I was stunned into silence and concluded she must be mad. Thankfully, the servant returned at last, carrying two pies bound in cloth. I thrust them out to her, closing the door firmly before she had even stepped back.

With the door closed, I shuddered, remembering how her hand had almost bitten mine. How her touch had left me sickened. If witches truly walked amongst us, they must do so in old rags and dirty caps. They were the old crones with paper-thin skin and exposed gums, rotting teeth. The ones whose skin burnt when it touched yours. Why did Sara associate with this woman?

With haste, I walked towards the kitchens, in search of Ruby, or a servant – anyone who might be able to help.

When I found Ruby, busy chopping carrots, I asked her to go to the stable boy so that he might carry out the task.

'Tell him to find a stray cat and snap its neck. It needs to be dried, wrapped and placed within the chimney breast.'

She looked at me, questioning, and I tried to compose my face, hoping I might pass the notion off as a whim. I'm sure she could see the fear in my eyes, the tension that gripped my jaw as I pictured Awen crying, hungering. I couldn't help but imagine her, coiled in blankets wrapping tighter and tighter, snaking about her neck.

'He'll be discreet?' I asked then. I didn't want Hywel to know about this. Though Kathryn Lewis had frightened me to my core, if I spoke to Hywel about this, he was certain to have her arrested too. I couldn't carry the responsibility of her arrest, couldn't let her rot in gaol with Sara.

'He'll be discreet,' Ruby said, clasping my hands, trying to stop them from shaking.

The case against Sara was set in motion quickly. The villagers were asked to gather at the parish church one afternoon, where the magistrate would collect evidence against her.

'Or evidence in support of her plight,' Hywel reminded me one evening as we were readying ourselves for bed. 'If she's innocent, I'm sure the people will speak in her favour.'

His words should have been comforting, but he spoke with a smirk – he was teasing me. Fury burbled in my stomach, like a pot of boiled water threatening to erupt, I had to still myself, not trusting I would reply calmly.

I held Awen to my chest, focussing on her face to steady my temper. Her long, dark eyelashes fluttered against her cheeks. Her lips moved in and out in her sleep, as though she was suckling in her dreams. I hooked one of her tiny fingers in mine, and took a deep breath before responding to Hywel.

'You know as well as I do that the magistrate will be looking only for damning evidence.'

The beggar woman's words echoed in my mind. *No one is freed once the bishop puts a case to the assize judges.*

Hywel shrugged off his jerkin, draping it over the chest beside the bed.

'It's out of my hands.'

'Is it?' I asked, quietly. I was careful not to disturb Awen, knowing she would be looking to suckle again the moment she woke.

'I am neither magistrate nor bishop. I am not a justice of the peace. Yet. Her case does not concern me, Doli. Nor should it you.'

'That's not true!' Though I was speaking in hushed tones, my words were needle sharp. 'Of course the case concerns you. You said yourself, you wanted to see Sara hanged as a *witsh*.'

His nostrils flared. His reply was curt.

'That may be so, but as I say, whatever becomes of that Godless woman is out of my hands.'

I took a step towards him, and made an effort to soften my voice once again. I knew I needed to be careful. If I was too bold, he would be angered beyond reason and our conversation would be swiftly ended.

It didn't used to be this way. Hywel used to listen to me, to treat my thoughts with keen regard, to argue with me in enjoyable debate. To read poetry to me. We used to laugh.

He wouldn't care about Sara's fate, I knew that. But perhaps if I spoke about Awen....

'Hywel, darling. Our daughter is sick. She cries without end. She hungers. I believe – I know – Sara Gwen is the only person who can help. If she perishes in gaol, or ends her life at the gallows, we'll be doomed too.'

Hywel reached out a hand to smooth my brow.

'Doli, I know you're worried. But babies cry. If she hungers more than you can bear, we'll employ a wet nurse. If indeed there is something wrong, it will be the result of a curse at the hands of that wretched woman. Her conviction will only serve to improve our situation. When she hangs, the curse will be lifted. You'll thank me then, *cariad*.'

Knowing there was nothing I could say that would change his mind, I chose to stay quiet, bundling Awen into bed. I prepared myself for another long, disturbed night, and wondered if Hywel was right. Perhaps there was nothing wrong with Awen. Perhaps the problem did lie with me, with my inability to feed her, to comfort her, to mother her as God intended.

We gathered on a stiflingly warm day in early August, the church filled with sweating bodies. Sara's name was hot on everyone's lips, villagers clamouring to tell their stories, to share their tales of witchcraft and malice with one another.

The magistrate commanded the room well, his voice deep and

booming, silencing everyone with ease. Jacob Lloyd stood at his side, silent and watchful as a hawk. Through the long afternoon, they took statements from each person, the clerk writing furiously, translating the depositions to English for those who were unable to speak it themselves.

'How do they know what they're signing?' I asked Hywel quietly, as we watched a woman scrawl a shaking cross alongside her name at the bottom of a piece of paper.

'They trust the clerk to do his job as instructed,' he replied. His words seemed unnecessarily curbed. I was only curious about the legal proceedings.

A woman, her belly bulging beneath a cream smock dipped her head and spoke quietly about how Sara Gwen had soured her milk and caused mould to grow all over her cheese. How her home was infested with fat spiders. How she could not sleep at night because an owl would try to swoop through her window slats, scratching at the walls and hooting as it tried to get inside. The woman's voice was familiar, but I didn't recognise her until she turned towards me, and I was able to fully see the face beneath the brim of her cap. It was the drunk woman from the summer festivities, the one we had seen outside of church not long after Awen was born. She smiled at Hywel with familiarity, and from the corner of my eye, I saw him nod.

The heat engulfed me, a sudden sickness overcoming me so that I had to push my way through the thick crowd to lean against one of the walls. The cool stone calmed me, and I focussed my eyes on the faint outline of an outstretched hand, visible where the whitewash had thinned and faded. The church must have been so beautiful before the murals were painted over, hidden from view.

Hywel didn't follow me. I saw him make his way quietly towards the front of the room, where he spent a great deal of time hovering near the magistrate and Jacob, whispering in their ears.

By the time the sun was sinking into the moors, glowing hot and angry across the dried, yellowing grass, we had heard countless tales of revenge, malice and sorcery. Sara Gwen poisoned somebody's cattle. She swore to help another person find their best mouser, who had wandered off with the night and not come home, only to lead them astray in their search. She had broken the arm of a yeoman who had spoken badly of her. Stolen money from desperate parents who'd asked the fairies to help heal their child. She had used magic to deform a litter of goats. Jacob claimed to have accidentally brushed her with his arm, only to find his shoulder lame and limp the following day, a bruise blooming where his arm had touched hers. I remembered the way he'd shoved her, barging his way into her home, and snorted at his use of 'accidentally', provoking a glower from Hywel. Perhaps the worst accusation of all, was that Sara had conspired with Kathryn Lewis to murder little Bess Evans. Had spent the night muttering curses over her under the guise of healing.

Bess' mother, who had told me only a fortnight ago that Sara had tried to help her daughter, was nowhere to be seen. She had no defenders. The accusations came from villagers whose names I did not know, faces I did not recognise. Some stayed quiet until asked to come forward, then practically frothed at the mouths with their convictions.

The Villagers

Sara Gwen repeats the names of the father, the son, the Holy Ghosts. She calls for the three Marys. *Yn enw'r Tad, y Mab, a'r ysbryd Duw glân, a'r tair Mair.* She crosses herself. She does this when she curses. We have seen her do it. Now, she sits in gaol, awaiting trial. She will not confess. We heard that, under the eye of the deputy justice, Sara Gwen began to sweat. Told him her trade was no more than enchantments and words. The justice, tingling with the thrill, asked Sara about her familiars. *Do you have a fly that does your bidding?* Of course Sara denied it. Some say, she lied.

I chose a day when Hywel was away on business to ride to Tretower Court. He'd gone to meet with Thomas Mostyn, and made no efforts to conceal his excitement about the trip. Now that I knew where Sara was, now that I'd heard first-hand the vitriol from the villagers, I felt I had to see her.

Ruby warned me not to go, but given that Hywel wouldn't return until the following evening, I knew I needed to seize the opportunity.

'Then I'm coming with you,' she said, her face set like a carving.

The ride was long and tiresome, and I was hot with the extra weight of Awen bound to me with a shawl, Ruby pressed behind me on the horse. Beneath me, the ground rushed by like a river of dust. The smell of leather was inescapable. Eventually the manor loomed over the horizon, the singular tower huge and dark against the sky. That must be where they kept prisoners. We dismounted at the bottom of a grassy incline, and walked towards the guard who was standing at the gate of the tower.

'I need to see one of your prisoners. Sara Gwen, of Llynidwen,' I told him. 'I believe she's being kept here.'

He looked at me blankly, as though I'd spoken another language. Then he grunted.

'Can't let you in,' he said, simply.

I'm not sure what I expected to happen when I set out that morning, but this wasn't it.

'I only need a moment, to speak with her,' I said. 'Please. *Mae'n bwysig.*'

He chewed a fingernail carelessly, and repeated himself.

'Can't let you in. No one is to speak with the prisoners. 'Specially not prisoners that's witches.'

I looked to Ruby, who shrugged and said, 'I told you it wasn't a good idea. Let's go.'

I glanced around hopelessly, my initial confidence entirely deflated. I considered trying to appeal to his sympathies, telling him that my daughter's life may depend on this conversation. That the only person who might be able to help her was trapped in the dark under the castle tower with the thieves and the liars. That she was innocent of any wrongdoing and shouldn't be down there. But I could see it would be a useless endeavour. The man was brutish. Stupid. Following orders.

I reached into my satchel for a silver coin and pressed it to his palm, meeting his eyes as I said again, 'please.'

Again, he grunted, and for a moment I thought he was going to take the money and turn me away regardless. But he stood aside, letting me pass.

'I'm going for a piss,' he said. 'You better be gone by the time I get back. Or I might lock the gate and leave you down there with the rest of 'em. *Dallt?*'

The moment he was gone, I untied the shawl that was holding Awen to me and handed her to Ruby. She began to cry immediately.

'Wait here,' I said before descending the stone steps down into the pits of the earth.

I'm not sure what hit me first – the firm press of darkness or the sickening smell. The air thick with faeces and urine and sweat and death. It reminded me of the time I found a rat carcass rotting in the stables behind the horses, lodged in the hay. The cloying, sickly sweet smell of it. The smell of decay. My stomach churned and I had to stop myself from retching.

As I approached the bottom of the staircase, the darkness was so intense that I had to use my toes to feel ahead for the next step. It was so dark, I felt as though the hangman's sack had been placed over my head. Thank goodness Ruby had come and I'd been able to leave Awen outside, away from the depths of this dank pit. I couldn't believe human beings were kept here. When there were no more steps, I turned around, trying to force my eyes to see something, anything, in the darkness.

'Sara,' I hissed, under my breath. 'Sara, where are you?'

The voice that came back was faint and croaky, like a voice that hadn't been used in some time.

'Doli Maredudd? Surely you haven't come all this way to see me?'

Relief flooded my core. A small slice of hope.

I felt my way towards the voice, one hand stretched out before me, one to the side, feeling blindly for the wet slime of stone wall.

Finally, my hand landed on something cold and hard. An iron bar. The gate keeping the prisoners in.

'Sara,' I called again.

When she replied, her voice seemed to be much closer this time. So close I could feel her breath near my face, though she was pressed to the other side of the gate.

'How are you? Have you got enough food? And blankets for warmth?'

A cruel, barking laugh came from somewhere up ahead, which very quickly became a hacking wet cough.

'Doli. Why have you come here?'

She sounded beaten, as though she had already given up all hope of acquittal.

'I've come for you, Sara. This isn't right. You shouldn't be here.'

She laughed then, a sad, tired laugh.

'And Sara? It's Awen. She's sick. Pale. Starving.'

A cough in the darkness, whether from Sara or someone else, I couldn't tell.

'And I suppose you think I've caused it? Cursed her with my wicked ways? Implored God and the devil himself to take her from you?'

I was startled by the bitterness in her tone, stunned into silence. Was there a part of me that believed it? Meeting Kathryn Lewis, hearing what the villagers had to say about Sara, had left me questioning my conviction in her innocence.

'Of course not,' I said. 'But Sara?'

She said nothing, waiting quietly for me to go on. The darkness pressing in around us made everything else bigger – the lump that was forming in my throat as I tried to speak. The hurried breathing that was coming from the cell ahead of me. The door to the outside was open and Awen's phantom cries spun down the stairs towards me.

'The villagers said such awful things.'

It was not what I wanted to say.

'And you, Doli? Did you speak in my favour?'

In that moment, I was glad of the darkness. Glad that she couldn't see my cheeks redden in shame. I hadn't said everything Hywel had wanted me to, but it would have been a lie not to nod when the magistrate asked if I'd taken a charm. To contradict Hywel when he said the midwife had broken her ankle during the birth. To say Sara had not put her lips to Awen, nor taken the afterbirth away with her.

I tried again.

'Tell me. How did you learn your skills? Is it magic?'

'Why does it matter whether it's magic, or God, or a trick? If it works, there's no need to question it.'

I thought about this for a moment.

'Sara, please. I need to hear you say it. Did you do what they say you did? Any of it?'

She responded only by muttering something.

'And Bess Evans? Did you harm her?'

'I did nothing but try to heal that poor girl.'

I was scared to speak again, scared to move, to break the stillness that had fallen over the dungeon. But I had to.

'And Awen?' The question came in a quivering whisper. 'You don't know why she's so unhappy? There's no curse?'

She didn't answer, so I pressed her. I had to.

'Is it because the charm was burned? Can it be undone?'

'Mistress. Doli. Please. I don't know.' Her voice was so small, so sad in that moment that she didn't need to say anymore. I believed her. 'I told you I might be in need of your help, mistress. Perhaps that time has come.'

'I'll do all I can. We must have faith in the justice system. You'll be found innocent. I'm sure of it.'

Even as I spoke the words, I knew they were untrue. Too many people had spoken against her. The magistrate's power was too great.

'I'd hoped, as the court is owned by the Vaughans, I might have been treated more fairly. That they might instruct the jailers to treat me with kindness. I was a fool.'

I didn't understand. She lowered her voice again, practically whispering now.

'The Vaughans are Catholic,' she said. 'I thought they might have been sympathetic to someone like me. Harbouring trinkets of worship is the only real evidence they have against me.' Her words dripped with scorn, like soured milk.

She was right. The line between those of the old faith and those practising witchcraft was slim.

From the world above, Awen's cries intensified, nudging me to ask Sara what I needed to. I felt rotten, asking Sara for help, when she was the one imprisoned and starved. But I had no choice.

'Sara, can you help me? Can you help Awen? It might be the best way to get you out. I'm sure if you are able to help us, Hywel will speak in your favour before the assizes. He will write to the judges and —'

It was Sara's turn to laugh.

'You truly believe your husband will help me? He's the one who put me here.'

'He doesn't —'

She cut me off before I could finish speaking.

'The bishop told me himself, when he came to question me. My name was given to the justices by Hywel Maredudd, master of Faen Maredudd.'

'Sara, I —' I stopped, unsure what to say to her.

She sighed, the sound of it echoing in the darkness.

'I can't do anything for Awen from here, Doli. I'm sorry. Truly I am. But I'm locked up in the darkness. How can you expect me to help her?'

I stayed silent, unable to form a response. I don't know how I'd expected her to help. I hadn't imagined such a dark, horrible place.

'I'll get you out,' I told her 'I promise.'

As I left, I heard the horrible rasping laughter once again. It followed me back up the steep stone steps. I could still hear it as I emerged, blinking, into the daylight.

Taking Awen back from Ruby was like taking a long drink after a bout of thirst. I nuzzled my face against hers, whispering to her, clutching her tight. Before climbing back on the horse, I unwrapped the shawl from Awen, handed it to Ruby, then looked around for the guard.

'Go down there and give this to Sara. It's icy cold down there. Hurry.'

As we drew close to home, I was relieved knowing that Hywel would be away on business until tomorrow. I wasn't sure I could have faced him now, having learned it was him, my own husband, who had Sara arrested, when I had told him so many times that she was innocent. That she had saved Awen's life, and possibly mine too. Telling him she may be the only one who could help Awen even now. If I tried hard enough, I could convince myself his motivations were the same as mine – to protect Awen no matter the cost. After all, he clearly believed Sara was capable of harming us.

But he was wrong. He wanted Sara to lift a curse she hadn't cast. Awen's condition was the result of Hywel burning the charm, it had to be. His actions had brought this on, and now he wanted to see Sara hanged as punishment when she'd done nothing but help us. If she was killed, we'd have no hope of stopping whatever dark magic plagued our daughter. Why couldn't he see that?

We dismounted outside of the stables, and guided the mare in through the wooden doors. Hywel's horse was already there, settled in amongst the hay, a fly buzzing about its ears. Why was he already back at Faen Maredudd? Ruby and I looked at each other, confused.

Slowly, we picked our way back to the house.

We agreed to go back inside as though nothing were out of the ordinary. If anyone asked, we'd simply say we'd been for a long walk.

'Do you think he's noticed we're not there?' Ruby asked, her voice low.

'I don't know,' I said. 'You go straight to the kitchens and get to work. Don't worry about Hywel.' We parted ways silently, avoiding each other's gaze.

When I found my husband, he was busy with his correspondence in the hall, his pen scratching furiously at the paper.

'Doli, where have you been?' His gaze was steady, his voice cold. I met his eyes, searching them for a hint that he already knew where I'd spent my morning.

'I thought you were away until tomorrow,' I said, trying to sound pleased, or curious – anything but irritated by his sudden early return.

'There was a change of plan.'

His eyes didn't leave mine once, not even when a servant came in to prepare the table at the far end of the room for supper.

'I'll go and change,' I told him, trying to smile.

Later that evening, we ate in silence for some time. The only sound was the clang of daggers and spoons against plates, echoing around the hall.

'I know where you were, Doli.'

I stopped chewing. Set my spoon back on my plate. I tried to shape my face into an expression of innocence while I waited for him to speak again.

I braced myself for the weight of his accusations to hit me, but he only speared another chunk of meat, placed it in his mouth and chewed. Steady. Deliberate. Blood seeped from the meat and covered his lip.

I kept waiting, scared to speak. How much did he know? I didn't want to implicate myself. He couldn't possibly know where I'd been. How could he?

He swallowed, continuing to stare quietly at me.

'Tretower is a strange place for a young gentry woman to spend the day, wouldn't you agree?'

My heart dropped. So he did know. But how? It didn't make any sense.

'Hywel, I —'

He raised a hand to silence me.

'No Doli, you've spoken enough recently. Far too much, in fact. Now I will speak.'

I stared at my lap, my heart pounding in my chest like a startled, trapped sparrow.

'I have been lenient. I have been kind. I have made allowances over the years, indulged you after so many losses. You were carrying our child, which I appreciate, of course. And yes, she has been a difficult child. She does cry relentlessly, I will admit it. And I know you've been worried. But your...' Here he paused, in search of the right word. 'Freedom ... has gone on too long. I can see that now.'

I stole a glance at him, peering up with my head still tipped downwards. His face was eerily calm. I looked away just as he began to speak again.

'I take responsibility,' he said. 'It's my fault, after all. I should have kept a closer eye on you. I shouldn't have let you roam about the moors as I have done. I should have insisted the physician make weekly visits once Annie was born, to take care of her, and of you.'

I opened my mouth to object – *her name is Awen* – but thought better of it once I met his cold, hard glare. His brown eyes were practically black in the dimming evening light.

'Can you imagine my embarrassment, my humiliation, when my good friend Jacob Lloyd stopped me on my journey this morning – and this, in front of Sir Thomas, no less – to ask why he had seen my wife and maidservant riding towards Tretower, with my daughter strapped to her back like a package?'

So I'd ridden past Jacob Lloyd. There were eyes all over Llynidwen; all over the county. Sometimes, it seemed as though the trees, the birds, were always watching. As though the river could take my secrets, like tiny stones, and carry them to every corner of the land. But no. The trees, the birds, the river were not the problem. Rather, it was humans who watched, who talked. It was humans who wagged their tongues and spilled lies and gossip.

'Doli. This cannot continue. It will not continue. You've made me look a fool within my own community. How can I expect respect from my servants, my tenants, the villagers, when I don't receive any from my own wife? How can I hope to secure a higher position, a seat on the bench? Your days of traipsing freely about the moors are over. You will no longer leave this house without my express permission. Is that understood?'

Protests boiled inside of me, threatening to spill out, but Hywel looked more furious than I had ever seen him, and I was cowed into silence. He would change his mind, once he'd calmed down. At least, I hoped he would. Surely, he must. He couldn't keep me here like a prisoner.

The hall door creaked open – a servant entering to clear the dinner plates. I'd barely touched my pigeon pie, but Hywel had somehow managed to clear his.

Through the newly opened doorway, I heard Awen crying softly, as though in protest. I'd left her sleeping in Ruby's arms, but she must have woken in search of milk. She rarely slept long enough for me to eat a full meal. Though usually her insatiable hunger was exhausting, this time I was grateful for the opportunity to escape. I began to rise from the bench.

'Sit down.'

I glanced at the servant clearing the table of plates and half-full jugs, and felt the heat rise in my cheeks.

I looked at him, hovering uncertainly.

'Sit,' he said again, commanding. I was reminded, for a moment, of the way he spoke to me on our wedding night, commanding then too but in a reassuring way. He'd spoken with confidence as we explored each other's bodies. That night felt like such a long time ago now, a memory that belonged to another life, another Doli. It was hard to believe the deep brown eyes that penetrated mine then were the same that glared at me from across the table now. I had been so sure that having a baby would bring that Hywel back to me, that things would once again be as they used to between us.

'Darling,' I said, softly. 'The baby.'

'Yes,' he replied, drawing out the word. 'The baby.' He rapped his fingers against the wooden table, his eyes flitting to the open doorway then back to me. I was desperate to stand, to go to her, but his eyes pinned me in place. 'The baby doesn't need you.'

Couldn't he hear her mewling? She was becoming more irate as I hovered here, caught between my daughter and my husband. Beneath my gown, I felt my breasts swell, milk beginning to pearl at my nipples.

'She's hungry,' I said.

He repeated his words again.

'She doesn't need you. I've taken the liberty of hiring a wet nurse for her.'

I could barely breathe. While the idea of another woman nursing my baby was perfectly unremarkable before she was born, the thought of it now that I knew the feeling of her suckling made me sick to my stomach, despite the pain and discomfort that often came with her feeds.

Did he want her to go and live elsewhere? Most wet nurses had other children to care for, and took the babies to live with their families. That couldn't happen. I wouldn't let it.

Hywel cleared his throat, answering me as though I'd spoken out loud.

'Don't worry. I don't want to see Annie sent away any more than you do. Emily will live here with us. Her children are weaned from the breast, and it's not as though we're lacking in space.'

I opened and closed my mouth uselessly, like a fish spat out by the river. How could he have done this to me? To Awen? She was only upstairs and along the passage but I felt as though we'd been ripped apart. Before she was born, I could never have imagined feeling this way – the physical tug and draw of a baby. The deep ache in my chest and stomach at her absence, or the stirring I felt in my very bones at her cries.

From upstairs, Awen's shrieks quietened and stilled. I pictured her latching to the breast of a faceless woman and beginning to drink. Tears stung my eyes. I turned away, not wanting Hywel to have the satisfaction of seeing me cry. The servant skirted around us, busying himself with the dressoir. He was astutely avoiding looking in our direction.

'Go to bed, Doli. Rest. I'll introduce you to Emily in the morning.'

Before leaving the hall, I glanced back at my husband one last time, astounded by his cruelty. Was that remorse on his face? Sadness? Or something else entirely? Perhaps I was simply seeing what I hoped to see there. Longing for a tenderness that seemed to be long gone.

The Villagers

We heard the baby was sick. Thin. Ailing. We heard she fed without end and cried when parted from her mother, from her milk. Some say it was caused by witshcraft. A curse. A charm gone bad. Some say Doli Maredudd sought help from Sara Gwen, was given parsley, wild carrot and dill to stir into a stew. They say that is how her baby came to be. Now, we look at her and wonder: what hope do babies made this way have? Will the poor child ever be welcome in God's kingdom?

Emily's body was round, full, her bust ample; on our first meeting the following morning, she described her milk to me as 'wholesome'. Her own children –there were six of them – were healthy, fit as oxen, she said, and strong too. She and Hywel must have seen this as proof that she would be a better nurse for my daughter than I was. She assured me Awen would be well in a matter of weeks.

'But how can it be that my milk is not enough to sustain her?' I asked, hating the desperation in my voice.

Emily looked at me, her eyes trailing along my body, from the tip of my cap to my stockinged feet, and back up again. She met my eyes before speaking.

'You are small, slight. Perhaps you're unable to produce enough milk to help a child thrive and grow. It happens, sometimes. Don't worry,' she said, not unkindly. I imagined my face was betraying the pain that was seizing my chest. I felt as though a hand were gripping my heart, and squeezing. 'You've done nothing wrong. It's simply the way of the world. Besides, wouldn't you rather occupy yourself with other pursuits? You're the first highborn woman I've met to actually want to nurse her own child. Most see it as a role far beneath them.'

'I saw it that way too, once.' It felt strange to admit. 'But as soon as she was born, I felt she needed me, and I needed her.' It was all the explanation I was able, or willing, to offer. I handed a grizzling Awen to the woman, and turned away as she stirred, searching for milk at this imposter's chest.

Back in my bedchamber, distraught, milk swelling beneath my dress, I did the only thing I could. I snatched up a quill, and my prayer book, and scrawled some lines of verse in the margins.

Through milk-stained stitches, heartache weaves its threads,
A song of sorrow softly spreads...

The ink seeped into the paper, black as a curse.

Later that night, I was awoken from a restless sleep, fire raging in my chest. The darkness pressed in hard all around me as I touched a hand to each swollen breast. They were hard as rocks. Sore. Bruised. I looked to my side, searching for Awen, eager for her to drain the pain from me, then remembered. She wasn't here. Her cradle had been moved into the chamber next to mine, where Emily was now asleep. I longed to watch her chest rise and fall in the darkness, to hear her rapid breathing.

I was alone – Hywel must have slept in another room, perhaps on the truckle bed. Good. I was still in disbelief at his actions. The fire in the hearth was burning low, the flames casting shadows across the rug.

Then I heard it again – the sound that had woken me. *Scratch.* I looked around, but couldn't see anything much through the gloom, beyond the outlines and shadows of my dresser, chest, and bedpost.

Scratch. Scratch.

The sound was low, persistent, like rats scurrying along the timbers. It began quiet and slow, but became louder and faster the longer I listened. I closed my eyes, trying to pin the sound to its location, but it seemed to be coming from all around me – first behind my head, then to my side, then near the fireplace. I held my breath, listening. The sound was met by my own heartbeat, pulsing in my ears.

It grew louder and faster still, until the scratching was accompanied by a horrible hissing. I pictured a cat, arching its back in anger. Baring its teeth and its claws. Could there have been a living cat in the room, pacing the floor, looking for a way out? It wasn't impossible – a cat could easily have snuck in through an open window, or sidled past one of the servants as they carried in vegetables and herbs from the garden. We kept a few mousers in the stables, any of them could have ventured inside.

I remembered, with a sinking feeling of horror and dread, what Hywel had said about witches transforming into animals and sneaking through keyholes. I thought of Kathryn Lewis, quivering in the doorway. Her putrid smell. Her anger.

I held myself still, trying to make my breathing as quiet as possible while I listened. There was no movement around me, but the noise persisted. *Scratch. Scratch. Hiss.* Unmistakable. It was exactly as I'd feared. It was coming from inside the walls.

I could hear the thud of my own heart as I listened, the blood pounding in my ears. It was almost as though ... but no, it couldn't be. It wasn't possible. And yet ... I lowered myself slowly, quietly, from the bed, gasping at the needle-sharp pain in my breasts. At first, it had seemed as though the scratching was all around, coming from deep within the walls of the bedroom. A relentless scraping behind the tapestries. But as I moved towards the fireplace, the sound seemed to travel towards it too. It was undeniable now – there was a cat trapped somewhere behind the fireplace, trying desperately to escape. It was shrieking so loudly I couldn't understand how it hadn't woken the rest of the household, and yet there were no sounds or stirring from any of the other bedchambers.

But surely the cat was dead. I was certain I gave clear instruction that the cat should be killed and dried out. The stable boy wouldn't have been stupid enough to place a still-living cat beneath the floorboards or in the chimney, and even if he had, it wouldn't have survived there, silent, for weeks as summer reached its peak. And yet, I could hear it now, clear as I heard Awen crying on waking each night, or my husband speaking, or the wind howling through the moors. Something had brought that cat back to life. Something which meant to do me harm, perhaps. Or something else. Could it be a message? From the old beggar witch? From Sara, who I'd left in the cold and the dark and the filth? I couldn't stop thinking of her, suffering there in the muck.

Hywel had given her name to the magistrates because I had involved her in our lives. The idea that I could be to blame for her imprisonment haunted me. I couldn't be responsible for her death as well. I had to do something. But what?

I climbed back into my bed, pulling the drapes tight and lifting the coverlet over my head. There in the darkness, I lay quiet, still, my heart pounding as I listened to the awful sound of the cat hissing and spitting. From somewhere along the passageway, came the sharp smack of a door slamming in its frame.

I must have fallen back to sleep, though I'm not sure how I managed it. When I awoke the next morning, the cat had quietened, but the memory of it was still loud and clear, scratching within my ears like an insect.

I winced as I moved my body. My chest was agony. My head ached and throbbed, and an intense pain had settled behind my left eye. I stared up at the canopy, my mind a tangle of dank cellars, milk, witches, crops, wet nurses, and the dried and stiffened bodies of cats.

I rose from my bed, dressed quietly, wincing at the pain in my breasts, and rubbed my teeth clean. With a final glance over my shoulder, I ensured that last night's events had left nothing disturbed in the room, and went down the stairs and into the hall, looking for Hywel.

Although it felt as though he'd hired Emily to punish me, I knew that he, too, had noticed the sallowness of Awen's cheeks, the way her skin seemed pale as the moon. The constant crying. The endless hunger. My husband truly believed that Sara Gwen was to blame, that her imprisonment and death would lift whatever curse he thought she'd placed on our child. He'd hired Emily in an act of desperation. He could see that Awen was unhappy, that my milk had not been good enough to sustain her small, fragile body. He had indulged me, allowing me to nurse Awen myself, and now, though I hated it, I had proved him right – it was a role better suited to somebody else.

Still, I hoped to find him in a better mood, planned to implore him to see reason, to allow us both to nurse Awen, so that she might have ample milk. That morning, I would have agreed to do anything he'd asked of me. I would even have agreed to stay at home in Faen Maredudd and seek his permission to leave the house, if I must. I only wanted my baby kept close to me.

I swung open the door to the hall, expecting to see my husband taking breakfast, but I found the large room empty. Perhaps the parlour, then. Hywel would likely be hunched at his desk.

But no, there was no sign of him. Then I saw it – it looked as though Hywel had been here this morning – a small stack of correspondence sat on his desk, a quill still dripping with black ink lay beside the papers.

At the very top of the pile, a note had been bound neatly to a small pamphlet, addressing Hywel.

I believe you may find the contents of interest. While Holland does not address certain intellectual debates, he does make a well structured case for the eradication of witchcraft from our lands. Perhaps something to share with your tenants? – JL

I opened the papers carefully, reading quickly. The pamphlet was written in the form of a conversation between two men – Tudur and Gronw. They spoke of witches and magic. Of curses and charms. Some passages had been underlined, for Hywel's benefit, I presumed.

There were passages about witch familiars – demons metamorphosing into cats and mice and fleas and hogs. The animals were, according to Gronw, fed on the blood of the witches that kept them. *The old woman showed us the spots and traces where she dropped blood to him from her breasts!* I was sickened, both by the idea of countless beasts feeding on the blood of old women, and by the sudden, painful memory of yesterday's events. The unexpected appearance of the wet nurse.

In another section, Tudur spoke of soothsayers and wizards and fortune-tellers, and told Gronw that even the gentry visited these people. I thought of Sara's charms and her herb garden. Perhaps this pamphlet would show Hywel that there was indeed a difference between the good village folk who used their magic to help others, and the sort of witches who appeared in rain-driven doorways to shriek their curses at the skies. Is that why it had been sent to him?

But no. Gronw told his friend that all magic came from the devil. Even 'good' magic. That the magistrate must implement the Hebraic laws and follow the example of Josiah by purging Wales of magic. Thick ink underlined the words:

> *God's word does show well enough*
> *everything necessary for our salvation.*

Elsewhere, a note had been scrawled in the margins beside a passage about church sermons, which stated that proper sermons were not delivered in Wales, and that the Bible was too expensive for the poor to purchase and keep at home.

The note, written by the same hand as the note that had lain on top of the pamphlet, asked, '*What can we do about this?*' I remembered the Welsh language Bible that Hywel had bought and given to the church as a gift. He seemed to feel it was his responsibility to educate the villagers. It occurred to me then who had sent the pamphlet – *JL* – Jacob Lloyd. Of course. There was noise from the entryway. Servants bustling about. Or perhaps even Hywel himself, back from wherever he had been. My hand itched to tuck the pamphlet away in my skirts, to keep it safe to read later. I wanted to stare at the etchings of withered old women mounted on their broomsticks. Dancing naked about cauldrons. But I couldn't – Hywel had likely already taken note of it on his desk. I couldn't begin to imagine how he might react if he missed it, and found it later with me. Instead, I placed it very carefully back amongst the other papers, using the thread to bind the note back to the pamphlet, and left the small pile of correspondence where I found it.

The Villagers

From the piss and the shit and the sweat that dripped from the stone walls, the devil himself took form. There in the darkness of the dungeon, he spoke to Sara Gwen. He told her how to claim her revenge. And outside, the stars disappeared from the sky, and all was black and still. We know this to be true. We will swear to it.

The days were long and strange now that Emily was living with us in Faen Maredudd. We swept by one another like ghosts in the passageways. I stole time in the gardens with Awen, afraid to venture any further with her, knowing that she would want to nurse before long, and need to be returned. I thought, more than once, about taking her with me for a longer walk along the moors, but Hywel had forbidden me to nurse her myself, saying it would take longer for my soreness to heal, and the temptation would be too great if she started to hunger, which I was certain she would – she still fed without end.

Despite this, her face was pinched. Starved. Something was wrong and I was helpless to do anything about it. I couldn't protect my daughter. I couldn't do the one thing I should have been able to do. I grew sallow too, and my hair began to fall out in thick, rope-like wads.

I begged Hywel to speak with the magistrate. To have Sara released from gaol, so that she might help Awen. I felt like we were sitting in a cart, hurtling towards the end of Awen's short life, with Sara the only one who might be able to prevent it. Of course, Hywel wouldn't hear of it.

I stayed at home, restlessly occupying myself with darning and pastry making. I played with the kittens that had been born in the stables, trailing ribbon for them, secreting them in my pockets. I knew the cook would want to drown the kittens – she saw them as a pestilence – but I'd asked Ruby to find good homes for them in the village, once they were weaned. I couldn't help but think of the dead cat clawing at the chimney breast when I looked at them. That poor stray that was killed on my orders. Finding the kittens a home seemed like a reasonable penance.

I made comfits for Hywel, ignoring the kitchen staff bustling about me as I steeped the fruit and flowers in sugar, then allowed them to harden and dry. I thought it might mellow his mood, that I might implore him to see reason.

Early one morning at the end of August, as I was dressing for the day in my bedchamber, I heard a commotion from outside. Clutching my gown in my fist, I looked through the window, searching for the source of the noise. In the distance, trees bent to meet the river, blackbirds and magpies circling over the moors, flitting back and forth. A lone red kite circled high above them. There was nothing out of the ordinary to see, though the noise persisted. Perhaps it was coming from the back of the house.

The sound was of people shouting. Panicked voices. There was grunting, snorting and shrieking – a pig? It sounded as though it was in pain.

I finished pulling on my dress, snagging my stockings and forgetting to rub my teeth in my haste, then rushed outside, following the noise to the small holding area at the rear of the house.

Ahead, I saw a wall of servants near the pigpen. They were crowded around, as though to witness a public spectacle. The crowd was so excitable, it was like they were anticipating a hanging or a performance of some sort. Some had their arms outstretched, forming a barricade. As I moved closer towards them, I saw Ruby leaning against the brewhouse wall, watching while the shrieking continued rising and falling.

I was about to call out, to ask what was happening, when Hywel pushed past me, his boots thundering against the hard-packed earth.

'What is the meaning of this?!' His voice was loud, booming, bringing almost everyone to a silent stillness. He had always possessed this power, to command any room, any number of people. I'd even seen gentlemen of greater rank than us rapt in silence at his speeches before now.

The stable hand spoke first.

'The gilt. She's gone mad,' he said. He was panting, his breath coming fast as though he'd been chasing the poor pig about her pen.

I turned towards Ruby, still standing unmoving at the wall. She looked to be muttering something under her breath. I edged closer, wishing I had put my cloak on. It was a grey day, the clouds hanging heavy overhead.

'What's happening?' I asked her, my voice barely more than a whisper, although it wasn't necessary – no one would hear us over the shrieking and wailing of the pig.

'It's as he said,' she replied, simply. 'Pig's gone mad. She started trying to break loose from the pen. Kicking the ground in a rage. Charging at everyone who tried to help.'

'Charging?'

The pig had always been docile, submissive as a kitten. We'd had her since she was a piglet herself, and soon she would be bred for piglets of her own. In the warmer months, I would lie with her in the grasses, scratching her belly. I couldn't imagine her in a fit of rage. Something must have agitated her.

'Is she hurt?' I asked Ruby.

'Something's riled her,' Ruby said. 'It's strange, you know. Agnes told me something similar happened to the pigs on the Garretts' farm. Not long before she left. They said Kathryn Lewis had done it.'

We were still pressed to the wall a distance away, and I could scarcely see over the heads of the crowd surrounding the enclosure. The servants had begun to raise their voices again now, some clamouring to tell Hywel what had unfolded, some shouting at the poor pig, who was still shrieking and grunting as though she were possessed.

All day, the men tried to soothe her, to comfort her, to calm her. She was given water and kitchen scraps. She was given straw and mud and shelter. She was given apples that had been picked fresh and stored in the apple house only the day before. Nothing seemed to work. All day, we could hear her screams, echoing through the grounds, seeping through the walls of Faen Maredudd.

Later that evening, in desperation, the pig was killed, her throat slit, her blood pouring into the fresh imprints of her trotters in the soil.

By now, Hywel had come back to the bedchamber after spending a few nights in another room. Night after night, he slept soundly in our bed, snoring, splayed like a cross on our mattress, while I lay next to him, uncomfortable, longing to hear Awen's soft breath coming in rapid waves beside me. I would've liked him to go back to a different bedchamber. I'd grown accustomed to the space.

'Was the pig ill?' I asked him, unlacing my shift in readiness for bed. My eyes were still stinging with the sadness of it.

'Ill? I don't believe so.'

'Then what caused her to become so...' I searched for the correct word, but Hywel found it for me.

'Savage?'

I nodded.

'Is it not obvious?'

I looked at him, wondering what he meant. Was she fed something poisonous? Was she attacked?

'Witchcraft, of course. This is more damning evidence against that ugly old *witsh* you let into our home, Doli.'

I knew then I'd been right not to tell him about Kathryn Lewis' visit, too. Though the very thought of her left me shuddering, I didn't want her rotting in a cellar beside Sara.

'You can't know the poor pig was lost to witchcraft,' I said, trying to convince myself as much as Hywel. 'After all, it was the farmhand that slit her throat, on your orders,' I reminded him.

'We had no choice, Doli.' He sounded tired, defeated. 'The wretched thing had been taken over by some sort of madness. You saw it for yourself. She was dangerous.'

I nodded, slowly, before continuing.

'Even so, Sara wouldn't do this.'

I was speaking too freely, but I couldn't hold my tongue.

Hywel rubbed all the more vigorously at his temple, scrunching up his eyes. When he spoke, it was as though he was addressing a simpleton.

'So you believe it to be mere coincidence, that Sara Gwen was taken to gaol, at my suggestion, and within weeks our best gilt becomes murderous overnight? With no other reason to speak of? Is that what you're telling me, Doli? Things haven't been right around here since you planted that curse. The house has been unwelcoming, unfamiliar ... Shadows lurking in the corners. Doors slamming all through the night.'

'But Hywel,' I spoke quietly, cautiously, not wanting to appear as though I was contradicting him. 'Sara is a good woman, despite what's being said about her. I truly believe she helped us to conceive Awen, she —'

'Be quiet,' Hywel said. 'Please. Stop.'

Perhaps I shouldn't have argued with him, but there was nothing more he could do to me. No more means of punishment. In appointing Emily, in bringing her into our home, placing Awen in her arms, he'd already taken everything from me. I had nothing left to lose.

'Have you forgotten what I told you? Witches don't conform to the same earthly restraints as people like us, Doli – people who embrace the Lord, that is. There is nothing to stop a vile woman such as Sara Gwen from whispering curses to her familiars to carry out into the night. She could have sent any number of curses from whichever dungeon she languishes in straight here to Faen Maredudd. Stone walls are no barrier to a true *witsh*.'

I wanted to ask him what the purpose of keeping her locked up was, if she could continue to inflict harm from the darkness of that dungeon, but I knew there was no sense in arguing any further. It seemed as though logic was now as useless as the poor dead pig.

At first, it was the midwife watching my every move. Now it was the wet nurse, following me from room to room. I'd done no more than walk in the gardens, not wanting to be too far from Awen, or challenge how sincere Hywel had been in his insistence that I ask permission to leave the house. I was almost certain she was reporting my movements to Hywel. I felt as though she was watching me at all times and I wanted to be away from her, but I was horribly bound to her because wherever she was, Awen was too.

Now that I was unable to nurse Awen, my breasts were filled with milk that had nowhere to go. They were tender and swollen, though I regularly squeezed the milk from them with my hands, filling a basin with the creamy white spray then pouring it on the earth beneath my rosebush. A constant, painful reminder of her absence. I begged Emily to let me nurse Awen, if only a little, to relieve some of the strain, but she refused, telling me Hywel had told her not to allow it.

Awen cried and hungered and called out more than ever. Emily assured me it would pass. That she would fill up, and settle, in time. But she was wrong. It was early September now and my daughter was still pale and sallow and hungry.

One morning, I said something vague about collecting some thread for my embroidery, which Hywel agreed to, and asked Ruby to come with me to the village. Together, we stepped outside. It was a relief to be alone with her, to be able to speak openly without the walls of Faen Maredudd leaning in all around us.

'Where are we really going?' she asked me, as we passed through the garden and came out onto the vast moorland.

I looked sideways at her.

'We have to find help. We can't keep trying to do this alone,' I told her, simply. I knew she'd understand. 'Did you remember to bring an extra cloak?'

She handed me a brown cloak, belonging to one of the servants. I draped it over my shoulders, hiding my own clothes beneath it.

As I looked at the leaves of the birch trees on the horizon, I couldn't help but think of how much had changed since last autumn. Then, I was still carrying the last child, the one I hadn't been certain had even existed, before losing it in a morning of pain and blood. Now, I was losing another child – though she was here, alive, breathing, she felt lost to me, lapping milk at Emily's breast, waning more each day. I feared she wouldn't last the winter.

We found Agnes in the first place we looked – the alehouse. She was sitting with her back to the door, but it was unmistakably her. Red hair cascaded down her back.

I sent Ruby to order a jug of ale while I went to sit with Agnes.

Last time I'd seen her was at Sara's cottage, when we were both hidden in the pantry. When I said her name I expected her face to be warm, welcoming, familiar. But when she saw me it was hard. Stern, even.

'What do you want?' She asked, turning away before she had even finished speaking.

'Agnes, I need your help.'

She scoffed, almost spluttering into her own drink.

'Why should I help you?'

Before I could answer, Ruby appeared behind us. She put a gentle hand on my arm, and spoke for me.

'Agnes, Doli's baby is sick. The physician can't help. He says there's nothing to be done.'

I thought I saw a look of sympathy pass over Agnes' face, before her expression hardened again, and she replied.

'Best you listen to him then.'

'Agnes, please.' I spoke in barely more than a whisper. 'I have come to learn that physicians aren't always right. There's something wrong with Awen, something that I believe can be healed, by the right person.'

I was about to tell her about my visit to Sara in Tretower Court, about the darkness and the cold and the endless wheezing and coughing, the stench of urine and death, but she interrupted as soon as I said Sara's name.

'I'll ask you again, mistress. Why should I help you? You are responsible for Sara's imprisonment, are you not? If she was not languishing in gaol now, she would be here to help you herself.'

'Agnes, I'm not responsible. Why would you say that?'

I tried to believe my own tone of defiance, but I knew there was truth to her words. Without me, Hywel would never have bothered learning Sara's name, let alone passing it on to the magistrates. Ruby was looking quietly at her own lap.

'Your husband gave the orders for her arrest,' she said, with a half shrug. She finished her drink and helped herself to the beer in the jug Ruby had placed on the table before us.

'My husband cannot give arrest orders —'

I was going to argue that Hywel was not a Justice of the Peace, nor a magistrate, that he couldn't give any such orders, but she interrupted me again.

'He is well respected. You know as well as I do that if he has given the magistrates a name, the matter is as good as done.'

I stayed quiet for a moment, staring at a knot of wood on the table. I didn't know what to say, so I said nothing for some time. Agnes sipped her beer, looking bored. Ruby continued to stare at her lap.

'I am not my husband,' I told Agnes eventually, though it felt wrong to speak against him so openly. 'I begged him not to pursue Sara. She has been so good to me, to us. She helped deliver my child. She breathed the life into her when she was born still and stiff.'

Agnes looked at me, considering my words.

'Even so...' she said. 'You're all the same. You landowning gentry folk reclining on your seat cushions, dining on the miseries of your tenants and the village poor. Sucking our sorrow like marrow straight from the bone.'

I wanted to argue – weren't we good to the villagers? Didn't we feed them, welcome them, care for them when we could? But before I could say anything more, I saw a familiar figure in the corner of the room. Wyn Evans, slumped over, his face pressed to a cup, his tunic filthy. I thought of the tiny round hovel his family lived in, the smell of urine and damp earth.

'I'm sorry,' I said. 'Truly.'

Agnes considered me again.

'Can you do anything for Sara?' she said.

'I've tried. I've spoken with my husband, I've begged him. He won't listen.'

'Make him listen,' she said. 'I'll help you find a cure for your babe, if you're able to help her. You believe she's innocent, don't you?'

211

I thought for a moment. I thought of the cat scratching in the walls, of the pig going mad. Remembered the blood sloshed across the courtyard.

'Agnes? Do you remember the woman who cursed Elizabeth Garrett when you were working for her – Kathryn Lewis? Ruby says she also cursed the pigs?'

Agnes smirked, but said nothing.

'Our pig. She went mad, too. I wondered...' I trailed off, unsure how to phrase my question, strange as it was. 'I wondered if it might have been witchcraft, that did it. The pig was well before it happened. It doesn't make any sense. And Kathryn Lewis, she visited us, not too long ago.'

'You think Kathryn Lewis cursed your pig?'

I shrugged.

'She is good friends with Sara, isn't she?' I asked. Since she'd stood, wretched and angry at our front door, I hadn't fully been able to shake the question from my mind. What was Sara doing with someone like that?

Agnes frowned, and swallowed a mouthful of ale before replying.

'Good friends? No. Sara is kind, she takes care of people that need her help. Kathryn has very little. Sara sits with her, sometimes. Takes her food. She's a better woman than I am.'

I chewed my lip, thinking. Perhaps she was a better woman than me, too.

'But Kathryn is vicious – cursing people and scaring them. The pigs. The stillbirth?'

'Oh, Kathryn is mad, no two ways about that. But she's harmless. She gets what she needs by behaving that way, then she goes back to her misery. She's been spoken to, by the authorities, more than once. They always let her go. They know she's mad. You can't believe Sara is guilty by association, mistress, surely?'

I thought of Sara, shivering and hoarse in the darkness. Remembered her cradling Awen after her birth as the colour came back to her mottled skin.

'No,' I said. 'Of course I don't.'

'Then find a way to free her. Speak to your husband. Do whatever it takes.'

I glanced at Ruby, who looked as worried as I felt. She knew Hywel's stubborn nature as well as I did. He was not a man to be convinced of anything. And it wasn't as though I hadn't already tried.

'I will. I've already given Sara my word that I will free her. And I meant it. But in the meantime, please, you have to help my daughter.'

Agnes scoffed again.

'I beg your pardon, mistress, but I don't *have* to do anything,' she said, before taking another sip of her beer.

I looked her in the eyes, searching for any hint of compassion.

Ruby spoke from beside me, her voice soft.

'Agnes?'

Agnes rolled her eyes, placing her cup back on the table and letting the beer splash over the rim.

'Is your daughter baptised?'

I nodded, remembering the priest with his bowl full of clean water, murmuring prayers over Awen. Hywel's hand pressed tight to my lower back throughout the ceremony.

'Well where is she?' Agnes' voice jolted me back to the present. She looked around the alehouse, as though I might have been concealing Awen behind my back this whole time.

I told her about the wet nurse, that Hywel had made it impossible to leave the house with Awen, that sneaking her out would do no good, as she needed to be at suck constantly. It was a small, subtle movement, but I was sure I saw her wince, before muttering something obscene under her breath.

Agnes sighed, and looked over her shoulder. The alehouse was fairly empty. Then she spoke again.

'Sara Gwen is a good woman. You've admitted as much yourself. There may be some who call what she does witchcraft. Others see it for what it is – soothsaying, herbs, charms. She's a healer. A *swynwraig*. She works with flowers and prayers. She's helped so many people, yourself included, mistress. Perhaps, now, you should do more than *try* to help her. She'll hang if you can't guarantee her release.'

The weight of her words sat heavy in my stomach, the panic rising in my chest as I thought of Sara at the gallows, of Awen writhing in Emily's arms.

I remembered what Sara had said to me all those months ago, as I was leaving her cottage.

'I believe I will be in need of your help, in the future. Hold your payment, until then.'

At the time, I'd thought it such a strange thing to say. But Agnes was right. I had to help Sara. What choice did I have?

I nodded at her, and told her I would do everything I could. As we left the alehouse, Agnes called after me:

'Take some cabbage leaves from your kitchens,' she said, staring pointedly at my swollen chest. 'They'll help with the pain.'

After speaking with Agnes, I left Ruby in the village and rode straight to Allt-Goras, in hopes that Rhys might be able to assist me. He was well versed in legal matters, and seemed, upon my last visit, to believe in Sara's innocence as much as I did. Even if he dismissed her as a fraud, I hoped he would help me. If nothing else, he would be a friendly face. A welcome source of comfort.

Of course, he welcomed me with his usual jovial air when I arrived, but it was clear something was troubling him. We spoke of Sara's arrest, and of the charges laid against her. That's how I learned that Sara had several indictments against her, following the gathering of evidence in the church, but that only one was for felonious witchcraft, carrying a sentence of hanging: the murder of little Bess Evans.

'What if felonious was struck from the record?' I asked Rhys. 'Would that lessen the sentence?'

Rhys frowned.

'Indeed it would, but I can't see how it's possible. If the grand jury could be persuaded to find something other than a true bill...' he paused, scratched his chin. 'But, no. I don't believe there is anything to be done, now that the sad affair has been set in motion. I'm sorry, Doli. Truly.'

I believed him. But my sorrow was not the reason for the frown playing about his brow. Something else was troubling him, I could tell.

As we walked about the gardens, my arm locked in his, I asked what the matter was.

He sighed, rubbing his hand over the back of his head, then lowered his voice. Perhaps he felt, as I so often did, that the trees could catch conversations, carry them along their roots and branches across the moors.

'Our old friend, Jacob Lloyd,' he said, but didn't elaborate any further.

'What of him? Is he unwell?'

'No. Quite the opposite, in fact. He's been spending an alarming amount of time with Sir Thomas, of the Mostyns; he seems to be doing rather well for himself. I'm a little worried about the influence he holds over your husband, Doli. Hywel has always been a pious man, but perhaps you've noticed that recently he's become almost obsessed with scripture?'

I thought of the new Bible, the nightly prayers, the insistence that God would grant us a child, that God would protect her now, and nodded.

'He prays more than ever, with great concentration and focus. Lately, he rarely looks at me with anything other than contempt. You think Jacob Lloyd is responsible for Hywel's growing piety?'

'I cannot speak to Hywel's mindset or motivations, but since Jacob Lloyd decided to make his home in Brecknockshire, Hywel has hounded him to accompany us on hunting trips, invited him to dinners, and implored him to speak publicly against witchcraft and other criminal affairs. He wants the minister replaced, and Hywel agrees with him. They say the minister in your parish hasn't done enough to dissuade certain ... ungodly behaviours.' Of course. I remembered the pamphlet I'd found in the parlour. The sketches of bare-breasted witches, their legs hooked over broomsticks. 'They say he has the Queen's ear. He will be made a magistrate before long. I believe Hywel will be offered the role, soon after.'

'Rhys,' I said, touching his arm lightly. 'Hywel truly believes Sara Gwen is a *witsh*. He's certain she cursed Awen. That she plagues the whole village. I can't reason with him.'

Rhys stopped, turned to me, and sighed, taking both my hands in his. The warmth of his palms seeped into mine, and I felt the spark of his touch travelling up my forearms. I should have pulled away, but the closeness and connection was welcome, after so long quarrelling with Hywel.

'I know, Doli,' he said. 'He's fearful. I've spoken to him at length. He worries about the consequences of inaction against witches who threaten the county. He's also trying to make a name for himself. Trying to come to the attention of higher ranking men – sheriffs and knights. He's been trying to invite Sir Thomas back to Faen Maredudd for months. Doli...' Here, he sighed again, looking deep into my eyes.

I bit my lip. I wished I could stay here, in the quiet tranquillity of Allt-Goras, with Rhys listening to my worries, understanding my concerns and clutching my palms like trinkets. But I had to ride home.

Before I left, Rhys said simply, 'Be well, Doli.'

And so, it was with this conversation in mind that I sat opposite my husband at breakfast the following morning, imploring him once again to dissuade the magistrate from sending Sara Gwen to the assizes. Though I didn't have high hopes of him listening, I had to make one final attempt to persuade him to do what was right.

'For Awen,' I said, searching his eyes for some compassion, some

216

understanding. Anything that might suggest my husband was still by my side, with me rather than against me. 'Please, she's fairing no better. Her time with Emily hasn't improved her condition at all. The physician has no answers. I know you don't trust Sara Gwen. I *know* you think she's a *witsh*. But Hywel, I promise you she is no such thing.' Again, I thought of Kathryn Lewis, the milky sheen that clouded her eyes, the scud of earth that crusted her skin. The true image of a witch, if ever there was one. 'She's a healer and she's the only one who can help us. She'll know how to cure Awen, I'm certain of it.'

'I don't know what's come over you, Doli. You seem to have become as mad as the pig since finding yourself in childbed. It's not right, all this insistence on behalf of such a wretched creature. A common whore,' he spoke calmly, almost happily, despite the cruelty of his words. 'You must find other pursuits to occupy your mind. Perhaps you could peruse the scriptures later.'

I stared at him. I hadn't expected him to concede, of course, but I'd anticipated anger at my request. Fury, even. Certainly not this strange, calm demeanour. It was very unlike my husband, usually so quick to anger, to redden at the cheeks, to raise his voice. His serenity was unsettling.

'Hywel, perhaps if you speak with —'

He put his hand up, smiling.

'Doli, my darling. There's nothing to be done. The matter is simple. Sara Gwen is locked away, as she should be. Soon, she will hang, and upon her death, all curses uttered by her wretched lips will be lifted. You must have noticed, since she cursed us, how the doors slam all through the night so that we cannot rest? Has the cook not mentioned how the meat has gone bad? How her chamomile and thyme and garlic have withered and died so that we cannot season a thing?'

He spoke with such simplicity, such certainty. If only I could find a way to make him understand.

'Perhaps the indictment for felonious witchcraft could be struck from the record? She could spend time in prison, but her life would be spared. We cannot be responsible for taking a life – only God can do that. If you are wrong about this Hywel, think of what it might mean for your own soul.'

'Doli, don't speak of things you clearly don't understand.' There it was. The anger. It had been brewing beneath the surface all along. 'Legal affairs. Indictments. The grand jury. These are all matters which don't concern you. Where is the sweet, simple woman I married? She had no concern for such tiresome things.' He steepled his fingers beneath his chin as he spoke.

'I don't view our daughter's life as a tiresome thing, Hywel.' Tears brimmed in my eyes as I spoke. 'It troubles me that you do.'

'Doli.' His manner was still calm, controlled, but there was an edge to his voice now, like the sharp side of a dagger. 'Enough.'

I looked down at my lap, interlacing my fingers. What could I say? What would persuade him that sparing Sara's life may be the only way to save Awen's?

'She cannot remain alive. We have lost our best gilt to witchcraft. I will not lose our daughter to her curses too,' Hywel scowled as he spoke, rubbing impatiently at his temple. It felt like we were speaking different languages – as though he was speaking English, and I, Welsh.

'Hywel, if we do nothing, Awen will sicken all the more. She feeds insatiably. She can't satisfy her hunger. Yet she remains scrawny as a skinned rabbit. It's as though she's consuming only dust and air, rather than milk. I won't see her laid in her grave, Hywel.'

I couldn't survive losing Awen. Not now. I would die myself, I was sure of it. Words of poetry began to form in my mind, intrusive and unusually unwelcome.

None craves to lay to rest in this locked, lonely cave,
nor longs for the sad sleep of the grave.

Hywel tore me from my thoughts.

'What more proof do you need of witchcraft and malice, Doli? Freeing that ... that woman,' he spat, 'from gaol will only enable her to inflict more curses. I'm confident that once she's hanged at the autumn assizes, her curses and wickedness will be lifted. Sara Gwen will hang, and Annie will return to good health. You'll see. And perhaps, whatever spell she holds you under will be broken too.'

Before I could respond, he spoke again.

'I suspect, once she is dead, the village of Llynidwen will have cause for celebration. Crops will thrive. Milk that has soured will restore itself. Sick animals will recover. Mark my words Doli, things will improve across these lands. The people will be glad to see her at the gallows.'

That night, I woke from a feverish sleep, the bed linen damp and heavy with sweat. It was a cold morning, the air cool on my cheeks.

I had dreamt of walking along the moors, rain pelting my face relentlessly, my boots sodden, sinking deep into the wet earth. In the dream, sheep shivered under bushes and shrubs, their dull eyes yellow and wide, their faces gormless.

As I moved past them, I stumbled on something clawing up from the surface of the earth – a chip of bone. I bent over and pulled at it, tugging hard, until it unravelled from the soil like a flower root. It was a sheep's skull, full and stark white. The eye sockets hollow.

Then two rectangular pupils appeared, and bloodshot yellow eyes rolled. The teeth snapped in the skull, trying to bite at me. The animal's head screamed, a deafening, blood-curdling noise that left me covered in sweat and shaking.

I threw it to the ground and tried to run but my legs wouldn't move, my feet sinking down into the wet earth. Somewhere nearby, Awen was crying, bawling, hysterical and the sheep's awful jaw was drawing closer.

I woke, shrieking in panic and that's when I saw her.

It was Sara Gwen. Real as the daylight, standing at the foot of my bed. I rubbed my eyes, certain I was still dreaming, or imagining things. But she stayed standing right there, solid as a rock, at the bottom of the bed. A living ghost. She was gaunt. Pale. Her hair thin and wisping. Her smock was torn and tattered, and there was a smell in the room – a cloying, hot, disgusting smell, like burning.

'Sara?' I hissed. 'How are you here? How can you be? Have you escaped?'

She didn't answer me, just stood, staring, then she began pointing at her mouth.

'Did they let you go?' I asked. 'But why —'

I stopped talking then, because she was still pointing at her mouth, frantically. Silently. I'd heard of the violence that sometimes happened in gaol, the way they might torture thieves and murderers. But surely, surely, they hadn't cut out her tongue? That would be too barbaric. I rose from my bed, taking a step towards her, as she grabbed her mouth, her lips, then pointed desperately at the nub of pink flesh.

Stepping nearer, I froze, horrified by what I was seeing. Her mouth hung open, slack, as blood poured from it, gushing over her chin and staining her smock. A downpour of thick red clots.

'Sara?'

Before I could reach her, she vanished. I touched my hand to my forehead, checking for fever. The smell of blood and burning lingered until the sun rose the next morning.

I lay awake for a long time after that, then spent the early hours in a dozing fretful sleep. When I woke properly the following morning, the memory of Sara's apparition crowded my mind, clamouring in my thoughts. Was she really here, or was it only a vivid dream? What did it mean?

Either way, the sight of Sara's blood-soaked figure, her crimson smock, had ignited a new sense of determination in me.

'We have to do something,' I told Ruby after telling her what I'd seen in the night. 'We have to find a way to get her out. There must be something we can do.'

Ruby paused for a moment, picking at one of her fingernails.

'I did hear about one woman,' she said eventually. 'Who was arrested for bruising a man's legs and hips. He begged her to put it right but she wouldn't – said she hadn't done it. Her neighbours defended her. Said it was slander. Told the magistrates the man was a drunk and a liar. After a fortnight in gaol, the man took back what he'd said and they let her go.'

An idea began to take shape in my mind, not quite graspable yet. *Her neighbours defended her...*

Even if most of the villagers had turned against her, there must be people Sara had helped, people who thought highly of her. Why hadn't they come forward to speak their truths? Where were Bess Evans' parents?

It suddenly seemed obvious to me. Why hadn't I thought of it sooner? I needed to find them, the people Sara had helped. People like me.

I told Hywel I was feeling unwell and would be resting in bed, and asked Ruby to keep him occupied.

'Distract him if he goes near the bedchamber,' I said, as I pulled on my cloak. She twisted her lips but didn't argue.

The cold of autumn had begun to settle over the moors now that it was midway through September. Though the grass was still yellow and brittle from the scorch of summer, the rowan trees were beginning to shed their leaves and the rabbits had long since disappeared. I was on foot, following the river towards the village. In my satchel I'd placed several blank pieces of paper, quietly taken from Hywel's desk in the parlour, as well as a small glass vial of ink, and an unused duck-feather quill. With these, I would gather the written testimonies of anyone who could bear witness to Sara's kindness. Somehow, I would show these to the assize judges, and she would be pardoned. I was determined of it.

I thought of beginning my search in the alehouse, but quickly dismissed the idea – I couldn't risk being seen by too many people. Besides, I imagined the only villagers likely to be in the alehouse at this time of day would be of little use to me anyway.

Instead, I walked towards the village, avoiding the copse of trees that hung like a thick curtain between most houses and the small circular huts of mud where the poorest people lived. I hadn't forgotten the way the ground had come alive, the branches coiling like snakes, so I went the longer way around, past Sara's cottage, which sat empty and dark, until I reached the home of little Bess Evans. I wasn't sure what I wanted to say. Her parents had already suffered so much. Perhaps I should have left them in peace ... But, no, I had to do this. They'd understand. They were the only other people I knew for certain would have kind words to speak about Sara Gwen. I still couldn't understand why they hadn't come to the church when the magistrate was gathering his evidence.

I waited for someone to answer the door. When it swung open, I was faced with the same little girl who'd pointed the house out to me last time. I hadn't realised then that she belonged to the Evans family. Her dress hung limp from her shoulders. She was clutching a poppet doll, made of nothing but sticks, twine and an old rag, the colour of which was impossible to discern through the dirt that smeared it.

She stared up at me with huge, dark eyes. Awen's eyes were beginning to brown, their blue hues darkening. Would she grow to be the same age as this girl in front of me? To clutch a poppet doll to her chest and play outdoors amongst the catkins and the birds? Before I could ask to speak with her mother or father, they both appeared behind her, blinking in the sudden daylight.

Her father spoke first. Wyn Evans.

'Mistress. How can we help you?'

'May I come in?' I asked, not wanting to be overheard.

The man nodded and stood back, pulling the little girl aside to let me pass. I glanced back over my shoulder, trying to shake the creeping sensation of being watched.

Inside, the house was just as I imagined it from the outside. No more than a single room with a mound of charred wood at its centre where a fire had been recently extinguished. There were two pallet beds heaped with straw, a large pan filled with water and several items of clothing strewn around. The girl crossed to the far side of the room and busied herself with a small pile of conkers that lay on the ground near one of the beds.

'Well? You've come in. What do you want?' His foot bounced up and down, his eyes darting about.

'Yeoman Evans, I am sorry to intrude, truly,' I began. 'But there is something I'm hoping you and your wife may be able to assist me with.'

He scoffed.

'No need for the formalities. I can't be called a yeoman any more.' His words ran into each other, slurred, as he gestured around.

'That may be so,' I said, looking down at my shoes. I hadn't known how to address him, and felt silly now for using 'yeoman'. 'But please, I need your help.'

They listened quietly, the girl still playing happily with her conkers and strings, while I told them about how Awen was sick. Dying. That Sara was the only one who could help. How she breathed life into Awen when she was born stiff. A witch with malice in her blood wouldn't have done that. When I was done speaking, they both looked at me, silent. Even the little girl lifted her head from her play.

The wife spoke first.

'Forgive me mistress. I understand your need to help your daughter, if she's suffering. *Iesu*, I understand it better than most,' she said, her eyes flitting to one of the pallet beds. 'But what if there's some truth to the accusations about Sara Gwen?'

It took me a moment to digest what she'd said.

'But last time I was here, you said Sara helped you. You said she'd tried to heal Bess.'

Wyn Evans interrupted.

'Aye. But how can we be *certain*? How can we know that her salves, her balms, her whispered words, were Godly ones? For all we know, she might have been muttering curses the entire time she was here.'

'No ... No. I'm sure...' I trailed off, looking to the wife, hoping desperately for reason. The lines around her eyes and mouth ran deep as tree roots.

'We believed, at the time, that she was doing her best for Bess,' she said. 'We wouldn't have had her here, in our home, otherwise. But we can't know. How can we be certain? I'm sorry, mistress, but we can't help you.'

'But my daughter —' My voice was quiet, quivering like a thin branch beneath the weight of a magpie. 'An innocent woman might lose her life to the gallows. My baby,' I said again. 'My baby...'

I couldn't even hold her without her rooting for milk, nuzzling at my chest in search, eventually crying so intently I'd have to hand her straight back to Emily. It hurt more and more each time.

'We've lost everything,' Wyn Evans said. 'Everything that was precious to us. First, it was our land. Our crops grew mould. Our milk soured. We couldn't meet our rent. Your husband gave us grace for several weeks, but, eventually, we had to take our animals to market. First the cattle. Then the sheep. Then even the chickens. Now look at us.' He hacked, then spat at the ground, a dirty, dark brown wad of spittle. 'We have nothing left now. Nothing. Not even our Bess. We are good, Godly people. When things go so badly wrong, there has to be a reason. Don't you see that? There has to be.' He met my eyes with a quiet sort of fury. The smell of ale carried from his breath.

I remembered what Ruby had told me about the yeoman's enjoyment of card games, his long days at the alehouse once the farmlands and animals were gone, and the leather gloves and buttermilk sold. Could he really have been blaming his losses now on Sara, rather than on his own vices?

I was steered towards the door of the hut. Before they shunted me through it, I noticed the doorframe was covered in strange markings, slashes as though someone had angrily taken a knife to the wood.

Outside, a scuffing from behind stopped me, but when I turned,

I couldn't see anything that might have made the noise. Still, I felt uneasy, exposed, as I knocked one door and then the next. The trees around the houses seemed to rustle and move, and by now, I was sure someone was following me, so I turned and circled back, re-emerging behind a dark figure. A familiar cloak.

'Ruby?' I called.

She jumped, turned, flushing pink as she lowered her hood.

'Were you following me?'

'I came to warn you. Hywel knows you're not in the bedchamber.'

No. This was terrible. He would be furious with me for lying.

'Hywel ... How?'

'He knocked the door. I tried to stop him.'

Ruby's cheeks were pink, her eyes flitting to the side. I wanted to believe her, but it gnawed at me. The dark figure, the rustling in the trees.

'Ruby, if you were coming to warn me, why were you sneaking about, following me?'

She flushed pink again, then spoke calmly.

'Following you? I wasn't?'

I closed my eyes momentarily, caught my breath, considering what was most important in the moment.

'Let's go,' I said.

Again and again I was turned away. Door after door was shut with claims of Sara's wicked sorcery, her malice. One woman even told me she'd seen Sara sneaking about at night to meet with the devil in the thick quiet of the forest. Another claimed that, since quarrelling with Sara, her doorway had suddenly been overtaken with witch's butter, though I saw no trace of the yellow jelly. Some simply stared past my shoulder, as though looking at someone behind me, shaking their heads. I couldn't tell whether they were remorseful, or secretly enjoying my plight. The more angry I became, the less I cared what they might think of me. Doli Maredudd, wife and mistress, come to plead at their doorways. Like a common beggar.

The paper, quill and ink pot I'd packed into my satchel so hopefully that morning sat, unused, at the bottom of the bag, rattling around like forgotten toys. By the time I dragged myself home, the sun was setting, dipping down behind Faen Maredudd, leaving the gardens deep in shadow.

'It's hopeless,' I told Ruby as we approached the house. 'We've knocked on nearly every door in Llynidwen. Nobody will speak to me.'

'I worried that might be the case,' she said. 'Doli. I don't want to speak out of turn, but —'

I placed my hand on her arm.

'Please. You know the people of this village far better than I do. You saw how stubborn they were today. I want to hear your thoughts.'

She hesitated, spinning her fingers around each other like reels of thread. It wasn't like Ruby to keep her feelings to herself.

'That may be part of the issue,' she began. 'You don't know the lives of the people of the village. Not well, at least. Yes, they see you at church. You host feasts and invite them into your home at Christmastide. And they are grateful, I'm sure, but you must understand, your lives are so different to theirs.'

I thought of poor Bess Evans, of the small, dark hovel where she'd taken her last breath. The curved mud walls and the pervading smell of urine. Even the yeomen, with their strips of land and their herds of livestock, or their small businesses selling leather gloves, or the alewives and the women who took in others' clothes for darning and mending, had very different lives to my own. I had servants to work the ground, tend the animals, bake the bread, light the fires and brew the ale. They had to do it all themselves, for the most part.

'You think that's why they won't talk with me?' I asked Ruby.

She nodded, and we continued walking, passing under the great elm at the bottom of the garden.

'I think that's part of the problem, yes. But...'

She hesitated again, trailing off. I could tell there was still something she was holding back.

'Ruby, please. What is it?'

'They're frightened, mistress.'

'Frightened? Of me?'

'No, not of you.'

'Of Hywel?' Something in my chest stung.

She looked up towards the trees, then back to me.

'Maybe ... But mostly, they're scared of the way things are. If Sara Gwen is accused of practising witchcraft, then those that seek her out or support her could be accused too. They don't want to make their associations known.'

'I suppose that makes sense. But if all they've done is asked for a salve to help their stiff limbs, then they have nothing to fear.'

Two blackbirds emerged from the tree above us. A red kite followed them, swift and huge above our heads, so close that I flinched.

'Maybe not. But even so, times are troubled. Nobody wants to risk speaking out. And there are many who've gone to Sara Gwen with greater concerns than stiffened knees and swollen elbows.'

She looked pointedly down at my stomach.

'Like me, you mean?'

She stayed quiet, looking off into the distance for a long while.

'Like me,' she replied, eventually.

I let out a small gasp.

'Ruby?'

She continued looking towards the distance, but gave a small, almost imperceptible, nod.

'There was a time. Not so long ago. I found myself in a position I didn't want to be in. Couldn't be in.'

I felt as though I was holding my breath, listening to her speak. I hadn't realised, until that moment, that babies could even be made outside of a marriage. I hadn't thought God would permit it. We were hovering at the far wall now, near the gate to the moors. I didn't want to venture further until I'd heard what she needed to say.

'I see. Go on.'

'I had to do something about it. I went to Agnes. She didn't have enough of what was needed. She told me to go to Sara.'

'And did you?' I already knew the answer. She wasn't with child. Her belly had never grown round and swollen in all the years I'd known her.

Another subtle nod. I felt sick.

'I did. I had to ask some of the servants to keep quiet when they noticed there were less bleeding rags in the laundry. But I went to her, before the quickening. She gave me belladonna, turmeric, mugwort.'

'I see,' I said again. How could she have kept this from me? How could I not have known? How could she do it – end a pregnancy, when all I'd wanted so desperately for so long was to maintain one?

'Is this why you didn't want me to meet Sara Gwen? You didn't want me to find out what you'd done?'

She sighed, running a hand over her face. It was confirmation enough. 'Who was the father, Ruby? Who put the baby in you?'

'Does it matter?' she asked.

'It matters to me.' I wasn't sure why I said it, wasn't sure why it mattered who she'd lain with. It was none of my business, and of course, there were things I kept from Ruby. But this was so unexpected. I struggled to picture her doing much more than drinking at the alehouse on her days off. The thought of her, wrapped about a man, sneaking about the stables at night, was too much.

I tried to conceal the hurt on my face, but it must have been written there clear as scripture. Hywel had always told me my face could hide nothing. He said it gave me away as though I was speaking the very words in my mind aloud. Besides, Ruby knew me well enough to know what I was thinking, with alarming precision.

'Doli, there's no immortal soul before the quickening. It's not a sin. Wise women can make babies stick in the womb. They can unstick them too. It's not witchcraft. But the magistrates may not see it that way, not now.'

'I don't know what to say to you,' I told her.

Ruby's actions stung. I felt as though I'd been struck by a horse fly.

With her words ringing in my ears like the drag of wind through trees, I turned and swept back through the gardens, back into the house, back to the relentless sound of my daughter crying.

I crept up the winding stairs, back to my bedchamber, my stomach tight. Sick. Dread had settled within me at the anticipation of Hywel's cold fury, along with the sting of Ruby's betrayal and the frustration at the reluctant, useless villagers. I found my husband sitting on the bed, hunched over, his head pressed to his hands.

'Hywel?'

He snapped his head up, looked at me, his face pale, his cheeks sallow.

'Not now,' he said. 'I have nothing to say, Doli.'

The way he spoke – quiet, tired, sadness hovering at his edges – was worse than any amount of anger could have been.

It wasn't until he got up and left the room that I noticed our bed had been replaced.

The new bed was similar to the last, with posts and curtains, but the headboard was like nothing I'd ever seen. Beautiful, intricate patterns were carved into the wood. Daisies at the centre of circles. Overlapping 'V' shapes. Knots. *Witchmarks.* I'd seen drawings like this, scratched or burned into fireplaces or doorways, but these were different. Deliberate. Careful. It was clear they'd been put there with the sculpting of the wood, the building of the bed. They were as much a part of the design as the canopy above it.

Whatever his other motivations, Hywel must have been terrified, to have commissioned a new bed complete with protective markings like this. It must have cost a huge sum. I flung myself on it, and howled the force of it wracking my chest.

By now, Emily had been with us for more than a month, but still Awen continued to cry. She was as unsettled as she had ever been.

Her eyes grew bigger in her face every day. She scowled. There was a part of me, a wicked part that lay deep in the pits of my belly, that felt relieved. I wasn't the problem after all. Emily and her 'wholesome milk' hadn't cured Awen of whatever ailed her. She was not, despite appearances, a better mother than I was.

I told Hywel this, implored him to dismiss Emily, to let me nurse my own child, before my milk stopped coming and it was too late, but he wouldn't hear of it. He insisted Awen wasn't improving because she was cursed, that she wouldn't recover until *that witsh* was hanged, but despite his conviction, he maintained that Emily was best for Awen.

'Emily is a remarkable woman, Doli. I made enquiries. She came well recommended. It's likely Sara cursed you too, your milk is not enough for Annie. Besides, I can't trust you with our daughter. Not after your blatant disregard of everything I've said. Everything I've tried to do to protect us. All we can do now is keep our faith, and pray.'

I tried.

I tried to work at my embroidery, to tend the rosebush in the garden, pruning it of its dead leaves, and to sew more gowns for Awen, but nothing could distract me, or ease my agitation. I paced the passages of Faen Maredudd, staring through the windows at the grey sky, listening to my daughter crying and crying and crying, milk pearling at my nipples and dampening my dress each time she was near. Her wailing had driven me to despair when I felt as though it was aimed at me. An attack. Confirmation of how poor my attempt at mothering her was. Now, coming from another room, carrying under the door and along the passageway, it hit my heart like one of Hywel's hunting arrows. I wanted nothing more than to go to her, to heal her suffering, to let her drink from me until there was nothing left.

Then, one dull afternoon in late September, Emily appeared in the parlour doorway, clutching Awen to her chest. Her cap was askew on her head, her cheeks flushed pink. Dark shadows weighed down her eyes. She was gaunt, pale. Small sores had started to appear around her mouth.

'Where's the master?' she asked me. There was a quiver in her voice, as though she were trying not to cry.

I stood up, reaching out for Awen. What had happened to my daughter? What had Emily done? My face must have betrayed my worry, because Emily reassured me that Awen was well, but asked again after Hywel.

I told her that he was in the hall, speaking with a tenant – a yeoman from the west side of the village. Hywel was arranging to buy one of his gilts, to replace our poor dead one.

'Can I help you with something?' I probed. 'Or perhaps, would you like to sit and wait with me a while?' I sat back down, pushing my sewing to one side.

I wanted her to sit, to stay, so that I could be near Awen. Now that Emily was with us, I hardly saw her. At first, the wet nurse would let Awen fall asleep at her breast, then hand her to me, pearls of milk still glistening on her lips, wetting her chin, but with being passed over, she would inevitably stir and begin to search for milk again. If I held on to her, trying to settle her myself, her cries would become so intense that I would feel my own heart breaking, and practically throw her back to Emily, often leaving the room to spare myself. Eventually, Emily began to anticipate this endless ritual of feeding, and wailing, and writhing, and stopped bothering to seek me out.

'I'll wait,' she said, lowering herself onto the chair beside mine. Now that she was closer, I noticed her bottom lip was inflamed and red, as though she'd been chewing on it. 'I really must speak with the master.'

'Emily, what is it?' I set aside my sewing – a blanket I was embroidering for Awen. 'What's wrong?'

'I, well —' she paused, looking down at Awen scowling in my arms, then back to me. 'There's no need to worry, mistress. Awen is well. That is, she is as she was when we first met. But something *is* wrong.'

Before she could continue, Hywel entered the room.

'What's this? Something wrong?' He strode towards us, lifting Awen from my arms and inspecting her closely. A small cry came from the material, before she stretched her little arms from inside her blankets, one fist trailing free like a loose thread.

Emily looked like a rabbit caught in a snare. What had come over her?

'Master. The child nurses constantly. My breasts are bloodied and sore. Sometimes, it feels as though her mouth is filled with daggers. I've given it much thought, and I'm afraid I can't continue in this position any longer.'

Her words were a pail of cold water. I'd felt it too, the sensation like a wolf's teeth biting down. I thought there was something wrong with me, with my body, with my inability to mother my child correctly, but now Emily, with her six healthy children, was describing the very same thing. The relief of hearing her say it was immense. I wasn't mad, or wrong, or incapable. No more than she was.

I looked towards my husband. I'm not sure what sort of expression I expected to see on his face – maybe irritation, anger, disbelief – certainly not fear. But he looked deathly afraid, a small muscle jumping at his temple.

'It's this house,' he said, quietly.

'The house? What do you mean?' Emily asked.

Hywel looked down at Awen, drinking in her small, pale face. Her eyelids twitched as she dreamed, her scowl tight across her forehead. When he spoke again, he kept his eyes on our daughter, but his whole body jittered.

'It's this house. It's cursed. The issue isn't with you, Emily, and it's not with Awen.' I noted how, confronted with deep fear, he had used our daughter's real name, rather than Annie. 'It's not with my wife, either. It's this house. Awen must go with you, to live at your home.'

Emily's face paled then. She began to respond, to say *no*, at the same time as I lunged forward and snatched Awen from Hywel.

'She can't go, Hywel. You can't send her away.'

'I must, Doli. I want to keep her here as much as you do but this house isn't safe. It's become a cursed place. It's the only explanation. Sara Gwen has cursed this home, this land. It's why the gilt went mad and why the milk sours. It's why the walls speak at night. Why the doors slam when there's no one around. It's why Awen is at suck all day and night but never seems full. Milk must turn to ash in her poor mouth.'

His voice was soft, gentle, and yet, there was a feverishness in the way he spoke. He was agitated. He knew how much pain this would cause me. I was about to argue with him, when Emily spoke.

'Please master.' She turned to me, and added, 'Mistress. I'm in pain. Awen is discontented. It's been five weeks and I can't settle her, no matter how much I let her suck. Surely taking her from one home to another won't make any amount of difference.'

'I'll pay double,' Hywel said, his voice curt. 'Take her to live with you. I will pay you double what you are paid at present.'

He looked at me then, and I found myself silently pleading with him not to do this. I kept my eyes fixed on his, refused to look away. He held my gaze, speaking as though to me, rather than to Emily.

'My wife may visit the child, one afternoon a week, until she is weaned from the breast, at which time she may return to us here, as long as the curse has been lifted by then. There isn't long to go now, before the autumn assizes. The *witsh* will soon hang.'

Emily's eyes widened. With six children to support, doubled wages must have been an enticing offer. She nodded.

My chest heaved. I couldn't breathe.

The house was quiet without Awen. More quiet than it had ever been. The passages seemed endless and draughty, the rooms vast and cold as deep lakes as autumn settled to winter. Hywel spent much of his time with Jacob Lloyd, occupying himself with business, leaving early in the mornings and returning as the sun set for the evening. Each time he returned from somewhere beyond the marches, he had a new notion about how to protect ourselves from witchcraft, how to lift the curse he was certain had fallen like a thick coverlet over Faen Maredudd. He hid thorn branches near the doors and windows – he said the thorns would frighten off the witches, who were scared of sharp objects. Then he suggested removing the thorns, all except one, to fashion a witch axe, and asked the servants to scatter the thorns like seeds across the windowsills and mantels. He took his dagger to his hair and hid a huge clump of it beneath the floorboards. He spoke of witch bottles, his eyes shining with the intensity of the hearth's flames, his voice cracking.

Beyond that, we barely spoke to one another. Occasionally, he nodded at me as we walked by each other in the passages. I stopped asking about his trade, the tenants, I wasn't interested in anything beyond bringing my daughter back home. If she was going to die, I wanted it to be here, with me. Not in a stranger's house. I spent my days counting down until I was next permitted to go to her, wondering how many more times I would get to see her before she perished.

As the days passed, I obsessed over what could be done, trailing the cold moors without her in my arms, sheltering beneath the dense canopies of elm and oak trees watching the breath rise like a spectre from my mouth. The kites swarmed above me, circling the moors as though they were searching for something. I didn't ask Ruby to come with me. My anger with her had grown like a fire, hot in my belly, since Awen was taken away to live with Emily. I knew the importance of forgiveness, I knew what the Bible said about it, but I couldn't imagine how she could knowingly choose to end a pregnancy when the pain of having Awen ripped away from me was so all-consuming. In truth, the idea that Ruby had a life so separate to mine, a life she chose not to share with me, stung. I thought she told me almost everything and was surprised and hurt to learn that wasn't the case. I felt more alone than ever.

I didn't quarrel with Ruby often, but when I did, the ache of it was almost more than I could bear. She was almost as stubborn as Hywel, and wouldn't ever be the first to apologise or admit defeat, despite her position beneath me. She wouldn't speak out of turn, as such, but she would usually find ways to avoid me; she would be needed in the kitchens, or too busy polishing the silverware to come with me on walks, or to sit with me in the parlour.

I remember a bitter few weeks, not long after I was married, in which Ruby and I barely spoke a word to one another. She'd had far too much to drink at the wedding festivities, and became overly familiar with some of the guests. I saw her, at one point, stroking Rhys' arm, and sent Hywel to scold her – I hadn't wanted to do it myself. The next morning she tried to behave as though none of it had happened, but the atmosphere between us was tense and we ended up bickering about something trivial – I can hardly remember what it was, looking back now. What I do remember is that it took weeks before things were right between us again.

Now, I wasn't sure I could withstand weeks without Ruby by my side, not with circumstances the way they were. In the days since Awen had been taken away, I was shrouded constantly in grief. I felt as though I was walking on pins, unable to settle or be still. If I let myself think too much about Sara, trapped in the cold, damp dungeons, my breath would come too quickly, and I'd find myself hunched over, barely able to get my breath out. Everything seemed to be falling apart around me.

When it was finally my afternoon to visit Awen at Emily's home, I left immediately after breakfast, leaving most of the sweetmeats on my plate to be cleared away by the servants. There was something I had to do first.

When I reached the Jones' farmstead, I made my way to the front door, expecting to speak with the mistress of the house, but before I got there, I spotted a familiar tumble of red hair disappearing into the cook house. I changed direction, and picked my way across the yard, past the buttery and the hen house, to follow her.

Agnes was hunched over the butter churn, the outline of her

shoulder blade cutting sharp and stark through her gown, as though she were about to sprout wings.

'Agnes,' I said, my voice low, tentative.

'Why are you suddenly appearing everywhere I go?' she asked, without turning around. She sounded disinterested, almost too bored to be irritated. 'I've already told you. I can't help you.'

'You *won't* help me,' I said. 'There's a difference.'

She sighed, and stopped churning to turn around and look at me.

'Even if I wanted to,' she began. 'I wouldn't come anywhere near the big house. Not now I know what your husband is capable of.' Her voice dropped with disdain as she uttered the word: *husband*, and something about it made me wince, too.

'Agnes, wait —' I was about to tell her there was no need to come to Faen Maredudd, that Awen was no longer there, but she interrupted me before I could finish speaking.

'I know exactly what will happen. I'll fail to cure the girl, she'll get more and more sick, and your husband will have me arrested on witchcraft charges, just like he did Sara. He'll say I've cursed her, caused her to worsen.'

I wanted to argue, but she continued, her voice high and quick, picking up pace like a horse's canter.

'Or, I will help. She'll improve. And still I'll find myself beside Sara in a dark cellar awaiting trial. He'll say I used witchcraft to heal her. I'm no fool, mistress. I'm sorry for you, truly, but I can't be involved in this.'

I took a step towards her. I wanted to tell her I wouldn't let any of it happen, that she would be safe by my side, but I couldn't make that promise. I'd learned that now. I had far less power over my husband than I ever thought. Instead I said,

'Agnes. I don't think you're a fool. Quite the opposite. That's why I've come to you. If Sara can't help me, then —'

Agnes interrupted me again. I had never known a person beneath my rank to be quite as insolent as she was.

'Your husband may own most of this village, mistress, but we do not all exist solely to serve you. Contrary to what you may have been led to believe.' Her words were muttered, angry.

'If Awen were not sick, would you still be trying to save Sara from the gallows? Or would you have forgotten all about her?' She dropped the handle of the butter churn, staring straight at me. I was aware I'd been preoccupied with Awen, begging Agnes to help me find a cure for her, but I was concerned for Sara too. Of course I was. Perhaps I hadn't made that clear enough. 'Would you be leaving her to rot, holed up in the dark, and the cold, waiting for death to be brought about by men in collars and ruffs who think they've the right to tell us who we must worship? Who we must bow down to? What we can and cannot do with our own lives? In our own homes? Our own beds.' She spat at the ground and I felt my cheeks redden with shame. I shouldn't have been surprised by her anger, but her words cut through me; I felt the sting of them in my bones.

'Agnes, please. My baby is dying.'

Agnes softened a little and reached out a hand, as though to touch my arm, then dropped it back to her side.

'Of course your daughter is your priority,' she said. 'It's only natural that you would lay down your own life for hers. But someone needs to fight for *Sara*. She's a good woman.'

Once again, the words Sara spoke to me last winter swam in my mind: *I believe I will be in need of your help, in the future.*

It had seemed so little to ask in return for giving me a child. I finally understood, in that moment, the true weight of the words. A life for a life.

I nodded.

'You're right. Sara's life *is* important to me. She wouldn't be languishing in gaol if she hadn't helped me. If she hadn't already saved Awen once. And she wouldn't be there if it weren't for my husband.' I stopped, brushed my hands over my skirts. 'I don't believe she's a *witsh*. I've tried everything I can to free her, but my power is limited. Perhaps more limited that I'd realised. I can't do it alone, Agnes.'

Agnes nodded, seemingly satisfied. And there, beside the butter churn, we devised our plan. First, we would go to Awen. Then, we would do what we could for Sara.

Afterwards, I waited until Agnes had finished her duties for the morning, so that she was able to accompany me to Emily's home. I even helped her beat the curtains and feed the hens, in an attempt to get her away from the farmstead sooner. Together, we walked along the stony pathway from the farm, our dresses dragging through the dirt. We would have made quicker progress, but Agnes stopped every once in a while to take cuttings from the verge. I didn't ask what they were for, but by the time we reached Emily's home, her apron was stuffed with heather and cornflower and thick knots of moss.

She stood back, waiting for me to knock. It had been several days since I had seen my daughter. I should have been banging at the door like a magistrate come to make an arrest, but I was hesitant. Something stopped me, as though my fist had been grabbed mid-air before it could descend on the door.

What if Awen was somehow happy here? What if she had settled, comforted by Emily's humble home, surrounded by the other children? My heart wouldn't withstand the blow.

Agnes, clearly bored of waiting for me to announce our arrival, stepped forward. She rapped the door, sharp and confident, then stepped back again. I gave her a grateful smile. As soon as the door swung open, I heard Awen crying. My heartbeat quickened at the familiar sound of her, mewling like a kitten.

Emily opened the door, a small boy clutched to her waist. Before she had even greeted us, another child came to stand at her side, a thumb wedged firmly in his mouth. He took her hand in his when he saw us.

'Mistress, come in,' she said, shuffling the older boy to one side. Her face seemed paler than when I had last seen her, and there were purple shadows deep as bruises blooming beneath her eyes.

Once she'd led us through to the kitchen, I said, 'Emily, you look tired. Is everything alright?'

I looked about, taking in the mound of clothes piled haphazardly on the kitchen table – stockings, rags, little gowns. There were marbles scattered across the floor and stew bubbling away in the pot above the fire. A small girl weaved her way into the kitchen, then back out again, clicking her tongue and pretending to gallop. It was no wonder Emily looked so pale, so tired. I thought nursing and cradling and shushing Awen at every hour was utterly exhausting. She was doing it now, while keeping house and caring for a horde of small children. But no ... her grey pallor, her waxen skin – she couldn't possibly be nursing and cradling and shushing every hour. Not here, in this home, with these children and this workload. It simply wasn't possible.

'I would like to see my daughter now,' I told her, a lump forming at the back of my throat.

'Of course,' she said, absently, wiping her hands on the front of her smock. Then again, 'of course. Through there.'

She pointed with her elbow towards a door off the kitchen. I gestured for Agnes to follow me, then rushed through it to Awen.

She'd been placed in a cradle besides the hearth, a thin coverlet over her legs. Setting my eyes on her for the first time in days brought a confusing mixture of emotions all at once. There was relief – she was here, she was alive. My Awen. There was, of course, love, my heartbeat quickening as my hands stretched out to smooth her pale cheek. Then, there was regret. Fear. Guilt.

She was so sallow, her eyes huge in her skull. Her skin looked grey and ashen. Her cry came feebly and less often than it used to. She was quiet, her breath quick, then she emitted a small cry, like a kitten searching for its mother's milk, her fists stretching out. My breasts tightened and swelled in response. She fell silent once more. Is this how her life would be here, in Emily's home, amongst the other children? Quietly confined to her cradle, crying, calling, until she learned no one would come. That the crying did no good. That she would be better to keep quiet. The idea of it brought a horrible itching sensation over my skin and my scalp, left me feeling panicked and anxious.

I asked Agnes to examine Awen, while I went to speak with Emily.

'Mistress,' she said, when I re-entered the kitchen. 'You must think me so rude. I haven't even offered you a drink. Would you like some ale?'

I shook my head.

'Emily, please don't concern yourself with courtesies.' I gestured around the room, at the laundry, the toys, the children's shoes. 'But, I must say, I'm a little surprised. I thought you were paid well enough when you lived with us at Faen Maredudd to hire a maid to care for the children, and keep house while you were away. You are paid double now. What has happened to your maid?'

She looked down towards her feet, shuffling uncomfortably.

'When I came home, my husband thought – I mean, we thought it best – to let her go. There seemed no need for a maid once I was living here again.'

I took a deep breath. I didn't want to criticise her housekeeping, especially when I did little in the way of housekeeping myself, but I couldn't allow this to continue.

'Emily. As you and I both suspected, leaving Faen Maredudd doesn't seem to have improved Awen's affliction. In fact, she looks worse than ever.'

Emily looked as though she might cry, her lip trembling. I softened my voice, and took a step towards her.

'It's not your fault,' I said. 'But it's clear that she suffers. Whatever it is that continues to ail her, she needs to be at suck more often, and not left to cry in her cradle. Send for your maid. Appoint her again. Have her do everything else so that you may focus your time and energy on Awen. All of it.'

Emily opened her mouth to speak, whether to agree, or argue, I don't know, because I interrupted before she could say anything more.

'It won't be for long. And of course, we'll pay. I'll see to it that you receive enough silver to cover the maid's salary in addition to your own. But I want you to send for her immediately.'

She nodded. Good.

I spent much of the afternoon with Awen, holding her close to me, whispering to her, singing. I wondered if she remembered my voice, my songs, or if she might have forgotten the notes already. When Agnes and I spilled back onto the path outside, I turned to her, desperate.

'Well, can you help her?'

Agnes looked out across the moors, studying the heather and the bracken. A magpie flew overhead and disappeared behind an elm tree.

'Doli,' she began. 'I'm sorry. It's clear she suffers from some affliction. I think you're right. You need Sara Gwen.'

A sudden wind stirred, and grey clouds rolled overhead. Tears stung my eyes as the desperation took hold. I didn't want to walk away, to leave my baby again. Sara seemed so far away, so unreachable. I pictured her in the cold and the dark, stripped of her herbs and dried flowers, her pestle and mortar. Waiting for the assize judges to blow in with the wind and determine her fate.

We were drawing close to October, to the autumn assizes, and though I was still feeling the betrayal of Ruby's actions and wasn't certain I could trust her, I knew I needed her if I wanted any hope of helping Sara to get out of gaol.

I would have to apologise.

Later that evening, I followed her around as she greased Hywel's boots with calf fat. She marched into the parlour and began to move things about. I watched her pick up a pot of ink, move it to the oyster table, then move it back again. She was clearly only pretending to work now, like a child playing at copying the servants.

She smirked as I said again, 'Please. I'm sorry. I was so surprised, Ruby. I didn't know what to think. And things have been so difficult lately. I'm not myself.'

Finally, she stopped moving about and turned to me.

'I understand why my confession upset you,' she said. 'But *you* must understand, we live very different lives. There are things we will never be able to share, not fully.'

I nodded.

She turned her face, trying to hide her smile, and I felt a rush of relief to have her back at my side. For now, there was work to be done.

Later that night, sitting cross-legged on my bed like we used to when we were small, I told Ruby of the plan Agnes and I had hatched.

'So Agnes will gather the people she knows Sara has helped, and they will speak with her?' she repeated.

I nodded.

'And I'll write down what they say. The assize judges won't speak Welsh – we need a clerk who can deliver them the testimony in English.'

Once again, I found myself more grateful than I could ever have imagined to Hywel's father for teaching me my letters.

Ruby's eyes glimmered in the flickering candlelight.

'How can you be so sure there'll be enough people willing to speak to Agnes about Sara? Aren't they all afraid?'

'Of course they are,' I said. In truth, I'd had the same hesitations, when Agnes first suggested it. But she had a way with people. A way of drawing them in, of gaining their confidence and pulling the truth and the secrets from them, despite her brash manner. She was better placed than I was, at least, to persuade people to talk.

Our plan was simple. We would collect the testimonies the magistrate had failed to gather. We would take these to the assize judges, somehow – we'd ask Rhys for help, or maybe pass the papers to someone in the village to take to the judges somewhere on their circuits. If I could find out where they would be staying, I could have them delivered to their lodgings, ahead of their arrival.

Either way, once the papers were in their hands, they'd be so convinced of Sara's good character, they'd have to set her free. At least, that's what I told myself, over and over. There were women across the country who were accused of witchcraft without consequence – Kathryn Lewis, somehow, was still wandering the countryside begging for bread and salt and calling herself a *witsh*. She was free because she hadn't crossed the wrong people. Powerful enough people. Only recently, I'd heard a story of a woman who was arrested, accused of bewitching to death some ducks and causing a newly built wall to collapse, only to be released when her accusers withdrew the accusation. As long as we could get the right people to say the right things, there was hope. Sara would be freed, and then Awen would be healed.

By the following evening, everything was set and ready to go. Once again, I'd packed my paper, my quill and my ink in my bag, ready to sling over my shoulder. Agnes, being well known to the landlady, had secured a room at the back of the alehouse, and spread the word to the villagers. By a store of luck, Hywel had set out to ride to Bristol on business, along with Jacob Lloyd.

We stole our way out of the house, crept through the gardens and past the dovecote, where we found the stable boy. I instructed him to prepare two horses, hoping he wouldn't question where we were going at this time of day.

My heart pounded in my chest, my hands trembled and slipped as I fussed with the horse's bridle. This had to work. If it didn't, and Hywel found out what we were trying to do...

My mare hoofed the ground, turning her head away as I tried to soothe her, so I told Ruby to go ahead of me to the alehouse. I would meet her there, very soon. I wanted to calm my horse first.

I smoothed her flank and pressed my face against hers. Her heartbeat was clear and strong beneath my palm where I rested my hand against her chest. As I was about to mount her, I heard hooves pounding the ground. Had Ruby come back for me? But no. I saw the long, dark shadow before I saw him – Hywel, riding in atop his huge horse. Why was he back so soon? He should have been settling into his lodgings for the night by now.

'Hywel, you're back,' I said, cautious. I angled my body, swinging the satchel behind me to try to hide it, but it was no use. He knew I was about to mount the mare and ride into the night.

'Indeed,' he said. He stayed sitting on his horse's back, so that he was high above me, looking down. 'And it appears I've caught you about to leave?'

'Oh, no.' I tried to keep my voice level, light. 'I'm just spending some time with my horse. She's unsettled this evening.'

I avoided eye contact with the stable boy, who turned his back and busied himself with a pile of hay in the corner.

'With your satchel and riding cloak? Fascinating.'

He spoke quietly, calmly, his eyes boring into mine until I was forced to look away. Before dismounting, he spoke again.

'I will see you inside.'

I hurried after him, ready to hear his onslaught.

Once we reached our bedchamber, his calm demeanour cracked like shattered glass.

'Where were you going?'

'I told you,' I replied. 'I was comforting the horse.'

He stared at me, silent and intent. His face remained unreadable, but the rise and fall of his chest was quick, palpable. I knew my satchel had given me away, but all I could think about was whether Ruby had made it out of the grounds before Hywel returned. If she did, it would have been by a hare's whisker. But she must have – he hadn't mentioned her, and surely he would have had he seen her. I would not be surprised had he dragged her and her horse back into the stables. I closed my eyes, hoping that she was with Agnes by now, gathering the testimonies we so desperately needed.

We both remained silent for some time. When eventually Hywel spoke, his voice was quiet, his shoulders slack.

'I don't know you anymore, Doli. What's happened to us?'

He sounded miserable.

'What do you mean? I'm the same woman I've always been.'

He shook his head, almost imperceptibly. Shadows circled his eyes.

'Yes, I am. I'm the same woman you married. Only now,' I took a step towards him. 'Now, I have more to care for. We have a daughter.' For a moment I thought he was going to let me lay my hand on his chest, but he stepped away. 'I have more to fight for. More to lose.'

'No,' he said, quietly at first, then louder and louder. 'No, no, no, no. This cannot be. You don't listen, Doli. You openly defy me, for all to see! No. I knew something was wrong. I knew you were plotting something, that's why I turned around before reaching the old road. I had a feeling in the depths of my stomach. And Jacob said – well, anyway, here you are, satchel in hand, poised to leave our home. Where were you going? Were you planning to return?'

'Hywel, please.'

Before I could go on, he left the room, mumbling under his breath. My heart sank. A sudden clicking noise. The door had been locked from the outside.

Hywel left me locked in that room for the rest of the evening. I spent a long while pounding the door with my fist, crying, shouting, twisting the handle like a cockerel's neck until I was too exhausted to carry on. I stared through the window, focussing on the hook of the moon in the night sky. Waiting. He didn't come back. I heard the house settling around me – the soft creaking of floorboards quieting, and footsteps coming to a stop as the servants collapsed on to their beds in the hall. Where was Hywel? Why hadn't Ruby come to me?

I wondered if he'd warned the servants not to come near our bedchamber.

Seething, I rose from where I was sitting, staring through the window, and paced the room, too angry and exhausted to cry. Despite my weariness, I knew I wouldn't be able to sleep, so I pulled the prayer book from under my bed and started reading the poems I'd scribbled in the margins. Crossing through words and writing new ones in their place:

I would drive a dagger through your heart's stone,
slanted to reach your breast bone.

The sky was growing lighter by the time my eyes became too heavy to keep open, and I dragged myself to bed, falling asleep still clothed above the coverlet. I dreamed of Awen, saw her thinning, scattering to dust in my arms.

I didn't have the opportunity to speak with Ruby until nearing suppertime the following day. Hywel had unlocked the bedchamber door in the morning, wordlessly swinging it open and walking away. Good – I had nothing to say to him.

I wandered about idly, restless, desperate to be alone with Ruby. Had she got the testimonies we needed? Would they be enough? My stomach twisted in knots but I felt more hopeful than I had in a long time, excited at the prospect. If Agnes and Ruby had succeeded, Sara might be free before the month's end, and Awen back in my arms.

Ruby was busy at work, jumping from one task to the next. At first, I worried she was avoiding me, but when we finally managed to speak, she told me she'd been trying to finish the tasks she was unable to complete the night before, to avoid anyone questioning why she hadn't managed to do them.

Once Hywel was occupied at his books and ledgers in the parlour we sat together, cross-legged on the bed, and she told me how things had unfolded in the alehouse the previous evening.

'Agnes spoke, mostly, and I listened. I wanted to make sure I could remember everything, so that you could write the stories down.'

I was ready to write everything down, to gather a pile of written testimonies that I could take to the judges. I was so sure of the plan. But what Ruby told me was crushing. They'd only managed to find two people willing to say anything good about Sara, and both had refused to give their names.

'We knew who they were, of course,' Ruby said. 'But we can't use their names when they've asked us not to. Can we?'

I groaned, sinking into my bed, wanting to bury myself in the coverlet, my whole body racked with worry, the guilt dense as a stone in my stomach. How could this awful situation have come this far?

'People are scared, Doli. No one wants to be the only one to defend a *witsh*.' She lowered her voice to a whisper. 'Even the other servants are suspicious ... of you ... of me. They see what's going on. They hear you and Hywel arguing. They heard you last night, said you were wailing in your bedchamber like a madwoman.'

I spent the following morning tending the rosebush in the garden, pruning it back for winter, turning the dirt over in my hands until the creases in my palms were lined thick with soil. I dug and dug until my hands hurt. I thought about the meagre amount of testimonies we'd gathered. Was it even worth trying to get the papers into the hands of the assize judges? All we had was a couple of sentences with no names attached. It was a pitiful attempt. It wasn't enough.

The sun was warm as I worked, so I went back inside, passing the kitchen and heading straight to the bedchamber, looking for a rag to wipe my brow.

I stopped still in the doorway. Hywel was standing by the bedside, the papers clutched in his hands. I'd hidden them in my prayer book, which was now lying open on the bed. He was bound to tear them up, to scrunch them in his fists and throw them to the ground. To let the pieces cascade like snow. Not that it would matter, I knew by now they weren't enough to save Sara.

'This is, truly, adorable. Doli, *fach*. Did you really believe this would work? How did you ever plan to get these letters to the assize judges? And even if you were to manage it, did you think they would be swayed? Testimonies need to be witnessed and recorded by magistrates, not by common whores and servants. These papers are worth nothing. You must realise that. Or are you, in truth, stupider than I believed? I would be cross, were I not so embarrassed on your behalf.'

'I —' I began, but I found I couldn't speak, my words tumbling over each other as I stared uselessly at Hywel's smug face.

I grew so desperate, so angry, that I hit my fist against the window, smashing the glass. Blood smeared my knuckles, dripping down towards my wrists, but I scarcely cared.

For just a moment, Hywel looked startled, scared even. His eyes flicked briefly to the blood on my hands, then back to my face. Then he started to laugh. He turned and left the room, his laughter carrying behind him.

'*Cer o ma*!' I shouted, finally finding my voice. 'Go! You traitorous ass!'

It felt good to call after him, my words filled with venom. With every passing moment, Awen was inching closer to death. She was starving to a wisp. In a matter of weeks, Sara might be quivering on the gallows, breathing in the sack that would cover her face in her last moments, the burn of rope like a necklace at her throat.

In the days that followed, Hywel and I barely spoke a word to one another. I wandered around with a grief and sickness following me like a crow at my shoulder. I no longer yearned for the days in which all was free and easy between us. I had seen another fragment of Hywel, as though he had drawn back his doublet and revealed a part of himself he'd been concealing for years. It meant, at least, that he had stopped watching me so closely, and I was no longer living like a prisoner in my own home.

He seemed content to ignore me, shuffling meat and marzipan about the table each evening as though I wasn't sitting opposite him. Then finally, over supper one evening, the tension still thick and claggy between us, he finally spoke to me. His voice broke the days-long silence, and I flinched at the unexpected sound of it.

'I might not be able to control what is in your mind, Doroli,' he said. 'But to commit your verse to paper? To write it down? And often in strict meter no less? No, it's not appropriate.'

He'd seen the scribbled verses in the margins of my prayer book. I chewed my food slowly while I thought of how best to respond. He had taken so much from me. I would not let him take my words, too.

'It's only poetry, Hywel. What harm can it do?'

'Only poetry?' he said. 'And of what do you write, Doli?'

He looked at me then, his face still, as though trying to decide whether or not to believe me.

'Hywel, why did you look in my prayer book?' I asked him.

'Why indeed. It's not a suitable pastime for a gentlewoman.' He set down his spoon and dagger, and looked at me for so long that I wanted to shrink back from the table. 'Read the Bible, if you must read. Listen to the bards when they come. But writing your own verse down...' he trailed off, looking about the hall as though he might find the words he was searching for up on the dais, or hiding on the trestle. 'It's a peculiarity. People will talk.'

'No they won't. Plenty of women do it. Besides, nobody knows about it.' *Except Rhys.* It crossed my mind, fleeting as a hummingbird's wing, to confess to having shown Rhys, to tell Hywel about his support, but it wouldn't have been wise. 'I haven't shown the poems to anyone.'

This didn't seem to deter him.

'That doesn't matter. People have ways of learning about these things. If you are writing poetry, what else might you be writing?'

I looked at him, struck silent by the absurdity of his question.

'There is a rather large difference between writing rhymes, and writing curses, if that's what you're implying,' I said, my voice flat and careful. *Don't argue with him.*

'I'm only saying what others will. Doli, you must understand, I am trying to protect you. To protect us. Our reputation.'

Fury flung my body upright. I couldn't stand it any longer.

249

'Damn our reputation,' I said, my voice breaking. 'What good is our reputation when our daughter is dying?'

I ran from the room, leaving him in stunned silence behind me.

The Villagers

The young maid only looked because she was frightened. They say she peeled a lid from a box beneath the bed, found strange markings scrawled over the pages of a prayer book. Loose pieces of paper covered in symbols. Penmanship that looked like it belonged to the mistress. Not long later, she heard them arguing – the master and the mistress, quarrelling. The word *inappropriate*. She says the master was irate, red as a beet in the face. She says the mistress insisted she should be allowed to go on writing her curses. Perhaps she threatened her own husband. Perhaps his tolerance is born of fear.

Several days after I had argued with Hywel about my poetry, Rhys came to the house, unannounced. I found him sitting in the parlour with Hywel, enjoying a cup of wine.

I was heading outside to look at the dovecote when I heard the voices from within the parlour. It sounded as though they may be bickering, their voices low but quick and heated. When I entered the room, however, both men looked up, Rhys smiled at me warmly, as though everything was wonderful. The falsity was unnerving.

'Doli! I wondered when you might appear,' he said.

I strode across the room to him, kissing his cheek, before taking a seat beside Hywel. I was glad to see him.

'We weren't expecting you, Rhys.'

'Ah, yes, well, that's my fault. I called in on passing. I've been down at Glancaiach, arranging some business affairs, and I was tired from the journey. I hoped seeing my oldest friends might revive my spirits a little.'

'You're always such a charmer, Rhys.'

I regretted the words the moment they'd left my lips, *charmer*, and looked over to Hywel to see whether or not he'd noticed the turn of phrase, but his face remained unchanged.

'I'm sure only you are charmed by me Doli. No one else seems to be,' he said, jovially enough. I glanced at Hywel, willing Rhys to stop talking.

'Only that's not true, is it Rhys?' Hywel replied. 'Plenty are impressed by you.'

Rhys rolled his eyes and sat back at the settle, crossing one leg over the other and reclining a little.

'I've made my decision Hywel.' I looked at him, the question forming on my lips. 'I've been invited to dine with the sheriff. I've heard he might offer me the role of justice,' he told me. 'A role I am inclined to turn down.'

'Nonsense,' Hywel said, and suddenly it was clear what they'd been arguing about when I entered. 'You must accept. Why you would choose not to is beyond me.'

Rhys shrugged.

'I'm not particularly interested in governing,' he said simply. 'I can put your name forward in my stead, if you would like me to.'

Hywel sat up a little straighter then, setting his cup down, his mouth twitching.

'Well, yes. Perhaps,' he said. 'If they're in need of someone.'

He worried at a thread on his trouser leg for a moment.

'I'll go and see about that kitten for you, Rhys.'

'He's promised you a kitten?' I asked, after Hywel had left the room.

'Yes. We're in need of a new mouser.'

'Well, we've plenty to spare,' I said, before glancing over my shoulder towards the door. I couldn't hear Hywel's footsteps. Now was the time to speak. 'Rhys. I don't understand. Why would you turn down the role of justice? There is so much good you could do. You could help Sara, and then Awen —'

Rhys reached forward and touched my arm, lightly, before I could finish my sentence.

'Doli. I would so dearly love to help you. But I can't accept the role. For numerous reasons. I am not like Hywel. I've no interest in enforcing our laws.' He paused, looked around quickly, then turned back to me. 'Did you know, Jacob Lloyd has also been made a magistrate for the county, as I predicted he would. I won't work alongside someone like that. I can't enforce laws I don't believe in. I won't help landowners take from the poorest in the county when their crops have failed and there is no money. I won't condemn men who've done no more than steal a loaf of bread to feed their children.'

'But Rhys, we need Sara free to help Awen.' I looked at him intently. Silently pleading, willing him to see reason. 'Awen is dying. And think of Sara rotting behind bars having done nothing but help me. It's not right Rhys, you know it isn't.'

'Please, Doli. I'm sorry. Truly. I cannot do it. Besides, I can't accept a political position to fulfil personal agendas.'

I knew, to some extent, that his reasons were fair. But in that moment, I felt more alone than ever. It seemed as though the solution was so close, sitting before me in a starched doublet, blue eyes gleaming in the light. And yet, Awen continued to sicken and Sara remained out of reach.

'Very well,' I said, hotly. 'Don't become a justice. But Rhys, could you speak with the sheriff, at least?'

He raised an eyebrow, but said nothing.

'Rhys, you know this situation is ridiculous. Sara Gwen didn't hurt anyone. She didn't curse us and she hasn't harmed Awen. I need her out of gaol before Awen's body fails her. Sara is the only one who can help, and she'll hang soon, if we do nothing.' I shivered at the memory of the dungeon's ice-cold seep. I had to speak quickly – Hywel would be back with the kitten at any moment. 'It's all gone too far. And now, because of my attempts to rectify the situation, Hywel is hardly acknowledging me. He behaves as though he can't see me, unless we're in company, of course.'

I hated the bitterness in my voice. I didn't care that Hywel was ignoring me, not really. But I despised the pretence he could put on so easily as soon as we had guests.

Concern creased Rhys' brow. His hand moved, as if to reach for mine, but instead he stood up, and went to the window, quietly looking out at the gardens. As he looked over the rows of clover and basil, his shoulders slackened. He'd always loved the gardens here, the hours we used to spend in them when we were younger. Everything had been so much simpler then. At last, he turned back to me, held my gaze.

A glint lit his eyes. It was an expression that took me back to our younger years, when he would stay late playing card games in the parlour with Hywel.

'I can't help, Doli. Not directly, at least. I'm afraid the sheriff won't have much time for me, once I've turned down his offer. Besides, there are tens of justices over the county – I am but one man. My influence wouldn't be great enough.' He paused.

Hesitated. 'But I know of a man ... An apothecary. He brews salves sometimes, too. Works with fairies. He may be able to do something for you.'

'By consulting with fairies?' I asked.

'No, no. I'm sorry.' He sighed, ran a hand through his hair. 'No, not quite. He's provided his services to many men of high social standing in the past. He may even have connections to some of the assize judges. I believe he knows the Deputy Lieutenant himself. Perhaps I could speak with him, on your behalf?'

An inkling of hope began to unfurl within me. I went to him, grasped his hands in mine.

'Oh, Rhys, thank you,' I said, looking up at him. His warm eyes met mine, and squeezed my hands lightly in return. 'What will you say?'

He looked about for a moment, his eyes eventually settling on the desk in the corner.

'Actually, you shall say it,' he said, decidedly. 'Write a letter and I'll carry it to him for you.'

I glanced at the door again, before scribbling something short and hurried, imploring the man to help us. 'You must get it to him quickly. Urgently. The assizes are only weeks away. Our time is nearly up.'

Rhys took the letter from me, tucking it safely into his breast pocket. I felt as though he had tucked away my final hope, placing it squarely beside his heart.

Two days rolled by as I waited, impatient, for the apothecary's reply. Every afternoon, I stole into the parlour to look through any correspondence at Hywel's desk, but there was never anything interesting to be seen. We were approaching All Hallows' Day, and a great number of our beasts were slaughtered. The vast grounds of Faen Maredudd smelled sickeningly of coins because of it, while the meat was salted, dried or smoked and put away for use over the winter.

That afternoon, I wrapped myself in my riding cloak and set out across the moors, trying to escape the stench of the animals' blood, but the frightened bellowing followed me, carrying with the wind. The temperature had dropped considerably over the last few days and the air was sharp, cold.

I followed the river as I had done on so many occasions, without any sense of destination. The sun was high and bright, glistening on the water's surface like jewels. Something compelled me to keep walking. Along the bank, overgrown and prickling now with heather and moss; down past the bridge that led over the river and into the village; along the lane and past the small cottages scattered at the river's edge, until I reached the lake that gave Llynidwen its name and sat down on the cool, stiffening grass.

When I was younger, my father told me a story about this lake, and an enchantress called Ceridwen. He said this was her cauldron, where she brewed her remedies and spells. It shone in the sunlight, like a huge looking-glass in the middle of the land. I looked at the reeds around the water's edge, and then at the distant hills. Over the whistling of the kites above, and the gentle rustle of wind in the grass, I could still hear the awful keening of the dying animals.

Only ... that was impossible. I was far enough from home now. I looked around but couldn't place where the sound was coming from.

Then, something landed nearby. At first I thought someone had thrown down a full brown satchel, but it was no satchel – it was a red kite, wings tucked at its side like a riding cloak. I held my breath, scared to move – I didn't want to frighten the bird away. It looked straight at me with deep, golden eyes, before turning its head and beating its great wings, soaring off silently across the lake. My eyes followed it to the other side of the water, where it hovered above the trees, sweeping about in circles. A group of black birds came pouring out soon after, chattering angrily.

I stood up, dusting off my skirts, and began to follow the trail around the edge of the lake, thistles tickling my ankles.

As I approached the area of trees where the bird was circling, the keening sound grew louder. It was human, a woman crying. Whimpering.

I followed the sound and found her heaped on the forest floor, dress torn and covered in mud and leaves. She looked as though she'd sprouted from the shrubbery, her legs like roots holding her firm to the ground.

'Agnes?'

She looked up. Her face was red and puffy, tears streaking a clean line in her otherwise dirty face. I rushed to her side.

'What's happened?'

'Nothing, I'm fine.'

She sat up properly, wiping her face roughly with the backs of her hands. She was embarrassed to be seen this way, I could tell. I imagined it pained her all the more that it was me who was seeing her so upset.

'I'm fine,' she said again.

I waited quietly, letting her gather her composure.

'There's a man, helping to repair the well at the Jones' farm, where I work,' she said.

I nodded.

'He wanted to come with me to the lake. I've been picking heather before it's gone for the winter,' her hand pointed loosely to her satchel, full to the brim with clippings.

'I see?' I said, though I didn't. Not really.

'He,' she sniffed. 'Well, he...' She gestured loosely around again.

'What did he do to you Agnes?'

'He did what all men do. Tried to take what wasn't his.'

I nodded again. I didn't want her to have to say anymore. I'd never seen Agnes like this, so vulnerable and upset. It was jarring.

'Are you hurt?' I asked.

She wiped angrily at her eyes, and rubbed her nose. I handed her my handkerchief.

'Here.'

She didn't seem able to speak.

'Agnes?'

'I —'

More tears gathered at the corners of her eyes, rolling down her cheeks like rain drops. She took a deep breath, tried again.

'Not really ... A few bruises. But, Doli. I'm worried about something I said to him.'

'What did you say, Agnes?'

Her reply, when it came, brought a sourness to my mouth.

'He brought it on himself,' she muttered darkly.

'What did you say?'

'I shoved him away, said he'd regret it. I said I'd make him regret it. I said I knew people who could ... curse. It was stupid. I was only trying to get rid of him.'

I nodded again, then offered her my hand. She grabbed it and pulled herself up. Once she was on her feet beside me, dusting off her skirts, I tried to reassure her, though worry gnawed at my stomach while I spoke.

'He won't take your threat seriously. It's obvious you were only defending yourself. And if he does say anything to anyone, you'll be able to say what he did to you.' The words sounded false even to me.

'Tried to do.' She spat at the ground, a hint of the Agnes I knew returning to her voice. 'He must have believed me. At least enough that he ran off and left me alone.'

'It's not right. Agnes, you should tell your employers. They'll dismiss him.'

She glanced sideways at me. 'I doubt it. They need the well fixed, don't they? Let's not talk of him any longer. Please.'

I nodded again.

We walked in silence for a while, Agnes stopping more than once to pluck thistles and weave them into her hair.

'Agnes, there's something I need to tell you,' I said as we emerged onto the path towards the village. 'It might sound strange.'

'Sure I've heard stranger, mistress.' She picked dirt from beneath her nails as we walked.

'A few weeks ago, I saw...' I paused here, trying to find the right way to describe what I'd seen in my bedchamber in the dead of night. 'I saw Sara. Only, it wasn't really Sara. It was like she was a ghost. She appeared while I was sleeping. I woke from a dream and she was there. I thought for a while perhaps I was still asleep, but now, I'm not certain. I think it might have been real. A visitation.'

Agnes gave me a searching look, but to my relief, didn't laugh, or scoff. I hadn't even spoken to Ruby about what I'd seen. I worried she'd think I was going mad.

'What did she say to you?'

'Nothing at all. She couldn't. She was pointing at her mouth, as though she was in pain. She started to bleed. I'm worried they've cut out her tongue, to stop her speaking.'

'They wouldn't do that,' Agnes said, so quietly she could have been talking to herself. 'How could she confess, if they took her tongue? No, this is something else. Something important.'

She stopped walking then, and looked around as though she'd misplaced something, before looking up to the sky and muttering, '*ble'r wyt ti Sara?' Where are you?*

'Agnes?'

'When you took me to see Awen with the wet nurse, I had a suspicion...' she trailed off, thinking. 'I thought then that maybe the problem was physical. Her tongue.'

I wasn't sure what she meant. I couldn't recall ever having seen Awen's tongue. It wasn't until that moment that I realised how strange that was. Didn't babies coo and lick their lips? Didn't they poke their tongues out and smile?

'Exactly!' Agnes said. 'You've never seen it have you? I didn't say anything last time because I wasn't certain yet ... I've never seen a case leave a child looking quite so sickly. But if Sara's trying to tell you it's her tongue, then we must believe her.'

I could scarcely keep up with what she was trying to tell me.

'But what do you mean? What's wrong with her tongue?'

'I think it's bound. From beneath.'

259

'Bound? Why?'

'I don't know. Because she was born that way. Because God made it so. It could be magic. Or a curse. But these things don't always have a reason, mistress.'

I couldn't comprehend it, there had to be a reason. I was sure that somehow, I was to blame. I'd angered God. I'd played with forces I shouldn't have, using a charm to help me to conceive, to help the baby grow and be born alive. Then Hywel had burned the charm, which seemed as likely a cause as any for Awen's sickness.

But none of that mattered now.

'Can you help her?'

'I'm not sure. I wanted to wait until Sara was freed. I was so sure our plan would work. But, I suppose, we may be waiting some time.' She chewed her lip, and I thought, with irritation and anguish, about the apothecary and his refusal to reply to my letter. 'Maybe ... can you speak to a physician?'

I considered for a moment, before brushing the thought away.

'No. Not again. I trust you, Agnes,' I said. 'So, can you do it?'

'If the bind is thick, I might struggle to free it, but I can try. If you take me to her, and promise you won't let your husband accuse me of anything.'

I knew it was a promise I couldn't keep. I knew, but I was desperate. So I nodded.

'I'll need to gather some things. Can you meet me there, later today?'

We made arrangements to meet at Emily's home in a few hours. I would quiet Emily with silver. I couldn't risk her saying anything to Hywel about Agnes being there.

I let myself wonder, for a moment, how things might be if Agnes was able to cure Awen. If she could come home to us at Faen Maredudd, would Hywel's spirits lift? Would his step lighten? Would we laugh and play as we used to? It was impossible to imagine.

If Awen was healed, would Hywel admit that perhaps he'd been wrong about a curse? Or would he continue to be fearful of witches, and of the influence they could have? The havoc they could wreak on us. Since he found and burned the charm in our home, his fear was palpable, the worry sitting heavy on his brow, sweat dripping from him at night like meltwater. I couldn't imagine him calm, restored. Not now.

When I got home, Rhys was there. He came on the pretence of wanting to thank us again for the kitten we gave him, gifting me a beautiful pair of kid-skin gloves he'd bought in London. For a while, he regaled us with tales of London Bridge – of bakers and tailors, and the boats that travelled along the River Thames, and the plays and performances. All the while, my heart pounded and I squirmed where I sat, desperate to hear any news he might have. Once we were alone, he looked to the rug, and, without looking up, told me the apothecary was unwilling to help us.

'I'm sorry, Doli. I truly am.'

'You've done all you can Rhys,' I told him, offering a small smile. 'Did he say why he wouldn't help?' I asked, though I supposed it didn't really matter now.

'He was sympathetic,' Rhys told me. 'But he was frightened. He didn't want to draw attention to his own practices, not in the current circumstances.'

I nodded. I understood his reasons. I would be afraid to help too. I *was* afraid, but it was too late for me. I had no choice, if I wanted Awen to live through the winter. I had brought Sara to Hywel's attention, and in doing so, had delivered her directly to the magistrates. It didn't matter that she hadn't been carried there by my horse; she might as well have been.

Sara's fate would be at the hands of the assize judges, now. I only hoped they would be merciful.

Rhys cleared his throat.

'There's something else, Doli,' he said, his eyes shifting to the rug again.

'There is?' I wanted to let myself feel hopeful, but he couldn't meet my eye.

'I will be going to London, for a year or so.' I looked at him, taking in the details of his face – the pale blue of his eyes, the freckles smattered like stars across his nose. He couldn't leave. Not now. 'It's for the best,' he went on.

I didn't want to accept it. Couldn't. My heart thundered and I felt the sting of tears, the creeping sense of panic. He was the only person other than Ruby that truly saw me.

'And Doli?' he said.

'Yes?'

'I'm sorry to tell you, but ... I believe you know Agnes Griffiths? Ruby's cousin?'

I nodded, and he continued.

'She's also been arrested. I saw it on my way here.'

I made no noise. I was incapable of responding as I tried to process the words, to make sense of them. I couldn't. I'd been with Agnes only a few hours ago.

'Arrested?' I repeated, stupidly. 'On what grounds?'

'She's accused of causing harm through witchcraft,' he said simply.

'But how —'

'I spoke with the men taking her. A farmhand claims she threatened him, earlier this morning, down by the lake. They've acted very quickly. He says he saw her pricking a poppet doll by candlelight. And that he saw her meeting with the devil himself. Her and Sara Gwen together. He claims he's become impotent, since he saw it.'

'That's slander,' I said, my voice shaking. 'It's not true.' I was too angry to say anything more.

I was supposed to be meeting Agnes at Emily's house near sundown. What hope was there for Awen now? I'd failed her. Rhys didn't say anything either. We stood that way, staring around us uselessly, until Hywel bounded back into the room.

'I've asked the cook to fetch us some pies,' he said, merrily.

I found Ruby in the kitchen, gazing at the wall as she stirred a pan of milk.

'Ruby?'

She didn't answer me. The milk was beginning to bubble, threatening to spill over the rim of the pan.

'Ruby – your milk,' I said, touching a hand to her arm as it began to spit.

She blinked, wordlessly taking the pan from the flames and setting it on the table.

'So you've heard?' I said, uselessly.

She looked at me then.

'I begged you,' she said, as the milk calmed to a simmer. She paused, but before I could begin to dissect her meaning, she went on. 'I warned you not to go to Sara Gwen. I pleaded. I told you this would happen.'

'Ruby,' I said. 'You can't blame me.'

'Why can't I? If you hadn't involved yourself, the master would have let Sara be. And Agnes would be sitting in the alehouse now, singing or laughing. She wouldn't be locked up in gaol.'

I cut across her. She knew how terribly I felt about my role in Sara's arrest. How I walked about with a sickness in me because of it. I wouldn't let her blame me for what had happened to Agnes. I couldn't bear the weight of that, too.

'I'm doing everything I can,' I said, aware my voice lacked any conviction.

'It's not enough.'

I took in Ruby's pale complexion, the utter defeat in her cat-like eyes.

'I know,' I said, quietly. Hopelessly.

She took off her apron and gestured for me to follow her towards the buttery.

'There's talk,' she began, once we were safely inside the room. She stared at a point behind my head, as though she didn't want to look at my face. 'The way you knocked doors, asked about Sara Gwen...' she paused, licked her lips. A quick dart of the tongue. 'It didn't go unnoticed. The villagers have much to say. The servants too.'

'About me?' My chest seized, and I felt it again: the little sparrow, beating her wings in my breast.

Ruby nodded.

'But I've done nothing wrong?' I focussed my eyes on the rows of wine bottles that lined the shelves, the glass smooth and beautiful as emeralds.

'Since when has that mattered?' Ruby said. Her voice was growing louder now, I glanced beyond the buttery door to ensure no one was lingering nearby. 'They see how eager you are to help a woman they believe is wicked. They talk about how you can read and write. They say curses have been found in a box beneath your bed. That your prayer book is full of strange lettering and symbols.'

What did she mean? Curses? Who had been under my bed?

'My poems? No one would think they were curses Ruby. That doesn't make sense.'

'There's one woman in particular. She lives in one of your properties. She's not long been in childbed. Unmarried,' she added. 'She certainly has enough to say about you.'

The woman she was describing ... Could she be the drunk from the summer festivities? She was a tenant, and her belly had been swollen with a baby on that awful day we'd gathered in the church, the villagers telling the magistrate their stories. I thought then, of the night I'd given birth to Awen. How the woman had snored against my shoulder on the dais. Hywel's unexplained absence. How they had seemed familiar with one another. I shook the thought from my head – it wasn't important. I couldn't bring myself to care about who Hywel was taking to bed, not now. Surely ... I was a woman of some influence. A woman of rank. The villagers could talk all they liked. After all, I was a Maredudd.

I told myself that would be enough.

With Agnes gone, I had no choice but to act.

Before he left, I asked Rhys for directions. Of course, he warned me not to go. Begged me to forget Sara and take care of myself, but if he thought I was going to pace the grounds of Faen Maredudd, doing nothing but watching the doves shed their feathers to the dovecote floor, watching the roses wilt and curl, he didn't know me at all. Eventually he relented.

I mounted my mare as evening settled over the moors, thinking about what I might find when I arrived. I made two false turns, and had to go back the way I came. I rode over grasslands and heath, listening to the gentle clip-clop of my mare's hooves on the earth. The smell of peat moss, wet soil, pine and rain were my constant companions, growing stronger as the evening drew in. By the time I arrived, darkness had descended, as though a huge bat had spread its wings before the sun, blocking its light.

I expected to come across a cottage, or a small farmstead – something humble, like Sara's home. But the house that stood before me was almost as large as Faen Maredudd, with a storied porch and a huge herb garden at the front. It must have been the right place; Rhys told me I would recognise it by the sudden turn in the road, which split beside an abandoned wagon.

It was dusk now, the sky indigo and purple like a beautiful gown embroidered with stars. It was late to be out unaccompanied. I took a deep, steadying breath, inhaling the outside air one last time, before sliding from my horse and striding to the front door.

The woman who answered it looked confused when she saw me, but she showed me inside and led me to a small room where I was instructed to wait.

'Your wall tapestry is beautiful,' I told her, more for something to say than anything else. My voice was hoarse. She thanked me, smiling awkwardly, and left to find her husband.

I sat on the settle, then stood up, then sat again. I was not sure what to do with my body. After some time, a man entered the room. He was thin, pale, with shadows circling his eyes. His movements were quick and sudden, like a hare being chased by hounds.

'Ah. I feared you might come here,' he said. 'I cannot help you, mistress. I'm sorry. Truly I am.'

I blinked, taken aback for a moment. How did he know who I was?

'Master Hepsworth,' I said. 'I understand that you feel unable to help. But I also understand that you hold a certain amount of influence. And what *you* must understand is that I've grown tired of people telling me that they cannot intervene, when I know that they can.'

I was surprised at my own words. At the anger and frustration that bubbled inside of me like boiling water, before spilling from my mouth, threatening to scald anyone who stood too close.

John Hepsworth looked over his shoulder, as though someone was standing behind him, though it was just the two of us in the room. When finally he spoke, his voice warbled.

'It's not that I don't want to help your friend, mistress. As I've already conveyed to Rhys, I can't be involved. If I were seen to be meddling, if I were to draw too much attention to myself from the wrong people, the repercussions would be too great.'

I laughed.

'Repercussions?' I didn't mean to speak with such hostility, but my anger, my incredulity, my fear, couldn't be contained any longer. 'The repercussions for my friend Sara Gwen will be death, if you don't intervene. She will hang, for doing nothing but good. For helping me and my child. Agnes Griffiths too. Guilty by association. Dragged to gaol for defending her own honour. I am sickened. As any good man or woman should be.'

I stared deep into his eyes, imploring him to understand, to do what he could. My whole body quivered as the last of my strength, my hope, poured from me, uncontrollable, like birth water pooling on the rug. I would have liked to have spoken these words to Hywel, rather than to the apothecary. He was the one who should be standing before me, pale as ash in the candlelight, crescent moons blooming black beneath his eyes. But John Hepsworth would have to do.

He blinked.

'Did you say Agnes Griffiths?' he asked, quietly.

'I did. Do you know her?'

'I don't. At least, not personally. But my wife —' He stopped talking to look around again, craning around to face the door, as though expecting his wife to burst through it. His left eyelid twitched. 'My dear Catrin. Agnes helped her, during a very troubling time, when my own skills failed me. She knew more about the way a woman's body worked, gave her mugwort, cared for her,' he trailed off. 'Anyway, we are, undoubtedly, in her debt.'

Perhaps I should have been surprised at this revelation. That Agnes' kindness, her ability to heal had reached this house, miles from home. That she had helped these two people, who were clearly so much grander than she. But I wasn't.

'Then repay her now,' I said. 'She needs help.'

A lump travelled the length of his throat. It was as though he was swallowing his own words, the letters bulging from him.

'But why Agnes?' He mumbled. 'She's no *witsh*?'

'Neither is Sara Gwen. I've come to believe there are no witches, John. At least, not in the way the justices would have us believe. There are only people. Only women. Some are good at heart – most, I hope. Some are wicked. Some go to church and some don't. Some worship with prayer, some speak with our Lord, some pilgrimage. Some wish ill on others. Some make bold claims of witchcraft through malice, or spite, or fear. Some hang. Some do not.'

John sighed. It was a deep, rattling noise that made his whole body tremble.

'Mistress. I want to help, I do. But —'

I raised my hand to him, in much the same way as Sara had raised hers to me all those long tiresome months ago.

'There's no need of that,' I told him. 'As I understand it, you have the means to prevent the wrongful death of two good women. If you should choose to do nothing, that's between you, and God.'

With that, I took my leave, passing his wife in the entryway. She stared silently at me, her eyes wide and troubled. My hands were shaking too much to manage the buttons on my riding cloak, so I mounted my mare with it still undone, trailing behind me in the darkness.

As my horse galloped back towards Llynidwen, I'd never felt more hopeless. More friendless. More alone. I told myself over and over that if Sara and Agnes were innocent, there'd be no evidence against them, and they'd be freed. But I couldn't bring myself to believe it. Good women had been hanged on lesser charges. Charges that made no sense to me, accused of suckling their dogs and chickens, or of night walking. Of scrying and cursing and making men lame.

I arrived at Emily's house tired and cold, knowing that whatever became of Sara and Agnes was beyond my control now. There was nothing more I could do for them.

Emily opened the door in her nightdress, the grit of sleep still settled about her eyes.

'Mistress? It's the middle of the night?'

'Where's my baby?' I said. I'd lost all patience with formalities and politeness.

Emily showed me inside and I lifted Awen straight from her cradle, hurrying her back outside into the night, ignoring Emily's voice calling after me.

I held her close, rubbing a thumb slowly over the soft hair on her head, feeling the balding patch where it had rubbed away around her crown. She smiled up at me. It was the first time I'd seen her smile. She'd grown in length, but she was still thin as a skinned hare, her huge eyes bulging, round and clear as the lake. Her cheekbones cupping shadows.

Agnes had explained it all, before we parted ways. Before she went back to the farmsteads, the noise and the people, carrying the smell of rosemary with her, unaware of her impending arrest at the words of a vengeful farmhand.

Thanks to Agnes, I knew to look for the heart-shaped groove at the tip of Awen's tongue. I knew to search for the tight white knot

268

beneath it – as though someone had placed a daisy petal there. I could see now, for the first time, how the tongue didn't rise fully in her mouth, even when she screamed. I tickled her lips, but it failed to come out and rest there, tracing my touch as it should have. *My poor Awen.*

My whole body quivered. I tried to breathe deeply, to steady my nerves, but I couldn't rid myself of the wings that beat with a frenzy in my chest.

I didn't want to do it. Of course I didn't. But what choice did I have? I couldn't go to Hywel with this, he wouldn't listen to a word, and I wasn't prepared to go to a physician. Not again. The idea of a faceless man prying my baby's lips apart with cold, rough fingers ... And that was if he even listened to me, believed me. No. I'd had enough of husbands and physicians and prayers. If neither Sara nor Agnes could do it, I would have to do it myself.

I tucked her under my shawl and we set off across the moors until we reached a quiet spot. I placed her down beside a large tree trunk, listening to the soft shush of the river nearby. The ground was cold, beginning to frost over. Above us, a red kite perched on a branch, staring down, the moonlight catching its golden feathers. I murmured a prayer, then spoke the protective words Agnes had told me to. The more I thought about being careful, steady and still, the more my hand trembled and shook. I had to get this right. If I slipped...

I barely gave myself chance to think about it. If I had, I wouldn't have done it. She trusted me and this would hurt her. A deep breath. A trembling fist. I held Awen's head still with one hand and, with the other, pushed the dagger in, aiming straight for that white, daisy-like knot at the very same moment she lifted her tongue in a wail of indignation and showed it to me.

I'm sorry, Awen. I'm so sorry. Paid â chrio.

The skin was thick, like hide. Tough. But the dagger made a clean cut. There was far more blood than I'd expected. It poured from her mouth, as though she'd been drinking it. I thought of a hound, muzzle smeared red after a hunt. I thought, too, of Sara's ghost at the bottom of my bed. It must have hurt – she shrieked and cried. I did too. I cried with grief and pain and relief and joy and love. I put her to my breast to comfort her, and she sucked straight away, her blood smeared and stark across my skin. I'd been worried the milk might not come, after all this time, but the swell and sudden tightness in my chest on hearing Awen's cry reassured me.

That was how I knew I'd been right to do it. The scoop of her chin as she nursed. The easy guzzle. The deep, hungry swallows and swollen cheeks, puffed like blown eggs. Everything about it felt different. Right.

'It will all be better now,' I whispered, over and over. *Mae popeth yn iawn.*

We sat that way for a long time, while she filled her cheeks and I let the tears come. I didn't know what to do next. I wanted to take her home, to show Hywel what I'd done, but I didn't think he would forgive me for it, at least not until he saw the change in Awen for himself. Even then, he might continue to blame Sara and witchcraft and curses, might insist the binding of her tongue was the result of dark magic. Maybe it was.

I thought about taking Awen back to Emily, begging her not to say anything and leaving her there to fatten. If she continued to feed like this, she'd be round as a turnip in no time, and I could take her home, then. No one needed to know what I'd done, or how I'd learned to do it. She would be well, Hywel would believe the curse had been lifted, and we could forget these last, awful months.

But no. I was fooling myself thinking either of us would ever forget any of this. Things couldn't be the way they were between us, not now. For a long time we had simply existed, two people living in one, grand home, barely speaking to one another unless company dictated it. If Sara or Agnes hanged, I would never forgive Hywel for his role in their deaths. Besides, my husband was right – I wasn't the same woman he had married. I was far more than that.

Though I was cold, uncomfortable, I began to doze, with Awen nursing sleepily at my breast, the red kite keeping watch over us. I dreamed of Sara, calling to me from the gallows, wheezing. Choking.

When I woke, stiff and upright, my arms still tight around Awen, a dark, caped figure stood before me. I clutched Awen closer, made to stand up, trying to centre myself. It took me a moment to recognise him – Jacob Lloyd, the county's newest magistrate, telling me to go with him. Telling me I was under arrest...

The Villagers

We heard she tore into the house and snatched the baby straight from the wet nurse's arms. That her eyes were coal black and filled with malice. We heard she wanted to feed the baby to her hound. That she was taking her to sacrifice to the devil himself. Of course, we rushed straight to the magistrate, who happened to be nearby. Told him what had happened. We told him, too, of the curses found beneath her bed by a frightened servant. And then we saw her. The mistress. Doli Maredudd flying over the moors, a bloodied parcel in her arms. The parcel cried and squealed. The parcel dripped with blood. The parcel bled. The parcel; the parcel; the parcel.

I told Jacob everything, beginning with the miscarriage on the moors and I didn't stop talking until I reached the arrest. I told him about the charm, the long night in childbed, Awen's sickness, my desperation to heal her ... I told him what Ruby had said, about the villagers and their suspicions, the servants and their worries about my poetry. I wanted him to know my story, to see the honesty and truth in it. To know there was no malice, no harm intended.

When I finished talking, Jacob wrote something down, underlined it.

'I always knew there was something ... unnatural ... about you,' he said.

I flinched at his words, at the vitriol in his voice.

'You can think of me however you like,' I said. 'But please. Look at my daughter. She's all the proof you need that I'm telling you the whole truth.' I looked down at Awen, sleeping soundly in my arms. 'Sara is no *witsh*.' My voice shook as I spoke, and I felt the sting of my words in my throat. 'I may not know much about the law, but I know you can't hang a woman for selling salves.'

'Sara wasn't thrown in the dungeons for giving anyone a fertility charm. The accusations against her are far greater than that. As you know. A child lies dead in her grave, and more harm besides.'

I stared at him, desperate.

'What proof do you have?'

'You are the one under arrest here, Mistress Maredudd. Do not question me. Besides, proof is no longer an issue.'

He was still staring down at whatever he'd been writing, the ink dripping in thick black globules from his quill.

'What do you mean proof isn't an issue? Are we not law-abiding people? Isn't proof needed to —'

'Sara expired in the dungeons late last night. It's cold down there. Damp. The conditions are not good. Not everyone survives long enough to see the jury.'

'No. You're lying.' I stared at him. Silent. Pleading.

His smile was thin, stretched.

'I am a man of God. I do not lie, Mistress Maredudd.'

I looked down again at Awen, reeling with this new discovery. What sort of world would this be for her? How could I protect her, in a world where a woman could be accused of killing a child when she'd done no more than offer salves and prayers? Where evidence and proof weren't needed, as long as men with enough strength to drag her to gaol were around?

'What about Agnes Griffiths?' My voice was quiet, shaking. I tasted the salt of my tears as I spoke, wiped my cheeks with the back of my hand. 'Any fool can see she was only defending herself. Defending her honour. What woman can be blamed for that? Please, Jacob. I might have done the same thing myself, in her position.'

He brushed his quill against the table, back and forth. His face was calm, unmoving. What was he thinking?

'I don't doubt it,' he said. 'But we are not here to speak about Agnes. We are here to speak about you, and how you took this infant from her home —'

'Her home is with me.' Perhaps I shouldn't have spoken, but I couldn't hold back the words.

'Took her from her home,' he repeated. 'And inflicted serious harm. You were found in the trees covered in blood, Mistress Maredudd. The villagers were terrified, learning you'd snatched this poor babe under the cloak of night, seeing you flying over the moors, hearing the screaming. They feared you were taking her as a sacrifice.'

A wail escaped me, tears salting my lips and stinging my throat. My breath came shallow and rapid, my words stunted.

'No. No. I would never hurt my baby.'

Jacob only nodded, touching a hand to his own chest.

'May God have mercy on your soul.' He spoke calmly, though his eyes looked fearful, and I noted he'd inched backwards on his chair, as though to draw away from me.

'I would do it again,' I said, quietly. 'For Awen. It worked, didn't it? Look at her.'

I smoothed a thumb over her cheek. Before he woke me, and wrenched her from my arms, he must have seen how her mouth spilled crimson and cream, milk flooding her chin. While we were sitting together, beneath that tree, she sucked so much from me that her belly grew and hardened. Her sleep, for the first time, was deep. Still. Peaceful.

He said nothing, only looked at me with disdain. There was nothing more I could say. Nothing more I could do. I had failed Sara. I'd promised her my help, and I'd failed.

'I've told you all I know, Jacob. I've done nothing wrong.' My shoulders shook as I spoke. 'Punish me, if you must, but please, make sure Awen is cared for.'

He pushed back from the table, gathering his paper as he stood. As he turned to leave the room, I gathered my courage, spoke again.

'Perhaps, you could leave me some paper and a quill? I'd like to write something, for Awen. Something about these women I have come to know.'

The Villagers

Of course, the master ensured Doli Maredudd was released without charge. He stormed the hall, filled with fire and fury, shouting that his wife was no *witsh*. That she was a woman of God. We heard he scrunched his fists. That he and the magistrate nearly came to blows. Some say his rage was not about the mistress, but rather, about his reputation. Tarnished by her arrest. She went home, the babe clutched to her chest like a locket. At the autumn assizes, the jury said Agnes Griffiths had lied – threatened witshcraft out of anger, and fear. The way a dog might bare its teeth and threaten to bite. Stupid, perhaps, but no crime. She was pardoned. She lost her employ, of course. We heard the courts grumbled about their time being wasted. The mistress invited her to Faen Maredudd, where she polishes the silverware. The servants there say things have changed. The master and the mistress do not speak to one another. The master brings his whore to the house, says she's there to help the cook. The mistress is different, now. They say she can heal or hurt. That she mended her daughter with magic and sap. That she is always writing some verse or other, scrawling her words with utter abandon. They say wherever she goes she is followed by a great golden bird, the sunlight hooking its wings.

A note on the witch trials

Beginning with the publication of the *Malleus Maleficarum* in 1486, which claimed that witchcraft came from insatiable 'carnal lust' in women, the witch trials were, at their core, an attack on the female body. The *Malleus Maleficarum* is rife with stories of castration, orgasmic sex with demons, seed stealing and old women luring and corrupting young virgins, highlighting deep-rooted misogynistic anxieties about women's sexuality and insisting that the female body is innately perverse and deviant. The sentiment was echoed over a century later in King James' anti-witchcraft treatise *Daemonologie,* not long before he oversaw a retranslation of the Bible, which is still read widely today. Over hundreds of years, thousands of women were murdered on baseless accusations, founded in religious theology and medical theory describing women as inferior, made to pleasure men and bear male children. Those who didn't fit the accepted ideas of what femininity should be were targeted, penalised and killed. In 2025, women's bodies are still politicised, scrutinised and feared. Increasingly in the western world, women are being stripped of their bodily autonomy, having their reproductive rights removed and used as leverage in political campaigns. We've seen politicians in world-leading countries openly mock women, brag about sexual assault and brand women in their field 'disgusting' for requesting a medical break to pump breastmilk. These aren't isolated incidents, but rather, part of a trend of flagrant misogyny and systemic attacks on women in the public sphere — in 2017, the Turkish president likened childless women to 'half a person,' 'deficient' and 'incomplete;' the Russian senator said the only thing 'relevant' for women was 'being a mother;' a South African MP shouted a derogatory term for 'sex worker' at a female colleague, and a European MP claimed women were 'weaker and less intelligent' than men. The American Republican Party have even resorted to vilifying and attacking musicians, actors and other women of influence. As an outspoken, strong figure with a platform

278

of particular influence for women and girls, Taylor Swift posed a big enough threat to the US president that he felt the need to declare on social media, Taylor Swift 'is no longer hot,' while his senior advisor threatened to 'put a baby in' her. Our cultural obsession with women's bodies and what they do with them is a centuries-old overhang of the early-modern rhetoric on witchcraft, which convinced the world that women who were sexually voracious, independent, childless or otherwise not subservient to men were servants of a great evil.

A note on the text

Witch trials in Wales were sparse, with only thirty five cases on record, resulting in eight guilty verdicts and five judgements of death. Those sentenced to death by hanging were: Gwen ferch Ellis in 1594, Lowri and Agnes ferch Evan and their brother Rhydderch ap Evan in 1622, and Margaret ferch Richard in 1655. For narrative purposes, the novel implies more deaths in closer proximity and over a shorter period of time than is true. The character of Sara Gwen was largely inspired by Gwen ferch Ellis, the first woman to be hanged on charges of witchcraft in Wales. While Doli's story is imagined, I've tried through extensive research to remain true to the historical, cultural, shifting political and religious landscape inhabited by the characters, and attempted to imagine how a lay healer and soothsayer could be rebranded as a *Witsh* during the sixteenth century, particularly on the fringes of Wales. Llynidwen is a fictional village in the county of Brecon, near the border of Wales and the Welsh Marches, (now made up of Hereford, Gloucestershire and Shropshire) which saw a great fear of witches.

The poems included in this novel were inspired by the original works of Gwerful Mechain and the translations of these works by Katie Gramich. The snippets of Mechain's poetry read by Rhys and Doli are also taken directly from Gramich's translations. One verse borrows from a poem of unknown authorship, translated by Nia Powell.

During the time the novel was set, Tretower Court and Castle in Crickhowell was owned by the Vaughan family, and would have played host to bards and poets during lavish feasts. There is no evidence that it ever acted as a gaol for suspected witches or other criminals.

Acknowledgments

Witsh would not be the novel it is without the input of the following people, to whom I am grateful.

Eluned Gramich, Emily Vanderploeg, Katie Edwards and Emma Butler-Way, who read early drafts of the manuscript and offered endless insight, ideas and encouragement. Similarly, Natalie Ann Holborow, who is as patient and kind as she is talented.

I am indebted to the scholars and historians whose research contributed enormously to my understanding and depiction of sixteenth century Wales, its politics, culture and religious values. In particular, the works of Richard Suggett, who has transcribed the Court of Great Sessions records housed at the National Library and provided great insight into the circumstances that shaped the witch trials in Wales.

Matthew Francis and Cathryn Charnell-White believed in the novel from the get go and were always happy to listen to my ideas. Matthew's knowledge of early modern Wales and Cathryn's insight into the female bardic tradition were invaluable to Doli's story.

My wonderful agent, Laura Williams, who understood my vision and determination to tell a story about the dangers of ignoring women's understanding of their own bodies, worked with me on the manuscript before it went to publishers, and championed me when I doubted myself.

Rebecca Parfitt, whose unwavering passion for the project was always clear — I feel so lucky to have had her as my editor at Honno.

Finally, for my children, without whom Awen would never have existed.

ABOUT HONNO

Honno Welsh Women's Press was set up in 1986 by a group of women who felt strongly that women in Wales needed wider opportunities to see their writing in print and to become involved in the publishing process. Our aim is to develop the writing talents of women in Wales, give them new and exciting opportunities to see their work published and often to give them their first 'break' as a writer.

Honno is registered as a community co-operative. Any profit that Honno makes is invested in the publishing programme. Women from Wales and around the world have expressed their support for Honno. Each supporter has a vote at the Annual General Meeting. For more information and to buy our publications, please visit our website www.honno.co.uk or email us on post@honno.co.uk.

Honno
D41, Hugh Owen Building,
Aberystwyth University,
Aberystwyth,
Ceredigion,
SY23 3DY.

We are very grateful for the support of all our Honno Friends.